"I feel things with you, Bridget.

Things I didn't even feel with my wife. How can that be?" His eyes reflected remorse and confusion and something else. Could it be longing?

Her stomach gave a twitch in response. She had no answer for his words or the pain in his crystal-blue eyes.

"She's been gone three years," she said. "It's a long time for a man to be alone." He raised an ache in her, making it difficult to recall that his intentions were not honorable.

"You stir me and mystify me like no woman I've met."

His words vibrated through her. It would be easy if she felt nothing for him, but it was not so. His touch made her throb. But she did not trust his words.

His admission and her longings made him dangerous, and climbing the pass was deadly enough.

* * *

Outlaw Bride
Harlequin® Historical #883—February 2008

JENNA KERNAN

Outlaw Bride

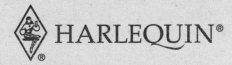

HARLEQUIN®

TORONTO • NEW YORK • LONDON
AMSTERDAM • PARIS • SYDNEY • HAMBURG
STOCKHOLM • ATHENS • TOKYO • MILAN • MADRID
PRAGUE • WARSAW • BUDAPEST • AUCKLAND

ISBN-13: 978-0-373-29483-1
ISBN-10:   0-373-29483-2

OUTLAW BRIDE

Available from Harlequin® Historical and
JENNA KERNAN

DON'T MISS THESE OTHER
NOVELS AVAILABLE NOW:

#884 THE WAYWARD DEBUTANTE—Sarah Elliott

Eleanor Sinclair is thoroughly bored by high society. Sneaking
out one night, dressed as a servant, to avoid yet another stuffy
party, she meets the most handsome man—but her innocent
deception will lead her to a most improper marriage....
Sarah Elliott's defiant heroine will enchant you!

#885 SCANDALOUS LORD, REBELLIOUS MISS—
Deb Marlowe

Charles Alden, Viscount Dayle, is desperately trying
to reform, and the outrageously unconventional Miss Westby
is the most inappropriate choice to help him. But Charles just
can't seem to stay away from her!
*Witty and sparkling—enjoy the Regency Season in Golden
Heart Award winner Deb Marlowe's sexy debut.*

#886 SURRENDER TO THE HIGHLANDER—
Terri Brisbin

Growing up in a convent, Margriet was entirely innocent in the
ways of the world. Sent to escort her home, Rurik is shocked to
be drawn to a woman wearing a nun's habit!
Surrender to Terri Brisbin's gorgeous highland hero!

This story is dedicated to my sisters,
Amy and Nan,
and my brother,
Jim,
who I know would climb
any mountain to rescue me.

Chapter One

Sacramento, California
November 1850

The jailor eyed Bridget Callahan with sterile blue eyes. "You carrying a weapon?"

"What?" she asked.

"Or anything else that would help him escape?"

"I just want to speak to the man, not hang beside him."

The jailor nodded and led her across the deck of the prison brig *Stafford,* moored on the eastern bank of the American River. Stripped of all rope and sail, the ship wallowed in the mud like a sow, left to rot along with those poor souls locked belowdecks.

Bridget's nose wrinkled at the stench. Stone or wood, the housing didn't matter. Unwashed bodies, urine and filth smelled the same, both sides of the Atlantic.

Keep your family together, and the rest of the world can take care of itself. Her father always said as much.

Bridget set her jaw. Mary and Chloe were all she had left of her family. She would not lose them, as well.

The jailor descended the galley stairs, disappearing into the gloom. Bridget paused on deck as apprehension prickled her neck. Nothing on God's green earth could convince her to go down those stairs. Nothing, she thought, except her family dying by inches in the freezing cold.

She shifted her attention from the decking to the long, straight street leading east to the rolling hills she had crossed alone. Beyond stood the jagged ridge of mountains. Low clouds hung over the peaks. She knew what that meant. The granite teeth devoured her family and the snow buried them alive.

"What's keeping you?" called the jailor.

Perspiration erupted on her face and neck as she lowered one foot and then the next to the steep stairs. Below, small pinpoints of sunlight broke through the green deck, glass prisms set in the deck, casting the narrow hall in eerie shadow.

"He's got his own cell. Moved him aft from the brig to the second mate's quarters, just till the hanging."

She followed him down the corridor. He halted before a sturdy wooden door with bars set in a square opening at eye level.

"Where's me keys?" He fished in his overcoat for his ring and then fanned them to locate the right one.

She peered into the darkness beyond the bars.

"Keep back. He's had some to drink."

"You let your prisoners drink?"

"Started his last meal early. Asked for four bottles

of whiskey and the mayor says he's to have them. Wants him to go to his Maker in this sorry state." The jailor turned to the darkness beyond the door. "Ellis, you awake?"

"Time already?"

Bridget thought he sounded eager, but that made no sense. No one was anxious to die.

"No, you stupid bastard, you got a whole day left."

The condemned man cursed.

"Got a visitor. Miss Callahan. She got trapped in your mountains. Her family's still up there."

Another curse. "Go away."

The jailor leaned closer, letting her know without words that Ellis was not the only one drinking on board. "He don't like to talk about it."

She stepped forward and spoke into the gloom. "I've some questions."

"Go away, damn you."

The jailor grinned. "Ellis knows all about them mountains. Rescued some, but not all." He raked his keys across the bars. "Right, Ellis? Couldn't save your own kin?"

He'd lost his family to the Cascades. Her worst nightmare had happened to him. Is that why he had fallen so far?

The jailor banged on the bars with the iron ring. "But *you* made it, all right. Didn't you, Ellis?"

His captive muttered something unintelligible and the jailor chuckled as he retraced his steps, pausing before the narrow stairs.

"Enjoy your visit," he called, and disappeared up the ladder.

* * *

Cole heard Meredith's heavy step on the stairs. Was the woman gone, as well?

He clutched the smooth neck of the whiskey bottle and tipped it back, longing for the burn in his throat and the fire in his belly.

Nothing.

He released his grip and the bottle clunked against the bunk, then the floor, rolling in a circle before coming to rest.

Three left.

Her voice drifted in from the cell door. She sounded young and Irish. His wife's people had come from the old country.

He squeezed his eyes closed tight as the guilt overcame him. His wife—dead and gone while he still lived. Never should it be so.

Angela.

Why had she left him? He should have died with her that day, but then he thought he might still save their daughter. He hadn't. The rage billowed inside him. Twenty-three-year-olds should not die in the snow.

"Mr. Ellis, my family is still up there."

"So's mine," he muttered.

What did she want from him? He was in here and she, out there. What month was it? Every damn day was the same in this miserable land—no seasons, just mild days and warm nights. Angela would have loved it here.

"Can't tell winter from spring," he muttered.

"What was that?" she asked.

He didn't answer.

"Mr. Ellis, they say they can't make a rescue until February at the earliest. The food won't last that long. You've been there. You rescued fifteen people in November."

"I left more than I saved."

"But you saved some, Mr. Ellis. There are three more souls waiting."

"Not for me."

"You know how to reach them."

"Ah, is that all? Just wait until April and then walk straight up the trail. They'll be there, unless the wolves get at them."

He heard a small sound. Did she gasp? "They've only one ox and no flour. Mr. Ellis, do you understand?"

He did and his gut coiled in tight knots. He wanted to tell her to forget them, but he could not muster the words.

"Can you give me some notion on how to proceed?" asked the woman.

She made him remember. He reached for the whiskey.

"Please, Mr. Ellis."

He paused before pulling the cork with his teeth. "If I tell you, will you go away?"

Silence. The little bit of baggage was considering his offer.

"If you answer *all* my questions."

A counteroffer. She was used to barter. He smiled, intrigued enough to lower the bottle.

"No man living can answer all a woman's questions, especially a man who's fall-down drunk. I'll give you five, then you scat."

She was quiet again, but finally, just when he had nearly forgotten she was there, she piped up again.

"Should I hire horses or mules?"

"Neither," he said.

Her small face pressed to the space between the bars of his door, showing him a sharp nose centered between two large eyes.

"I'm not following you," she said.

He hoped not, as he was traveling to the gallows. He bit back the sarcasm. His wife had never approved of that side of him.

"Pack animals mire in deep snow. Get snowshoes."

Her fingers clutched the bars. He glimpsed thin, pale appendages and staggered to his feet. Since the prison ship didn't move, he assumed the rocking was entirely internal.

He lost his tenuous hold on his equilibrium and stumbled against the door. His hand gripped hers. The heat of her skin registered first, and then, the sweet fruity scent of her drifted into his world like a soft breeze through an orchard. Had she been eating oranges?

She didn't draw back at his touch and that surprised him, but not half so much as her next action—she reached through the bars to capture his wrist. Her strong grip showed her vitality. If he didn't know better, he'd think she meant to drag him through that narrow gap and force him along on her mission. He could see the determination glowing in her green eyes and something else, something familiar—grief. She mourned them already.

"I didn't think of snowshoes."

The woman leaned in to catch his next words.

"And stay clear of the avalanche plane," he added.

"How shall I know it?"

Cole couldn't keep his jaw from dropping. Had she walked right through it, unknowing?

The woman blinked at him, her brow wrinkled in concentration. She'd been up there—on his mountain. How had she escaped? What quality did she have that his wife had lacked?

Was it all luck? Was that what decided who lived and who died?

It was a question he'd asked himself more times than he could remember. Why had they died? Why had he lived?

Bridget tried to regain Ellis's attention. "I thought canned fruit might do them the most good." It was, in fact, what she most craved, along with bread, but she could think of no way to bring that.

"No, no. Jerked meat and dried fruit."

"But coffee and…"

"Too heavy. Melt snow for drinking and bring a buffalo robe."

She would not have thought of that, either.

Bridget needed to learn all he knew, but minutes slipped by. This time tomorrow, he'd be dead and she'd be alone again.

It was a miracle she had survived her descent. She could not rely on luck on the return. This man had been there and back—twice. He knew things, things that she must understand if she was to succeed.

She needed more than words. She needed…him.

Her next idea so shocked her that it took her breath away. She stood frozen in horror as the idea took hold. Her heart beat against her ribs with such force she needed to grit her teeth against the pain of it. Part of her wanted to turn tail and run. The coward, she thought, the side of her that always sought to save its skin. Instead, she stood silently, battling for the courage to speak.

Her whispered voice rang with desperation. "Would you take me?"

His eyes narrowed as if she mocked him. His smile was sardonic. "I've a previous engagement."

She felt the noose tightening around her own neck. If he died, her only chance to rescue her family died with him. She knew it without question. "If I get you out, will you promise to come?"

Cole measured the woman. She looked that desperate. He was tempted to say yes, just to be rid of her. It was an easy lie, since the woman's chances of gaining his release were about the same as those of anyone reaching her family in time.

Still he hesitated. He didn't want to struggle any longer. That's why he'd stolen that pretty little mare. Jabbing his finger so far into the mayor's eye, not even he could overlook it. Too bad about the horse's broken leg. He had never intended that. His jaw clenched. Mark it down with his other sins, he thought.

"Please, Mr. Ellis. I need you."

He saw her face clearly now, earnest, thin and as pale as ivory. How long had it been since anyone had needed him?

Cole pulled free of the woman's hand. The heat of her still clung to him, as did the lush scent of orange peels.

"My family's lives, Mr. Ellis, for your liberty."

As if he wanted that. She couldn't provide him the release he sought and neither could he. He glanced at the three full whiskey bottles. Their respite was all too brief, so he'd taken the coward's way.

"No."

"Mr. Ellis, you are the only one who has been there."

He just wanted her to go away. A lie would make that happen, and what harm would it do? They'd both have what they sought. She'd have hope and he'd have peace. Likely she'd push off to plead with some judge. What was she willing to bargain for his freedom?

The first thing that sprang to his mind made him grimace, though he could not fathom why he cared what the girl did, so long as she did it elsewhere.

Let her weep and plead for his freedom. Then there might be one person in the world who would mourn his passing.

"All right," he whispered.

"Swear."

He didn't want to.

"I do."

"Swear on the soul of your wife."

He drew back.

"Mr. Ellis?"

He just wanted to lie down and rest, sleep. But she kept picking at him like a crow on a carcass.

"I'll not go until I hear you say it."

He could feel his wife's disappointment in him,

knew she would not approve of what he was about to do. But she had left him long ago. He clenched his jaw against the anger that glowed brightly for an instant before drowning in guilt. How could he hate her for dying?

"Mr. Ellis. Your vow?"

Oh, would this woman ever go away?

"Yes, on her soul, then."

The instant he said it, the fog of whiskey lifted and he understood what he had done. A cold chill seeped into his bones.

Pray to God, she can't do it. Please, God, don't let her succeed.

She shouted, "Mr. Meredith!" On the second call she heard his heavy step as he descended the stairs.

"What is it? Did the mongrel grab you?"

Bridget stood with her hands in tight fists. She couldn't believe what she was thinking, couldn't breathe past the enormity of it. She was risking all on the promise of a man who stank of whiskey.

Small hope is better than none.

"I…I…the heat." She lifted her hand to her brow for effect as the jailor drew closer, and then she stumbled against him.

"It's the smell what does it."

It was nothing to reach into his coat. The difficult part was doing it so that the keys came away soundlessly. But she'd had practice, years and years of it. Some skills stuck like tar on flesh. She threaded her fingers through the individual pieces and squeezed. The jailor held her now, supporting her weight.

"I'll get you out."

"No," she whispered, regaining her footing. "Some water."

He released her, but stood near, ready to catch her. He didn't appear to note the hand she kept behind her back.

"Water?" she whispered.

He dragged a stool from beneath the stairs. "Sit there."

She did and he rushed away. Bridget turned to the lock, now at eye level. She could feel Ellis standing above her, just inches away as she tried one key after another.

"Don't," he whispered.

You'd think the man wanted to hang. She stiffened as realization dawned and she shot to her feet, staring hard into his eyes. Yes, he looked that hopeless.

"Now, you listen to me, Mr. Ellis. You made a pledge."

"You tricked me."

"You'll be seeing it through. After that, what you do is your own damn business."

He looked surprised—at her language, she wondered, or something else?

"I won't lead you to that icy hell."

"You will. You vowed on her soul."

She slipped another key into the lock and this time the tumbler caught. The click brought them both to stillness, she on her side and he on his.

He glared at Bridget, but his face had gone pale.

"Damn you," he muttered.

"As long as you don't damn her. I've only seen Meredith—are there others?"

"Sometimes. Best lock the door or you'll be sharing my lodgings."

She couldn't help but flinch. He noted it and smiled. How quickly had he found her soft spot.

"Why, Miss Callahan, have you already been a guest here?"

She managed only to shake her head.

"Still time to change your mind, turn that key and walk away."

Oh, how she wanted to. Instead, she pulled the key clear of the open lock, flashing a challenge with her eyes. "I'll see Meredith is occupied."

His eyebrows rose. No doubt he assumed the worst of her, and why not, after what he had already witnessed? Well, let him. What did it matter what a horse thief thought of her?

But it did matter. The whys of it, she would not consider.

Above them, Meredith's footsteps marked his return.

Bridget aimed a finger at Cole Ellis. "You vowed on her soul. Mark that."

She met Meredith by the stairs, allowing him to assist her up as she slipped the keys back into his pocket. Above deck, she drank the water he offered, keeping her attention on the galley door as Meredith kept his attentions on her. She didn't like the way his glance slid over her like oil, lingering on her bosom before traveling back up to meet her gaze.

She allowed him to aid her down the gangplank to Front Street, where she sat upon a barrel with a clear view of the ship. She waited there, busying Meredith with a performance worthy of the stage. But Mr. Ellis did not emerge. Damn the man. Had he passed out in his cell?

At last she gave up. "Thank you, Mr. Meredith. I am feeling recovered."

"I can send for a doctor. We have a hospital in town, right next to the cemetery."

"How convenient." She rose. "Thank you for your kindness."

"You aren't going up the mountain again, are you?"

She smiled. "Don't be silly."

His grin was hesitant, but it came at last, a confident smile that said he fully believed a woman would not be so impractical.

She gave the brig one last furious glare and then rose. "Good day to you."

He doffed his hat, showing greasy hair. She headed directly up J Street, past the mercantile shops and eateries. Should she stop and buy supplies? Bridget hesitated in the street. But what to purchase? The task seemed so overwhelming. At least she had money. Her sister had given her all that was left from the sale of George's shop. As a wheelwright, he'd been in high demand, both in Kentucky and as a member of the wagon train.

She had been in this city two weeks already, recovering her strength and trying in vain to rally a rescue party. How much salted oxen had her family consumed already?

She stopped at Ned's Kitchen, knowing from experience that the food was hearty and fairly priced. She settled on the elk stew, knowing it was bound to taste better than the last elk she'd eaten. But that one had saved her life.

The meal arrived with a generous biscuit still steaming from the pan. She savored the first spoonful of stew, holding it in her mouth as the thick concoction coated her tongue. How Mary would love this.

She opened her eyes and noted two men taking more interest in her than in their meals, so she reached in her pocket and removed the Colt revolver, laying it by her coffee. The men returned their attention to their food, allowing her to do the same.

After she settled her bill and was once more on the street, she had to resist the urge to march back down to the river and throttle Mr. Ellis herself. Why should the hangman have the satisfaction? Instead, she headed back to Mrs. Dickerson's hotel. Mr. Giles, of the *Sacramento Transcript*, had kindly paid for her room, in exchange for her giving him an exclusive story of her ordeal. She'd thought it a fine bargain until he accepted without haggling, making her wish she had asked for board, as well.

Bridget mounted the second flight of carpeted stairs, her slow tread reflecting her mood. At the top she passed the little table and flanking chairs, noticing that the flowers in the vase were starting to drop their petals, making them look as tired as she felt. One chair was askew, so she righted it.

It must have been ten degrees hotter on this level. No wonder her room was stifling. She would leave the transom open again tonight, hoping to entice the cooler evening air. She glanced up, noting that she'd failed to pull it shut before leaving this morning. Not that it mattered. Everything of value, save her coat, was on her person.

She fished in her pocket for her key and slipped it into

the lock. The click sounded and she turned the knob, swinging the door inward.

Catching movement across the room, she hesitated on the threshold.

There, making use of her pitcher and washbowl, stood Cole Ellis, stripped to the waist, his skin glistening wet.

Chapter Two

Cole turned, still holding the cloth that Bridget had used that very morning on her own naked flesh, flashing her an expansive view of muscular male torso that nearly stopped her heart. She'd never thought of a man's body as beautiful. But she had never really seen one, had she? On her only opportunity, he'd never removed so much as his shirt. *Do you love me, Bridget Rose?* She had thought so at the time. *Then give me some comfort, girl. Can't you see I'm burning for you?* Sean had a flattering tongue.

No, don't think of him. She lifted her attention to Cole Ellis. There was no better distraction.

The golden light from the setting sun danced off his chest as if it, too, longed to touch those flat planes and enticing valleys. He looked powerful, beautiful…dangerous. She became aware that no iron bars separated them now and felt vulnerable in a way that made her nerves jangle like sleigh bells.

How had she not seen what a stunning specimen he

was? Imprisoning him in a dim, dank cell had been like caging a mountain lion. Suddenly his incarceration seemed unnecessarily cruel. How could they want to kill such a man as this?

She lifted her gaze to meet his eyes and she found his lips curved in a knowing smile. Was he used to women buzzing about him like bees? That notion irked her, but she couldn't muster any indignation. He held her with those crystal-blue eyes, making promises he'd never keep.

Their differences struck her hard. She had been curvy before she had lost so much weight, while he was solid muscle. His hair was straight, dark and in need of a trim, and hers was all riotous red curls. His eyes were frosty blue, whereas hers were green as moss on a rock. Was that why he stared at her with such intensity? Her breasts ached from his direct stare. He did this to her without so much as a word.

Her innards trembled as he took up the cloth once more, dipping it and then running it over his face. He squeezed the rag, sending water down his square jaw to bounce off his chest. The droplets formed a river, cascading down his belly and disappearing into the cloth of his trousers. That was when she noticed that they were soaking wet, as if he had jumped in the river.

Her brow lifted. Was that why she hadn't seen him make his escape?

Say something, you silly little twit.

"I—I didn't expect...expect to see you again."

He smirked. "Come to your senses, then?"

Now, that did irk her. She gave her head a vehement shake.

He sighed and reached for his shirt. She chewed on her fingernail and admired the bunch of muscle as he dragged the garment over his head. *Look away*, she warned herself, but instead she stood mesmerized by the play of light and shadow on his abdomen until his head emerged from the shirt's neck. He raked his long fingers through his collar-length hair, forcing it away from his broad forehead. It stayed, for it was wet, as well.

She pointed to the puddle at his feet. "You're dripping on my floor."

He grinned and reached for the button on his trousers. "Want me to hang them to dry?"

Her cheeks heated as he slid the button through the hole. "No!"

The smile faded from his lips, releasing her from the spell of their locked gazes.

"Did anyone see you?" she asked.

"No one."

"How did you get here?"

Bridget focused her attention on his shirt, hoping it would help her beat down the roaring excitement that she had no business feeling at all.

"I climbed down the stern rope and swam to the western side of the American, then had to get back across."

It didn't explain how he came to be standing, in his nothing-at-all, in her room. "But how did you get in *here?*"

He pointed above her head. "Over the transom. Used the hall chair."

"And you knew my hotel by…?"

"You should be careful what you say to reporters. Might attract the wrong kind of person."

They shared a smile at his jest.

He took a step in her direction and she backed into the hall. The man made her sizzle like bacon in a pan. But she'd not tread that road again.

He didn't stop until he stood right before her. "That was a neat trick with the keys. Looked like you've had some practice." He reached her now, grasping her wrists, turning her palms up. Did he feel her tremble at his touch? "Lovely hands." He glanced up. "Lovely little thief's hands."

His words and the cynical stare cut her like a cleaver. For reasons she did not wish to explore, she wanted him to like her, both inside and out.

"Well, at least I have the good sense not to steal what will be missed."

He laughed. "Oh, I'll be missed."

She hadn't meant that but had referred to the keys she had lifted, and his slow, beguiling smile told her he knew it. Still, his words caused her to clench her fists until her knuckles whitened. He brought them to his lips, dropping a lingering kiss on her fingers before moving to her wrists. The warmth of his breath and heat of his mouth caused a rolling tension to build in her like water in a pot the instant before it boils over.

She tugged, but he held her in an unyielding grip. Why didn't he release her?

She found her voice, such as it was. "Perhaps I should have left you there."

"Most assuredly."

She ceased her attempts to escape and, in turn, he released her. She tossed her head, feigning indifference to his disturbing kisses. "You prefer hanging?"

"Why else would I steal the mayor's prize carriage horse?"

Did he tease her? He could not be serious, but still…

"Drunk as a squirrel sick on fermented apples is how I heard it."

"That does make more sense."

More sense than what? She came back to her earlier notion and found it hard to draw a breath. Cole was still drunk and possibly crazy. Did she dare trust her life to such a man? She frowned. There was not a line of volunteers waiting to take up her cause. She only had him by trickery and that did not feel good.

He stepped even closer, dropping his voice to a whisper. "We're the same, you and I."

Bridget backed away until she stood on the hall carpet. "We're not, because I wasn't caught." *Not this time*.

"Not yet. But how long until they put two and two together?"

And run straight to her doorstep.

Voices at the foot of the stairs triggered her to action. She pushed Cole back into her room with both hands and followed him as she drew the door shut, throwing the bolt. It wasn't until it clicked that she realized she had trapped herself inside with Cole Ellis—a suicidal horse thief whose eyes glittered with desire. How long had they locked him alone in that cell?

He didn't grab her, as she expected, but neither did he move off, as she hoped. Instead he stayed close beside her, pressing an ear to the door.

She felt the heat of him and backed away.

"Just guests." He righted himself.

But the authorities were searching even now. Bridget knew it and panic turned her knees to water. She wouldn't go to that brig. She wouldn't walk to the gallows. She gaped at him. What had she done?

"Sweet Mary and Joseph," she muttered, then exploded into motion, rushing to her bed and dragging her woolen coat from the headboard. All her other possessions covered her or were secreted in the folds of her skirts. "You have to go."

He nodded.

The knock on the door made her jump clean off the floor.

She stared at Cole, hoping he'd say something, but he only ducked behind the door.

"Who's there?" she called, finding her voice did not sound like her own.

"Mrs. Dickerson, dear. I brought the papers. You're featured again."

Bridget cracked the door.

Her landlady beamed at her, clutching the *Sacramento Transcript* to her amply endowed bosom. Bridget could see Cole staring intently through the gap between the door and frame.

"So exciting to have you here."

Bridget forced a smile, but her stomach tossed like a stormy sea.

She extended her hand for the paper.

"Such an adventure. I'd love to hear about it. I've put on a pot of tea and laid out my own biscuits. We could have a nice sit-down."

"That sounds lovely."

The innkeeper brightened, handing over the paper. "I'll see you in a few minutes, then."

Bridget nodded. She would have agreed to anything, just to see the woman's wide back descend the stairs. Mrs. Dickerson had barely turned to go when the door swung shut with a thud, revealing Cole, pressed flat to the striped wallpaper. With the sunlight gone, the room was now cast in gloom. The nights came early now that winter had its grip.

He stepped from the shadows and she repressed the urge to scream. She was trapped between the gallows and the mountains with only this menacing stranger to help her.

"What will we do?"

"We? I'm going down the back stairs—alone."

"But we have to—you promised to help me retrieve my family."

"Like you promised to ask only five questions?"

Bridget lowered her chin, preparing for a fight. "You made a vow."

He glared. "We'll never do it, not there and back. You're marching to your death and taking me with you."

"I'll take that chance."

"You're stubborn," he accused.

She smiled. "I'm Irish."

They stood facing off, she determined to hold him to his vow and he desperate to break it.

"Three people and one ox and they've been there since October?" He shook his head. "We'll never reach them in time."

"You did it before."

"I was too late."

"Not for all."

The hopelessness in his eyes told her that he had been too late for all that mattered to his heart.

She squared her shoulders, ready to defend him, even to himself. "You did your best."

His voice turned hard. "My best? They died." He pinned her with a look of pure hatred. "And I'll not be responsible for another death. Do you hear?"

"If you don't go, you'll be responsible for three."

"Better than four."

But what chance did she have without him? More important, what chance did Chloe and Mary have without him?

"What's this, then?" she asked, pressing her fists to her hips and emulating her mother's stance when she was on a tear. "Did you not agree?"

He raised his voice now, despite their situation. "Because I never expected you'd do it. I didn't know you were a pickpocket. I thought you'd go begging to the marshal, maybe try to persuade some judge." He scanned her from head to toe, letting her know exactly what he thought a poor Irish girl would use as currency. "I was trying to get rid of you."

The truth of that cut her like broken glass and she bristled.

"So you vowed on your wife's soul on the hopes I would fail?"

"I was drunk! I couldn't think straight with your harangue ringing in my ears. I just wanted peace."

The suspicion she'd had on their first meeting

returned. She leaned in. "What peace is that exactly that you'd be seeking?"

He pressed his lips together and said nothing.

It didn't stop her. "Say it! You want to die. It's why you chose the mayor's horse."

He spoke not a word of denial, only straightened in defiance.

Her face heated as fury burned within. "You made a vow."

"It's why I'm standing here, isn't it?"

"I'm not anxious to face the mountain with a man seeking his Maker."

"Then release me from my promise. I'll take my leave."

"I will not!"

"Then you're as daft as I am, because two people alone—we'll die before we ever reach them."

"Then you'll get your wish. Surely freezing is easier than the drop."

The look he gave her chilled her as surely as the long nights she'd struggled through deep snow. Hanging was quick, while freezing…. She could read it there, how close he'd come to dying on that mountain. Had he come as near as she? But he'd wanted to live then. Surely he must have, because only someone with that kind of will could escape the Cascades.

"Don't do it," he whispered. "Stay here. Live a good long life."

"Like you? You lost *your* family and look what it's done to you." She saw her own wretched future glimmering in his grieving eyes. He stood as living proof of what would become of her, should she fail.

He couldn't hold her gaze. His words came raw and low, as if wrenched from some deep pit of despair. "I'm not bringing you to your death. I can't."

"Then they are dead."

"We can't save them. But I can save you by walking away."

Cole turned and desperation made her reckless. "Would you still be going if it was your family up there? A child *you* loved?"

He turned and gaped. What had she said to cause his about-face?

His shock faded; his gaze fell. He stood silent and still. She thought she had never seen a person look so bereft. Her heart ached just to look at him, so raw was his sorrow.

The urge to reach out was hard to suppress. What had happened to him? What had happened to his kin?

When he looked up again, there was a clarity in his eyes that she had not seen before.

"Is there a child in your party?"

Bridget grew cautious at his black scowl and found she could only nod.

"Meet me round back."

A moment later, he was gone.

Chapter Three

Bridget stole out of the hotel, like the thief she'd once been, the thief she had become again. All the years of honest work vanished as she fell into the familiar pattern of stealth. Had it been ten years since she had worked the streets?

Now she carried her old coat and wore her shawl, all that she owned save the revolver. It thumped against her leg, but she found the weight a comfort as she crept toward an unknown future.

The laundry hung in Mrs. Dickerson's backyard in long even rows, fluttering like sails in the evening breeze.

Was he here or had he abandoned her?

She paused, listening, but heard only the cicadas' buzz. Though she did not see him, she believed he saw her. She didn't call out, for fear that might bring unwanted attention. Instead, she walked on into the darkness feeling his presence.

His voice came low and quiet, to her left.

"Here."

She moved into the shadows, finding him leaning against the towering stack of firewood. Shadowy and mercurial, his face held none of its earlier warmth. He wore the night like a familiar cloak, completely comfortable in the darkness.

"Why didn't you say there was a child?" His tone was accusing.

"I would have if I had thought it would sway you."

"How old?"

"Nearly a year now. She's my—sister's first child."

He stalked back and forth before the neatly stacked cords, moving with a power and grace. As she watched him, the sense of danger returned to her.

"And they've been trapped since?" He paused before her, the anxiety clear on his face. Why this sudden state of agitation? She had the sensation of someone pouring cold water down her back as the realization struck.

"You lost a child."

His pale eyes rounded as her supposition hit the mark. Yes, so obvious, now.

She stepped forward and clasped his hand. He started to draw back, but stopped, choosing instead to lace his fingers through hers.

"When did they die?" Bridget asked.

He swallowed before answering.

"Three years ago come January. I can't believe it's been so long."

"What were their names?"

"My wife was Angela and my daughter, Laura, but we called her Lee-lee. She was six."

The information struck Bridget hard. A girl, he'd had

a girl and she had died. Tears welled in her eyes. But she cleared her throat.

"Laura," she repeated. "A lovely name."

"Your niece?"

She stifled the urge to correct him, but could not. "Chloe."

His fingers slipped through hers like fish escaping the net. "We have to hurry."

She stood battling the lump in her throat as he absently rubbed his jaw.

Chloe had done what she could not. Cole would help her now. She knew it without question. He would help because of Lee-lee, the child he could not save.

"Have you any money?"

She hesitated and the intimacy they shared was slipping away. She wanted to trust him, but experience intruded. Never tell a thief you have coins.

"Some."

"Enough for supplies?"

She nodded.

"Horses?"

She broke eye contact, laying her coat on the woodpile. To buy horses would be to spend the last of her sister's funds, the money that came from five hard years of labor. It was her sister's future and she'd not squander it.

"Have to steal them, then," he muttered.

She shook her head. "I'll not be convicted of horse theft."

"Then you best not get caught, little thief."

She paled to have her secrets bared, especially by this insolent man. He might even give her up to escape capture. It had happened before. The betrayal had taught her a lesson.

"So you've been caught," he said, staring at her with knowing eyes.

Was it her trembling that told him she'd seen the inside of a prison, or her habit of gnawing her thumbnail ragged? Regardless, she'd not admit it to him or anyone. Shame and fear kept her mute.

He touched her then, his hand coming to rest gently on her shoulders as he gave a little squeeze. She gazed up into his eyes. The cynicism had vanished, replaced by the sincerest look of concern. Either he was genuinely sympathetic, or the best actor she'd come across.

The man's mood changed faster than the weather on the plains.

"It was long ago," she whispered.

"How long?"

"Thirteen years."

His grip tightened. "What? But you couldn't have been more than a child."

She nodded. Not yet nine when apprehended and nearly eleven when released.

"Where were your parents?"

"You've not been to Ireland. My parents could not stop it." She had not meant to lose control, but her shoulders gave a jump as the tears choked her throat. He drew her in, enveloping her in strong arms against the solid mass of his body. Her tears soaked the soft flannel of his dark blue shirt.

"There was no work, no food. Stealing was the only way."

"Shh." He whispered. "Don't fret. I'll do the stealing."

Small comfort, she thought.

She needed to tell him about the horses, but somehow the words stuck. She tried again, clearing her throat.

"I can't ride."

His reply was a hiss, like a boiling teapot. "What?" He drew back. With him went the only comfort she'd had in months.

She dashed away the tears that showed her for the coward she truly was. Her pride returned and she spat her reply before he could find fault. "Not everyone grew up in the country, with servants and riding lessons."

"I grew up in Vermont, riding a swaybacked mule and herding sheep."

"Dublin."

"After that?"

The year of her release, her parents migrated, crossing on one of the coffin ships. She thanked God they had not left her behind and that they had all survived that dreadful voyage.

But families made sacrifices for one another. They did what they must to remain together and she would do no less for Mary and Chloe.

"Kentucky. My father and brother worked the mines, but a cave-in took Conor."

"I'm sorry, then."

Bridget glanced up at him and saw the raw pain reflected in Cole's eyes. It was something else they shared—the sorrow. He had lost his wife and his child. How much deeper did that heartache cut?

Bridget could think of nothing to say that could mend their hearts, so she fell to euphemism. "Well, it was God's will."

Cole snorted, his expression pure disdain. Bridget narrowed her eyes. The man seemed to have a grievance against God Himself.

"It wasn't God who led those children to that pass," said Cole.

The weight of guilt crushed the breath from her and her face felt prickly hot.

Cole met her gaze only an instant before glancing away. "I'm sorry." He fiddled with his thumbnail a moment. At last he lifted his head, his expression now tight with strain. "We need to steal two horses."

She struggled with her emotions, finally swallowing her grief as she had done so many times in her life.

"Horses again. I told you I cannot ride."

"I'll see you don't fall."

That prospect made her straighten. But instead of in-dignation, she felt a tingling anticipation low in her belly.

Her burning face must have given her away, for the smile he cast her was knowing. The raw passion glitter-ing in his eyes pierced her like a dart from Cupid's bow. How did he speed her heart with just a look?

She summoned her flagging self-control, shaking off her desire as if it were water clinging to her bare skin. When she finished, she still felt wet. She scowled at him, vowing not to yield to the promise in his eyes. She knew exactly where such lies would lead her.

Didn't they have worries aplenty without adding one more?

"If we ride double, why do we need two horses?"

He lifted his brow. "Because we have to move faster than the posse. That means changing horses and reaching the pass before they reach us."

The chill returned to her flesh. The mountains loomed before them and the posse nipped, like wolves, at their heels.

Cole extended his hand, hoping she would take it. She hesitated an instant before clasping her warm palm to his. Had the prospect of riding in his arms unsettled her as much as it had him?

"This way," he said, not looking back. The evening breeze swept her fresh scent to him, tantalizing him as he led Bridget away from the hotel, making use of the alleyway and then cutting through the backyards until he thought them well enough away for her not to be recognized. This city had grown to some 7,000 souls, but his likeness had appeared regularly in the paper. By tomorrow, every mother-loving one of Sacramento's honest citizens would be on the lookout.

Now that he knew about the child, he'd do what he could to see they had what they needed. How they went about procuring those goods depended on Bridget.

"We need supplies."

"It's too late for a mercantile." When he did not reply, her look turned wary. "You'll not be stealing them. I said I'll buy what's needed."

It was a foolish thing to say to a thief. If he was another kind of man, he might be inclined to press his advantage. The devil emerged within him, that irksome, playful boy he had once been. How had she roused that part of him which had lain dormant so long?

He paused in the dim light next to a large mercantile. Above the building's front door, a barely visible sign read Von Broch, Merch. He released her hand, already smiling in anticipation.

"How do you know I won't just relieve you of that purse in your skirts?"

She didn't look frightened, which surprised him, considering he outweighed her by at least a hundred pounds. Instead, she cast him a speculative look as if measuring his will.

"How do you know it's in my skirts?"

"I can hear the coins clink." He challenged her with his smile.

Her eyes sparkled in response, but she did not return his smile. "It's not where I keep the bulk of my savings."

All sorts of possibilities rose at her words. His mouth went dry as he took in her glittering eyes and wondered again what kind of a woman she was.

"Might be interesting trying to find it." He stepped closer still, letting her feel the difference in their size and strength. He expected her to retreat, but she held her ground.

"Since you are so interested in my skirts," she said, answering his challenge, "perhaps you'd care to be guessing what I carry in my other pocket."

Her eyes shone dangerously, confusing him. His wife had been pliant and mothering. She'd never challenged him, except at the end. Angela didn't scrap like this woman. Bridget reminded him of a stray cat and it fascinated him. He glanced at the pocket in question, noting for the first time her fist buried deep within.

Before he could guess, he heard a familiar click that removed all doubt.

He gazed in utter amazement. "You'd shoot me?"

"I will do if you don't step back, you son of a bitch."

He did, astonished at her nerve and horrified by her language. This was a woman of a new mold. "I was only teasing you, Bridget."

Uncertainty flickered in her eyes for a moment and then the steely confidence returned. "Well, I'm not."

What had she endured to make her so ready to fight, even against a jest?

He decided to drop a topic that might cause her to blow away a part of his anatomy that was very dear to him. He retreated farther into the street until he stood before the dark storefront.

"If you're buying, I'll get the owner. He lives above his establishment."

She seemed uncertain about this course of action, so he offered a second.

"Or we could sit on his stoop until he opens and hope we're not spotted. What do you think they'll do to you when they discover how I got out of the brig?"

She gasped and he felt a pang of regret.

This woman had the courage of a bear. He admired her for it. Likely she'd spent her entire life dodging bullies and men who tried to take advantage of her. Any woman as lovely as Bridget would attract plenty of unwanted attention.

She certainly heated his blood. He never felt like this about any woman, including Angela.

And he'd loved his wife—treasured her, in fact. She was so good, so loving and kind. A better mother, a man could not find for his child. And she had never made him feel unwelcome in their bed. Their lovemaking had been deep and quiet and tender. He missed the comfort of her embrace and the soft kisses she pressed to his brow.

But this woman beside him had a determined tilt to her chin, fire glinting in her eye and a loaded revolver in her pocket. She would not be above using her claws to put out an eye. He'd never met anyone like her.

Bridget had not lain down and died when she should have. She had kept on until she reached the valley. A survivor—like him. Someone who would fight until the end and then fight some more.

He recognized the strength that he had never before seen in a woman and it called to him.

Bridget's gaze traveled from him to the darkened storefront.

"All right then."

With Bridget following him, he walked round the back and up the staircase to the second floor, where he knocked on a windowpane. Light flickered as someone approached carrying a lamp. A man appeared in the hall beyond the room that Cole now recognized as a kitchen. He wore a white shirt and vest, dark trousers and a frown that dragged his bushy mustache down until it completely concealed his lower lip. The lantern cast light beneath his chin, nose and brow, making him a frightening specter. Cole had chosen this man because he had never laid eyes on him. He hoped the shopkeeper would not recognize him from the drawing in the paper.

"Were you really prepared to shoot me?" he asked Bridget, even as he raised his hand to Von Broch.

"Aye." The lack of hesitation gave him pause. "My sister gave me charge of her funds. I'll not be giving them over without a fight."

The idea of a skirmish with her heated his blood, but he beat back the desire as if extinguishing a brush fire. But the trouble with a brush fire is that even when you think it's out, it burns along the roots and flares up somewhere else. He very much feared that this woman would do the same to him.

"Cole?"

He was staring at her like a lovesick elk.

He cleared his throat. "She must have had confidence in your ability to reach safety."

She gave a mirthless laugh. "Or she reckoned the money did little good up there."

It was true. If Bridget's assessment of her sister's situation was correct, they would not live to spend it. Better to send it where it might do some good.

Von Broch reached for the door and jerked it open.

"What do you want?"

"Supplies," said Cole.

"Then come back tomorrow." The door began to close. Cole felt Bridget step forward, even as he heard her draw a breath—whether to plead or argue, he did not know, nor did he discover, because he raised his hand, touching her stomach, staying her. She stilled, deferring to him for the moment.

"We'll do that, but we mean to spend over fifty dollars, and come morning we'll be spending it at Strauss's instead."

Von Broch frowned. "You won't get as good a price there."

"That's why we came to you first."

Von Broch considered for only a moment, then stepped out onto the landing and locked his door. "Follow me."

He led them down the stairs and through the back by the light of one kerosene lamp. Upon reaching the store proper, he hung the lantern on a nail from a crossbeam.

Bridget could not keep her attention from the large store windows. The dark glass reflected the room in vivid detail. Anyone walking by would see them inside.

Her stomach knotted as she moved to stand between Cole and the all-seeing dark pane. But when trouble came, it came not from her back, but from her front.

Von Broch studied Cole. "Haven't I seen you before?"

Chapter Four

Mary Callahan Flynn carried the gun with her everywhere she went now. Not that she was afraid of the bull elk—no, her fears ran deeper than that. It was the elk that should fear her. She'd missed her chance earlier, because she had left the gun with George.

Now she followed its tracks, feeling her energy dissolving like the snowflakes on her cheek as she floundered in thigh-deep snow. The elk, aided by stiltlike legs, seemed unimpeded by the drifts. How much advantage did it gain with each minute? Eventually, she gave up. There was nothing to do but hope it wandered too close to camp again.

The gnawing, fearful voice in her mind said it would not. She had seen no game at all, save that one elk, since the arrival of the heavy snows.

Chloe wiggled against her, making a familiar sound of frustration. At eleven months, the child still needed to be carried everywhere and the cold kept her close. Mary used her shawl to hold the babe to her breast and belly.

"What's the matter, darling?"

But she knew. Chloe had had no milk for three weeks and did not like the substitute of beef broth she was now forced to eat.

Mary gazed down, noting that Chloe's once fat cheeks had sunken as she lost weight. A spike of dread drove straight through her heart.

Chloe smiled. "Da!"

"Yes, Daddy's getting better, now. Perhaps he can kill that elk." George called it a sprain, but Mary was certain he had broken his leg. Six weeks had passed since the lame ox had caused them to fall behind the group, and then the snows had come and they had struggled to cross the pass. George and Bridget had pushed and Mary drove the ox. The wagon had slid sideways over George's leg. The gash had healed, thank God above, but still he hobbled painfully, unable to put weight on it.

As she adjusted Chloe's red knit hat, tucking a wayward strand of red-gold hair beneath it, Mary glanced up and noticed smoke. A frown wrinkled her brow as she gazed at it. Why had he built the fire so high?

Of course it was cold, but gathering fuel grew more difficult by the day, because of the snowfall and the ever-increasing distance between them and dead wood.

The scream froze her to the spot. The rifle slipped from her fingers and into the snow. Mary snatched it up in one hand, clutched Chloe in the other and ran.

The deep drifts tore at her flagging strength, and she saw how weak she had become. For a dreadful moment she felt she could not make the two hundred feet back to camp.

She rounded the line of pines and halted. Thick smoke and flames burst from the canvas roof, carrying smoldering bits aloft. The green log walls George had hastily laid for shelter now hissed as the sap beneath the thin bark boiled. The dead logs covering the canvas roof exploded into flame like torches.

"George!"

Where was he? Please, God, not inside.

She ran again, tired legs pumping as Chloe's fingers dug into her neck.

"George!"

She saw him then, his coat smoking—or was that his hair?

He staggered from the inferno of their crumbling shelter.

She dropped to his side.

He reached a blackened hand to take Chloe. "Get the blankets."

Sweet Jesus, all their quilts. She rushed forward, circling the structure and finding no place, no opportunity, to breach the wall of flame. What could she use?

Mary ran to the pines, breaking off the largest green branch she could manage and dragging it back to the shelter.

She shoved the limb inside, trapped the quilts between the branch and the ground, then hauled them through the gap. She had the log cabin quilt, but not the friendship quilt. She tried again, coming away with a pillow. The down spilled from a tear as she hauled it out.

The logs began collapsing now, caving in on the center. She used her branch as a club to beat at the unstable wall. Again and again she struck at the burning logs, until the needles of her own limb blazed.

Her efforts caused the dwelling to topple to the left and she rushed forward trying to rescue something more. She saw the second quilt. A shower of sparks now ate through the layers. She grabbed it, throwing it clear.

Mary retrieved the woolen blanket next, though it seemed nothing but a charred ruin. Finally, she dropped to her knees beside the sorry collection and sobbed.

How could this have happened? Hadn't she set the fire well away from their home?

She rose and turned to George. He lay on his back, holding Chloe to him. As she neared, she smelled the acrid stench of singed hair.

"Are you all right, George?" she whispered.

Soot streaked his face and the shell of his ear held a raw burn. He stared at her through bloodshot eyes and said nothing. His forlorn expression so worried her that it took a moment for her to notice his hands.

Mary gasped. "Oh, George!"

She grasped his wrists, turning his palms up. Both were a mass of growing blisters. Some of the sores had burst and wept with Mary.

"What have you done to your hands?"

He shook his head in dismay.

"Put them in the snow," she told him.

"I'm sorry, Mary."

"It's none of your doing, now, is it?"

His sad eyes said otherwise. She bit back the question that sprang to her lips.

"I was cold. So cold. I dragged a few coals inside.

Just a small fire." He broke the contact of their gaze as the shame grew too great to bear. "My fault."

She moved to grasp his hand, but recalling his injuries, she wrapped her arms around his neck and held him tight. "I shouldn't have left you so long."

His shoulders jumped and a cry came from deep inside him. They had been married nearly two years and until this day, she had never seen him weep. It frightened her worse than her hunger, worse than the fire, worse than his blistered hands. "Oh, Mary, what have I done?"

"Hush, now. We'll build another. Sure, it will be all right."

Chloe cried now as well and tugged at Mary's arm.

They huddled together, the three of them, weeping and hugging and mourning their losses—so many losses.

Bridget stood in panic as the shopkeeper eyed Cole. Bridget had seen Cole's likeness in the newspapers several times over the past few days and was certain Von Broch would recall him. She clenched her hand around the pistol and waited.

Cole's reaction was so transient that if she had not been watching him closely, she would have missed the instant's hesitation. He squinted for just the time it takes to draw breath and then spoke.

She realized it was his *tell*, the physical sign he gave when lying, and tucked that bit of information away in her memory.

"Not likely, we're just down from our claim," he said.

Von Broch nodded, but his frown made Bridget think he was still trying to place Cole.

Cole distracted him by setting about collecting goods, picking out a large sheet of tin, dried elk, buffalo, raisins and rolled oats.

"Coffee, sugar and flour?" she asked.

He shook his head. "Flour is too heavy and coffee and sugar are a waste of space. We'll drink melted snow."

Von Broch lifted his bushy brow. "You two headed to a gold claim?"

"Right up on the snow line," Cole confessed. "We might even need snowshoes."

"I got 'em."

Cole turned to Bridget. "What caliber is that pistol?"

She didn't know. It had been George's prize possession, purchased from a Texan who had fought in the Mexican War. Her gaze shifted from Von Broch to Cole. At last she lifted the pistol from its concealment and handed it, butt-first, to Cole. It was the first time the handgun had left her possession since she'd struck out alone. She felt stripped naked without it and stood in mute discomfort as Cole examined the firearm.

"Forty-four caliber Walker. That'll do." He handed it back.

She breathed a sigh of relief and stashed it again.

Cole turned to the merchant. "We'll take three boxes of cartridges, four pairs of snowshoes and fifty feet of rope, a buffalo robe, three blankets, six yards of canvas and I need a coat." He turned to Bridget, lifting a brow.

"I have one," she said, lifting the bundle she carried.

"Wool?" he asked.

She nodded.

He glanced at her feet, then back to Von Broch. "You

got men's boots small enough for her, wool trousers and mittens made of moose hide?"

"Got the mittens, but boots and trousers?" He shook his head. "Boys', maybe."

The supplies were finally tallied and the price negotiated. Bridget wondered how they would carry all of it out of the store, let alone all the way to Broadner Pass, but she reached for her purse and paid the sum without flinching.

It was more money than she had spent at once in her entire twenty-two years.

Cole gave her the smaller pack, helping her shoulder the weight before lifting his own. They headed back out into the night. Each of them had two sets of snowshoes strapped to their back along with the food. He carried the blanket, canvas and buffalo robe. But her pack was still heavy enough for her to wonder how she would manage on the icy inclines ahead.

They had not walked a quarter mile before the pack began to dig into her shoulders. She readjusted the straps and continued on.

"Who exactly is up there?" he asked.

"My sister, Angela, her husband, George, and Chloe."

"Then why didn't George walk out, instead of you?"

Why, indeed. Bridget prepared herself for a storm. "On account of the wagon getting mired on the pass and running over his leg."

Cole paused, forcing Bridget to do the same.

"He can't walk?"

"Not when I left them."

"When were you planning on telling me?"

Of course it was the kind of information one needed when buying supplies and organizing a rescue and she knew it.

"I thought if I told you, you would not come." She fidgeted with her ragged thumbnail. "I'm sorry."

He didn't belabor the point, which surprised her. She rarely said she was sorry and had found that most men, once they'd discovered an error, laid out in great detail how this mistake had done harm and then proceeded to point out several ways that she could have gone about handling the situation in a much more reasonable fashion. Cole only glanced her way. The frown faded and was soon replaced by a look of speculation. He drew a breath.

Here it comes, she thought. But he surprised her again.

"What else should I know?"

He hadn't tried to back out, nor make her feel stupid. She gazed at him in wonder. Whatever else the man might be, he was a man of his word. She rubbed the back of her neck as she thought what else she might say.

"Mary was in good condition, but she's having to fetch all the wood in deep snow. She's tending the fire and seeing to the baby. She's eleven months now. Ten when I left her." Bridget wondered if Chloe had grown and then remembered how Mary worried, with the milk gone, if Chloe would manage on solid food.

"Wait," he said and dropped his pack, returning the way he had come. He emerged a few moments later with the runners for a sled, which he strapped to his pack. They headed down the street, side by side.

Cole glanced at her. "Why did your sister stay behind?"

"She wouldn't leave him, though he begged her to take Chloe and go. Families stay together, she said."

Bridget had heard the same thing nearly all her life. But it was a lie, for when trouble had come to her and she'd needed her father the most, he had cast her out like rubbish. But Mary would not. Her sister meant what she said. Bridget recalled Mary's words.

"She told him she'd sooner die herself than leave him to freeze to death, alone on the mountain." Bridget had begged her to come as well, much to her shame, but for different reasons. At first she thought their best chance for survival was to abandon the wagon and try to escape on foot. But before she mentioned the idea to Mary, she made her first attempt to break trail and she had learned the truth. It had taken three hours to go less than a mile. The snow was too deep and she came to believe that— nothing without wings could get out of that valley alive. She had lived by sheer luck—by the storm that she'd thought would kill her but had given her those wings.

She looked at the man beside her. How had he done it?

"They sent you because you were strongest," he said.

"No, they were against my going."

"Why did you, then?"

What she thought was, *because I knew how much faster they'd starve with me eating a third of their ox.* But what she said was, "Because it was their only chance."

She slipped up by saying *their* instead of *our.* But he did not appear to note it.

"Small chance," he muttered.

"Better than none."

She had not expected to make it. That was why she had skipped back half the rations after her sister had fallen asleep.

"How did you do it?"

"Stubbornness," she admitted and then smiled. "And luck."

"Luck?"

She recognized the suspicion in his gaze. He didn't trust her, and why should he? She'd already tricked him once.

"Yes, just when I couldn't go on, I saw a raven. It called to me as it winged along and landed on a great brown mound that I hadn't noted. It was a carcass and it saved my life."

He frowned.

She smiled. "A bear, I think."

His scowl deepened further. "You found a bear carcass, just lying there?"

When she nodded, he scoffed.

"Bears hibernate. They aren't out in winter."

She thought back to the coarse brown coat and the size of the carcass. Could she have been mistaken?

"I thought it was a bear."

He halted, his expression dark as an approaching storm. "Who was with you?"

"What?"

"Who else was there?"

"I told you, I was alone."

"You said you came out alone."

"It's the same thing."

His eyebrows rose in astonishment. "No. It's not."

He went silent then, leaving her to ponder his words. What the devil did it matter if it was bear or moose or a unicorn—so long as it sustained her?

He did not speak for what seemed an eternity. His cold gaze assessed her, trying, it seemed, to read her very soul. "You came out alone."

She nodded, knowing he implied something, but not able to grasp it. His sour expression said he did not believe her.

"You walked over the pass, *my pass*, without snowshoes and with only five days' rations, with the snow twenty feet deep in places. You should have sunk up to your armpits. But you made it out in…"

He lifted his brow in question, waiting for her to finish his sentence.

"Nine days."

"Nine days, without rations or snowshoes."

"That's right."

His cold smile froze her like the mountain winds.

"You, Miss Callahan, are not only a thief, but a liar."

She gasped, not understanding his words or his expression. It looked like appreciation, but also contempt. His hot breath fanned her cheek. He whispered to her then, his words both a tender caress and bitter condemnation.

"We two are cut from the same cloth, you and me. Thieves and liars." His lips moved against her ear, sending a flash of desire scorching through her blood. "We've done things, things we'll never speak of. Isn't that right, love?"

She nodded. He knew. Somehow he knew about her secrets, because he had secrets of his own. It frightened her and thrilled her to know this man could see into her soul.

He stroked her cheek, staring earnestly into her eyes.

Had it been only a year ago she had vowed never, ever to let a man near her again? But this was no ordinary man—this was some mind reader who knew what she was and still wanted her.

What was she doing? Here she was fleeing the city with a man sentenced to hang, running for their lives. She had no time to moon over him as if she'd known him all her life, instead of a few short hours. She bristled.

"Don't be supposing that you know me, because you don't." She pushed him away. "We're strangers."

The guarded expression was back, firmly fixed upon his face with his familiar smirk. She didn't like it, but when she thought of the pain and the passion she'd seen when his mask had slipped, she thought she preferred this cold, cynical man to the one who fired her blood. She felt the walls around her heart forming, like ice encasing a tender pine needle, sheltering the needle and keeping it safe.

Had she learned nothing from her mistakes? Men could not be trusted. Not fathers or brothers or men who whispered promises in the dark.

Chapter Five

Together they reached the eastern edge of town, passing the hospital and halting before the graveyard. When Bridget saw he meant to walk through such a place at night, she drew up short.

"You're not going in there." It was not a question.

He slid his hands under the straps of his pack, telling her without words that he struggled with his load as well. He carried double her burden, making her marvel at his strength.

"I'll be quick."

It occurred to her then that he was not choosing the fastest route to their destination, but rather had reached his destination.

"She's buried here?"

He nodded, gazing off to the northern side of the cemetery.

"I just want to say goodbye. I haven't left her since her burial."

He'd brought her from the mountain, all that way, to

place her here. The love he had for his wife poked at Bridget like a sharp awl, pointing out all that he had once had and that she lacked. The man she thought she loved had not even cast her a backward glance. The shame and humiliation stuck and burned like hot pitch.

Cole removed his pack. "You wait here."

She certainly would. No telling what kind of evil spirits lingered about a graveyard this time of night.

Bridget lowered her burden and sat upon the bundle, watching him move off in the moonlight. A flicker of apprehension ignited in her belly and she stood as the idea took shape. She opened her mouth to call out and then stopped, issuing a low whistle instead.

Cole paused and turned. She motioned like a mad woman and, thank Sweet Mother Mary, he returned to her. His wrinkled brow showed he did not appreciate being summoned like a hound.

"They'll be waiting for you," Bridget whispered.

The frown deepened to a scowl.

"Don't be ridiculous."

"If I was looking for you, I'd send men here on the chance you'd be stupid enough to come."

Cole stiffened.

Another thought occurred to her and she leveled a finger at him. "And don't think to get out of your promise by walking into a trap."

Cole now craned his neck to look toward his destination. His body radiated uncertainty. At last he faced her. "I'll scout the ground first."

"They'll catch you."

"Wait here." He hunched over and headed in the

opposite direction, leaving Bridget with nothing to do but pick at the cuticle of her thumbnail until it bled. She pressed her index finger to the tiny geyser of blood, feeling the sting of her torn skin as she waited.

She listened to the wind rustle the leaves of the mighty sycamore as she crouched by the iron fence. Beyond, the headstones cast eerie shadows on the ground. One grave caught her attention for two reasons. The domed earth indicated a fresh grave and it was small.

She froze in horror, wondering what mother wept for her lost child. The pain of that thought threatened to sink her, so she concentrated on what she would do if her unreliable guide got himself apprehended. Here she was with two packs of goods and the strength for only one. She needed to hide his. That sent her dragging his gear into the row of bushes on the right side of the gate. Surely any visitors entering by the conventional route would not note it. That meant she might elude notice under the holly bushes as well. She returned for her own. The crunch of gravel beneath a foot froze her to the spot.

Moonlight shone behind him, casting his face in shadow. But she recognized the tilt of his hat.

"Bridget," he whispered from the place she had just vacated.

"Here."

He crept to her hiding place and crouched on his haunches before her.

"You were right. There were three of them waiting just out of sight." He shook his head slowly, like a hound too close to the fire. "I almost walked right in to them."

"Did they see you?"

"No." He grasped her hand and brought her palm to his lips.

Her breath caught at the warm pressure of his mouth.

"Thank you," he said.

She didn't know what astonished her more, the tingling delight of his mouth on the sensitive skin of her hand or hearing a man say "thank you." His gratitude meant something more, she realized. He was no longer hell-bound to stick his head in a noose. She smiled, as hope returned to her, peeking like sunshine through dark clouds. Perhaps, just perhaps, she might see her family again.

"Let's go," she whispered.

Quiet as grave robbers, they slipped into their packs and crept along the fence toward the east. It was some time before Bridget's heartbeat returned to normal.

They walked past the quiet outskirts of the city. Cole kept close to the buildings now, never venturing out into the moonlight.

Bridget had recently traveled this way, only in the opposite direction, and she recognized the livery used by the California Stage Company up ahead. The sizable corral lay on the southern side, protected by the barn. Here some of the best horses rested, awaiting the daily arrival of the stage from San Francisco. These horses were fleet and young and tended to better than most of the citizens in Sacramento.

Bridget's heart began hammering again as she realized what Cole was up to.

He pulled into an alley between a blacksmith and a saddler. Silently, he disposed of his pack, stowing it behind a large barrel. Bridget followed his lead.

"I'll try for two with saddles."

She could barely speak past the fear rising in her throat. "What if they catch you again?"

He gave her a grim smile. "They can still only hang me once."

That made her feel no better. His smile turned genuine and he stroked the soft skin beneath her chin in a gesture she felt he intended to lighten the moment. Instead, his touch galvanized her. Had she gasped? She must have, for his gaze raked her, his eyes glimmering with such fierce intensity that she thought she should retreat. Instead, she lifted her tired arms and looped her hands about his neck.

He needed no further invitation. In an instant he had her pinned against his body. She had only intended to give him a kiss for luck. But it was a lie. She'd wanted to fall into his arms since she'd first seen him half-naked at her washstand.

He pressed his mouth hard to hers, taking possession of her, his lips demanding she return the passion he gave. She closed her eyes and obeyed. Her stomach fluttered and then lurched, as if she were falling. His mouth, that silken decadent mouth, made her giddy with desire. He set her gently away.

"You've the worst taste in men, Bridget," he chided.

"So my mother tells me." Had she really said that aloud? Oh, no, he'd made her lose her wits. Would he guess what her words implied?

Instead, he chuckled. The sound was new to her ear and she smiled at the rich, earthy tone. He smiled at her now, not the familiar belittling smirk, but a true, warm and glowing light that warmed her to the core.

"You are a most unusual woman, Bridget Callahan." His smile died as he glanced over his shoulder.

She grasped his elbow. "Please be careful."

Their eyes met. "I know you're worried about my skin. It's the whys that plague me."

He turned to go and she let him. He made it one step before turning back.

"If I'm caught, go to the hotel and forget you ever saw me. Understand?"

She nodded, gnawing her lower lip as he slipped into the shadows and out of sight.

Bridget tried to stay put, but she'd never been good at waiting. Her impatience had caused her much difficulty and tonight seemed to be no exception. She blew out a sharp, frustrated breath.

It was noble of him to let her hide in safety while he took all the risk of getting their horses. He was a brave man.

Suddenly, a more suspicious thought struck her.

"He wouldn't dare," she muttered. But why not? What was to stop him, after all?

She followed Cole Ellis and found him a few minutes later, in the barn. He had a horse bridled and set a heavy saddle upon its broad back. Nothing seemed amiss, except that he only had one horse.

She glanced about the dark interior, wondering why her neck tingled. Bridget pressed her back to the wall, resisting the urge to escape the way she had come. Something was not right.

A man stepped from a stall, not ten inches from where she halted. Did he hear her gasp?

"Hold it," he ordered.

Cole whirled about as the man drew back the hammer of his raised revolver. Bridget blinked, trying desperately to force her eyes to adjust to the dim light in the barn's interior.

"Deputies warned us you might be after a horse. You picked the wrong livery, Ellis." He stepped forward, standing right before Bridget, who now had her hand pressed to her mouth to keep from crying out. "I had the day off tomorrow, to see your hanging."

"Sorry to disappoint you," said Cole, as if they were discussing the weather.

"You won't. I'll have you back in time, unless I have to shoot you."

He certainly seemed prepared to do just that.

"On your belly."

Cole stared at the man but did not seem to see Bridget trembling in the shadows. He glanced about and the man aimed at the center of his chest. It was then Bridget recalled the revolver in her pocket. She could not shoot the man, because that would bring others, and if she used the handle as a club, the gun might go off.

Cole had no defense, since she held the gun. His captor waved the barrel at him and he dropped to his knees and then his belly.

"How'd you do it?"

Cole didn't answer.

"They can't figure how you picked that lock."

Bridget kept a hand over her mouth. They didn't know. She inched toward the door. If she slipped out, she could return to the hotel and forget this nightmare.

Tomorrow she'd try again to get assistance from the authorities.

There must be someone who would help her.

There was someone, but he lay in the dirt now with a gun pointed at his head.

Someone else, then.

Bridget slipped through the door and ran back to the alley. There she crouched behind the barrel and squeezed her eyes shut tight. She was away and no one knew what she had done. They wouldn't track her or arrest her or throw her in that godforsaken brig.

She hugged herself and rocked. Mary's voice shrieked at her from the past. *Run, Bridget! Run away!*

She clamped her hands over her ears to shut out her sister's voice echoing through her mind and making her blood run icy cold. She shook like a sapling in a winter storm as her past rushed back.

Funny old life, thought Cole, facedown on the livery floor. He'd been more than ready to mount the gallows steps. Anxious, even. Then that crazy woman tricked him into making a promise. His promise—his, a horse thief and worse. That's why it was so ironic that he still felt he needed to keep his word. She made him forget who and what he was.

She made him forget. She made him laugh, made him long for her in a way he never thought to experience in his miserable life. He could scarcely believe it himself. The worst part was that she made him feel. Bridget had given him back his desire to live, the day before his execution.

The stagecoach hand had him good and proper. Cole thought he might have a chance if the man was foolish enough to try and tie him. If he were smart, he'd holler for help.

"Don't you try—umph!"

Cole cocked his head at the thud accompanying that last utterance. An instant later his captor fell hard, landing right beside him. Cole pushed up onto his hands to peer in confusion at the downed man. He lay there with eyes closed, breathing through his open mouth as if he'd just decided to take a snooze.

Cole had only to turn his head to find the cause. Bridget stood clutching a chunk of firewood in both her trembling hands.

"Is he dead?"

Cole checked again. "Nope."

The wood slipped from her pale fingers, clunking to the earth floor. She crossed herself. "God forgive me."

Cole grinned. "He might, but this feller won't and now they'll know I'm not alone."

This news did not make her pause or quake. It was as if she'd considered all this before swinging that chunk of wood.

"Shall we tie him then?" she asked, as casually as if asking if he preferred his coffee black or with sugar.

The woman frightened him at times.

"Better do, I think," she said, answering her own question and then wandering off, possibly to look for rope.

Cole retrieved his hat, dusting the crown before collecting the man's firearm and tucking it into his own trousers. Then he replaced his hat and bridled the closest horse, a large dark gelding, with a chest as broad as an ox's. He had the beast saddled before Bridget returned with the rope, which she offered to him.

"My knots slip," she said, as if she regularly bound men hand and foot and so knew her efforts would be for naught.

He tied the man and laid him with the hay, and then thought to gag him as well.

Cole glanced at his work and then touched the brim of his hat. "Enjoy your day off."

Together he and Bridget led the horses toward the alley, where he secured their gear on the smaller gelding. He'd decided to ride the larger mount after noting the feathers on the legs and realizing it must be at least part draft.

Bridget stood holding the smaller gelding, her head swiveling at each sound. He hurried to secure the load.

That done, he gathered the lead line of the packhorse and stepped up into the saddle of the first. Finally, he offered his free hand to Bridget. Hard to believe that a woman who could pick locks, bust men over the head with cordwood and kiss like her blood were on fire had failed to learn to ride.

As she settled against his back, he was glad for the gap in her education. He was enjoying this, enjoying Bridget settling against him, enjoying life. It was something he never would have considered possible.

Chapter Six

Bridget wondered whether the authorities had discovered that the horses were missing yet. When they did, they'd know Cole was not alone.

"Dawn's coming." Cole's voice startled her. "We'll stop and switch horses."

Bridget allowed him to lower her to the ground.

"Do you think they are following us?"

Cole dropped down beside her. "Depends. They'll likely think I'm headed toward San Francisco."

"But the shopkeeper saw us together."

"Clear on the other side of town. Might take a while to connect us."

But they would connect them.

"I hit that man. They'll know you have help."

"That could be anyone."

"You're just trying to ease my mind."

He grinned, brushing his thumb along her jaw. "Maybe."

He looked like he might kiss her again. She stepped

back. This man was too alluring. She thought to herself that a woman with her experience would have better control, but Cole made her forget consequences and that made him nearly as dangerous as the mountains.

She looked down the road they had traveled, searching in the gray light for the hounds. "They're there somewhere."

He looped an arm over her shoulder and dragged her close. She looked up at him, surprised at the relaxed smile.

"You best look the other way." He thumbed over his shoulder. "The real danger is that way."

The Cascades—yes, that was right. She shivered and he squeezed her tight a moment before releasing her.

"I mean to reach the snow line before we stop. Take me a few minutes to change the packs, if you want some privacy."

Her cheeks heated, but she made her way off to the brush and out of sight. When she returned she found the horses munching their grain from sacks hanging from their necks and Cole nowhere in sight.

Her stomach clenched as she considered the dangerous path she had taken. Up until last night, there had been a very good chance that she would walk away from this entire mess and never look back. It appeared the jailor had not mentioned her visit to the authorities, or at least had not connected it to Cole's escape.

Had the guard seen her? She thought he'd turned his head as she struck him. The memory of the blow ripped through her. She had felt the vibrations through her wrists and arms and then again through the soles of her feet as he landed before her.

The decision to throw in her lot with Cole Ellis had been made the moment she raised that chunk of firewood.

"Reconsidering?"

Cole stood not four feet before her and she had not even heard him approach.

Had she been? Perhaps.

"I'm just wondering how we'll get away. I mean, they're sure to figure it out, and all they have to do is wait at the base of the mountain for us."

His benevolent smile froze her to the spot. She was not pointing out anything he didn't already know. He expected them to be waiting.

She gasped. "You want to get caught."

He removed his hat and spun it idly on his hand. "Only after we find your kin. And that may be never. Chances are still heavily in favor of the mountains."

"But why?"

His smile disappeared. "My business. Haven't figured out how to keep you out of it, but I will. I don't plan to share my execution with some Johnny-come-lately." He turned to their gear and drew out the small boots and heavy wool socks. "Put these on. They need breaking in."

She accepted them, giving him one last scowl before sitting on the ground to replace her footwear.

"Isn't it possible they'll give up?"

His somber expression made her shiver. He looked over her head, back the way they had traveled.

"They won't."

"But why?"

She thought he would not answer, but at last his gaze dropped heavily back to hers.

"The mayor's sister was with the Broadner party, with the group that tried to walk out. I made it. She didn't."

Her mouth dropped open as realization burned. "He blames you."

"He's got cause, though no proof."

He frightened her now, with his dour countenance and hostile expression. She realized she did not know what he had done up on that mountain to survive, but many terrible possibilities now cascaded in on her and she realized she did not know him at all.

She reached beneath her skirts and rolled down one black stocking, then decided to add the socks over the stockings and replaced it. After the first boot was laced, she paused to admire the new leather. That was when she sensed she was being watched. She glanced to Cole and found him staring, not at her boot but at the expanse of bare skin between her black stocking and skirts. She flipped down the skirt and glared. It still took a moment for his gaze to reach her face.

"I thought you said you loved your wife."

"I did. But what I'm feeling right now has little to do with that."

She felt her skin heat with shame. That was how all men saw her. No matter how she dressed or what she said, it always came back to their wanting. But in this case, she felt it, as well.

"No need to worry. That mountain ought to cool us down." He turned away to change the saddle and packs. The weary draft-mix looked only slightly more done in than the little brown mare.

Bridget quickly fastened the other boot and took them on a little walk. They did not pinch, but there was no telling. She'd likely have them on for days.

Cole mounted first and reached for her. "You'll ride before me now."

Bridget drew back her hand. She wasn't such a complete fool as to go sitting in a man's lap. "Why?"

"Because you were dozing off before we stopped. If you're before me, I can keep you from tumbling off."

"What about you? You need to sleep, as well."

"When we reach the snow line. I have a friend there."

She offered her hand and he pulled her up. She sat awkwardly, half on the pommel, and was forced to lean against him to throw her leg over the horse's neck. This allowed her to slide into the saddle proper, where she sat wedged between the ridged leather and the man.

"Rock and a hard place," she muttered and adjusted her skirts.

He chuckled. "Should have learned to ride, Bridget. Then you wouldn't be resting against me like a man's fondest desire."

She thought she could feel his "fondest desire" right now and it made her sit still before him. Could a man molest a woman on a horse? As if answering her question, his arm now came to rest on her thigh, holding the rein loosely as he gave a little clucking sound. The mare obeyed. Her gait was jarring, making Bridget wish for the smooth rocking glide of the big gelding.

They traveled up the gentle incline at a trot.

"Lie back and rest. We'll be walking again soon enough."

Minutes ticked by and his arm stayed relaxed upon her thigh. She spooned against him, resisting the urge to nestle tight. Fifty miles to the snowline. How far had they come? Surely it was thirty miles, at least. She tried and failed to stifle a yawn. She did not know whether the horse's jerking step or the man pressed snug behind her was more disturbing. As the sun rose, the lull of sleep came to steal her away. It was a fitful sleep with much nodding and jerking, and she awoke with the sun halfway to its zenith, feeling more exhausted than before she slept. But not as exhausted as she had been during those nine days. How many nights had she waken cold as the ice all about her, knowing that if she did not walk, she would die? Stumbling along in the dark, not knowing where the trail might be, lost... alone.

Death had lured her, promising peace and an end to her struggles. Then there had been the voices. First her grandmother, who had died back in Ireland, had called in her gentle lilting tongue. "Come, daughter, come and rest." Bridget had been so frightened she had rubbed snow on her cheeks to rouse herself and marched until the sun was well up. Only then did she sleep upon a fallen log, in the sun. The next time it was Conor, her older brother, buried by a cave-in far back east in Kentucky. "Bridget, it's not so bad, dying. I'll lead you to the others."

At such times, when she could hear them calling from the other side, she would think of little Chloe. Chloe, who had no milk and no chance at ever living if Bridget didn't reach help.

"You awake?" Cole's voice sounded gravelly and

deep. He'd ridden all night and into the day, with no stopping. When had he last eaten?

"Yes."

"There's a miner in the next valley. Sam Pickett. He'll help us."

Suspicions brought her awake. She straightened.

"How do you know?"

"He's a friend."

A little of the fight drained away and she accepted his decision.

"You need to rest."

He didn't deny it. His joints ached and his back throbbed with fatigue. But what plagued him most was why she hadn't done as he'd told her, back at the livery.

"Bridget, why did you follow me to the barn?"

He felt her muscles tense, but she did not pretend she did not know what he meant.

"Well, I was worried, so I crept up to see what you were about."

"You thought I would steal a horse and leave you," he corrected.

He smiled at the momentary silence that followed.

"It did occur to me. I'll not deny it. I haven't known you so long as all that, now have I?"

"How about now?"

He could not see her smile, but the humor rang in her reply. "I'm still making up me mind."

He chuckled. "Fair enough."

"So I stole into the barn and there was the guard not two steps from me, ordering you to the ground. He never saw me, so I went back the way I'd come."

To leave him behind? He wondered. It was what he had told her to do and now he was faulting her for it.

"I'll admit I was frightened half to death. All I could think of was landing back in prison."

She glanced over her shoulder for just a moment, but long enough for him to see the fear there, haunting her like a ghost. He could only imagine how she had suffered.

"I can't go back to prison, not ever. I won't."

"Why were you in jail, Bridget?"

The horse cleared the ridge and still she didn't answer. At last she spoke.

"They called it a workhouse, but it was a prison."

"In England?"

"Ireland, man. Do you think I'm a heathen Protestant?"

"I'm Protestant," he said, wondering what she'd do with that one.

"Well now, that explains more than you can imagine."

She had him laughing again. He enjoyed her tart tongue and cutting humor. They were so different from Angela's sweet disposition. Angela had reminded Cole of a day in August, where the insects buzzed and the land was warm and ripe. While Bridget more resembled an autumn day, when the air is crisp with frost and the leaves all bright with color. The kind of day that made your blood quicken and a body glad to be alive.

"They clipped me for pickpocketing, though they never found the purse, not that it mattered to the court. Off I went to the tread mill, picking oakum for twelve hours a day."

He recalled she had said that was thirteen years ago, but he must have mistaken her words. "And how old were you?"

"Nine."

"What!" Cole could not contain his outrage. "You were a child."

Bridget swiveled to regard him. "Life is often hardest on children."

Cole felt a stab of pain as he remembered his failure, his daughter starving to death while he struggled to reach her. "Yes, that's true."

"So I came back to the barn and hit the man with all I had. What else is there to know?"

"The whys of it."

She turned back and he realized the horse had taken advantage of his inattention by coming to a halt. He gathered the reins and urged it on.

"I need you."

"Your kin are more important than your own neck?"

"Weren't yours?"

They had been. But it hadn't been enough to save them.

He had failed, and since then he had been too sick at heart to live and too cowardly to end his miserable life.

Well, facing the mountain in November was certainly likely to kill him, but he didn't want it to kill Bridget. Her spirit and her self-sacrifice made him long for noble things. She made him recall when he had been a man that Angela had been proud of.

Could he be that man again?

Chapter Seven

Mary struggled to drag the last of the burned poles away from the charred wreckage that had been their only shelter. Already, the sun had crossed over the mountains, dipping toward the western sky. Night pressed heavily upon her.

They had no place to sleep, no protection from the cold.

She piled the salvaged logs from the shelter. George had cut them in those first terrible days when they recognized they could not cross the pass. Even with his foot broken by the wagon, he had chopped and sawed until he had them sheltered in the eight-by-eight cabin with a canvas roof.

There would be no recreating what was lost, not with the cloth gone and half the timbers burned through.

George had laid their dwelling beside the wagon on open ground, not recognizing that the snows fell deepest there. Walking back and forth from the pines, where she gathered wood, had become a struggle nearly past bearing, but at least it had beaten down the snow. If it kept snowing, any structure she built here would soon be buried.

She looked at the burned eight-foot remnant of canvas that had survived the blaze, wondering what to do.

Each day she collected firewood and retrieved meat from their meager larder, hanging in the ox hide high above her. She peered up at the hide swinging in the wind and a thought struck. Perhaps if she moved their shelter closer to the wood and food, she could better conserve her strength. She patted her middle. The coat and blanket did not fully conceal how her clothing hung on her. At this rate, she'd soon be unable to provide for George and Chloe.

Her husband coughed. The sound was sticky and as frightening as a shadow over a grave. His eyes followed her from where he huddled with Chloe near the salvaged pile of logs. She had never seen him laid so low. He coughed again and she cringed at the raw, wet sound. How much smoke had poured into his lungs?

Two at a time she dragged the logs to the tree line. Beneath the largest pines, the snow was not quite so deep. Once she had moved the timber, she stomped in circles about the tree trunk until she had packed down the snow. The side planks from the wagon would serve as a floor. Doubtless it would be cold, but better than resting on the snow. She considered digging down to the earth, but judged it ten feet deep now. They'd taken to crawling out from beneath the canvas roof of the other structure. They would likely do the same here.

After she had the floor set, she went to check on George.

"I'm sorry, Mary."

"Hush now. Let me see your hands."

He lifted them from the snow, showing her angry red skin and blisters, torn open and oozing. *Please, God, don't let them fester.*

"How do they feel?" she asked, stroking his forehead and not liking the heat she noted. Was it the burned skin or a fever?

"Numb now."

She had cleaned him as best she could without warm water, but some soot still streaked his face and the stench of singed hair and burned flesh clung to him. Chloe sat beside him, bundled tight in one of the surviving quilts against the bitter cold. She tugged on a button on his coat, gurgling at the game. Ah well, Mary thought, this cold keeps the snow away. She glanced at the gray clouds, trying to calculate how long until dusk.

"Best keep your hands under the blanket now or you'll get frostbite." She wrapped them with clean linen and then tucked them in place.

Chloe lifted her arms. "Mama, up!"

Mary stroked her cheek. "Not now, Chloe."

The child cried, but Mary ignored her, turning back to her work. She used the large pine as a center pole and laid the remaining logs against the trunk, making a conical structure like a tepee. The largest branches and poles came first and then she layered more and more evergreen boughs over this frame, filling in the walls.

Her hands burned from wielding the axe, but her shelter now took shape. Would it stand a strong storm…or a wolf? No, she decided, it would not. So she took the rope and lashed the branches to the tree and sewed the canvas to the branches to form a flap for a door.

Next she crawled inside. It was as dark as a well within. She gauged the circle of branches to be seven feet across at the base, but because of the center trunk, neither she nor George would be able to lie straight. Not that that mattered. Most nights were so cold, she huddled in a ball with her husband and Chloe.

Mary crawled out the door and propped it open, allowing for some light to enter. The wooden floor slats were ten inches wide and ten feet long. They extended out from the pines, making a porch of sorts where George could rest in the sun, on the rare day it stopped snowing.

It took only two more trips to bring the surviving blankets, pots and singed quilts into their new home. Mary plastered on a smile as she went to fetch George, trying not to show her bone-weary exhaustion. She acted as if they were moving into Buckingham Palace instead of a rude circle of sticks.

"All done. Come and see."

The effort of getting George to his feet cost Mary the last of her strength. He could not bear weight on his leg and now the burns harried him as well. They stopped twice on the short trip, when his coughing got too bad. He spat and the black spittle streaked the white snow. The ghastly sight stole Mary's bravado. How badly had he burned his lungs?

"Well, now," said George, regarding her work. "It looks fine."

Chloe wiggled to get down and Mary set her on the planking. She crawled into the little nest, gurgling before emerging once more like a kit from a foxhole.

George sat heavily on the wooden base, lifting the

structure slightly when he landed. Mary held her breath, fearing the entire hut might topple. It didn't.

"It's nearly dark," she said.

George glanced up and nodded. "Bring the shovel, Mary."

She retrieved it but kept possession. Her shoulders ached as she spoke. "I'll do it."

"You'll not. You've been slaving all day." George took the handle and she released it with a sigh. "Fetch some meat while you can still see and I'll start this."

She reached their larder and battled the icy rope. The stiff hide dropped to the ground before her. At its landing, the ravens appeared in the trees, staring greedily down at the butchered ox with beetle-black eyes.

"You'll not have it," she vowed. All the internal organs were gone now and both of the haunches. She still had the shoulders and ribs and all the bones neatly wrapped. It was torturous work hacking away bits of the frozen carcass but at last she freed three ribs, chipped icy meat into her pot and then returned the bones to the hide. Mary took great care wrapping their cache. The ravens, weasels and other creatures had all made their attempts to gain entrance, but none had breached the ox's thick hide.

Again she yanked the rope, dragging the cache high up into the tree, but not so close to the branch or trunk that a large animal could reach it. She had not seen so much as a fox in weeks, but she did not leave matters to chance.

Returning the way she had come, she found George still digging. He no longer rested on the wood platform, but now sat in a hole of snow that was four feet deep and showed no sign of reaching ground. Blood soaked the linen bandages covering his palms.

"Stop, George," Mary ordered, setting aside the pot and grabbing for the handle, but George pulled it away.

"We must have fire, Mary."

"I'll do it."

He cast her a defeated look. She couldn't meet his gaze, for the hopelessness.

"I'm nothing but a burden to you now."

His words alarmed her. "You're not."

"What can I do? Not gather wood or help you about camp. I should have died in the fire. You'd be better off without me."

She had not meant to strike him, but she felt her palm smack against his cheek. He gaped at her in shock as she fell to her knees before him.

"Don't say that, not ever again! Do you hear me? We are a family and we stay together. All of us."

He dropped his gaze and she stroked his red cheeks, then cupped his face, near desperate to reach him.

"You keep me warm at night, *mo chroí.*" She crooned the Gaelic endearment. "You tend the baby and you give me reason to live."

Their eyes met and she saw the change instantly. The purpose had returned. He nodded his acceptance, then patted the hand that had struck him only moments ago.

"All right, my love, all right."

Mary took the shovel and worked well into the darkness before she scraped the ice that covered the ground. Here she built her fire, melting snow into her pot. The smell of food lifted her spirits.

She filled two bowls, helping Chloe eat first, while George enjoyed his portion. She ladled a second serving into each bowl and offered one to George as she settled in with her own. It was not until she drained the last of the broth that she realized George had not touched his second bowl.

"What's the matter?" she asked.

"You're losing weight."

She blinked in astonishment. "We all are."

"You're doing all the work. You should have two shares." He extended the bowl.

"But you're bigger than I. You need more."

"I'll not eat it."

She recognized the stubborn set of his jaw and the determined expression. There was no changing his mind. So she tried a compromise.

"We'll split the share."

"No."

"We'll split it or I'll throw it to the ravens." She set her teeth and waited.

He held out his hand for the empty bowl. She gave it to him and watched as he poured off some broth but little meat into one bowl and handed her the other.

"Eat it, Mary."

She did.

Chapter Eight

The horses were lathered and trembling when they reached the ramshackle cabin of the miner just an hour before sunset. Bridget shifted to allow Cole to dismount. He stifled a groan upon landing but made no complaint as he lifted his arms to retrieve her.

She ached down to the bone, but the instant his hands wrapped about her waist, something happened. She couldn't breathe. Her face grew hot and her skin tingled beneath his commanding grip. Judging from the flush on his face, Cole was equally affected by the contact.

It made no sense whatsoever. She had just spent half the night and the better part of the day on a horse, pressed up against him as if he were her husband, but now, at this moment, the contact was thrilling. All notion of fatigue dissolved as she parted her lips, wondering if he meant to kiss her again.

"Who the bloody hell are you and what do you want?" The shout brought them both around to find a shotgun pointed out the crack of the front door and aimed in their direction.

Bridget crouched. "A friend?" she whispered.

Cole released Bridget and pushed back his hat, turning to give the man wielding the weapon a look at his face. "Sam. It's Cole Ellis. You know me."

The dull barrel of the shotgun vanished and the door flung open wide. "Know you! Damn it, Ellis, I've been trying to reach you for two damn years."

The miner wore dungarees several inches too short, giving a clear view of his muddy gray socks and worn boots. Black suspenders held his pants high on his narrow waist. A tattered woolen union suit completed his attire. He seemed unconcerned by his dishabille as he charged off the porch to hug Cole like a long lost brother. His dark bushy beard and agile movement told Bridget he was a young man and stronger than he looked, for he swung Cole clean off the ground before returning his feet to the earth. The thumping he gave her traveling partner raised a cloud of dust into the air.

Sam drew away. "I get no answers to my letters and I can't leave the claim. Damn me, you're a hard man to find. Where you been hiding?"

"Long story," said Cole. "Got arrested for horse theft. Sentenced me to hang."

"What? You could buy a hundred horses. That's what I been trying to tell ya'. I hit a vein." Sam grinned, clasping Cole's shoulders. "You're a rich man, partner." When his mirth was not returned, a look of confusion blanketed his eager face. "Did you say hang?"

Cole nodded.

"But they let you go?"

Cole shook his head, then thumbed over his shoulder at Bridget. "She sprung me."

Sam turned to Bridget, grinning. He had all his teeth, and a handsome face, from what she could see between the wild brown beard and long hair he'd tied at his nape. His dark eyes sparkled with devilment as he regarded her.

Bridget reached in her pocket for her gun, but Cole surprised her by laying a proprietary hand on her shoulder, marking his claim to her.

Sam's smile never wavered—in fact, it increased. "Oh, so that's how it is. About time, too."

Cole scowled. "She's not mine."

Sam slapped his knee and twirled. "Music to my ears." He peered at Bridget. "Paid off a judge, did she?"

Bridget's heart sank. Cole would now reveal her for what she was, a common pickpocket. She straightened for the blow to her ego.

"Something like that."

Had he just kept her secret? She gaped up at him and he winked at her. The only one she had ever trusted with her secrets had been Mary—until now.

Sam nodded his approval. "What's your name, missy?"

"Bridget Callahan."

"I know that name." He scratched his beard a moment and then stilled as his gaze fixed upon her. "You're the one Beaver Joe told tale of." He turned to Cole. "She's a survivor, too."

"My sister and her family are still in the pass."

His expression changed and he looked as somber

as a pallbearer as he and Cole exchanged glances. "Our pass?"

Cole nodded. "We need your help."

Sam's cheeks lost their rosy glow. "Cole, I…"

"Food and rest. I need you to see to the horses and watch our back until we can head up the pass."

Relief flooded Sam's expression. "Oh, sure. 'Course. Glad to do it."

"The horses are stolen, Sam. We're on the run."

Sam lost his beguiling smile. "Oh."

"We haven't eaten since yesterday. See to her and I'll see to the horses."

Bridget did not like being divided up as one of two chores to be done, but she kept her tongue.

Sam motioned. "Stream's good drinking for horse or man, and there's a paddock round back for my mules."

Cole led the horses along, leaving Bridget with the miner.

"Got coffee on," he said.

She smiled her thanks and followed him inside.

The cabin had been constructed of planks and had a dirt floor. Sam's narrow unmade bed showed a gray wool blanket hopelessly tangled with a red-and-white nine-patch quilt that had been hastily tacked. An unsheathed pillow lay on the bare mattress ticking and a crushed straw hat adorned one bedpost. The woodstove and a full box for logs stood at the foot of the bed. The rest of the cabin was spartan. Two chairs flanked a table on the far wall. Five gold pans littered the table, all partially filled with black sand and water. A wide plank served as a counter and caught the light from the single window. Judging from the supplies, it seemed Mr. Pickett lived on beans, salt pork, coffee and chewing tobacco. The rest of the cramped space was consumed by several large wash basins filled with filthy water.

"Don't have many visitors," he said, wiping his hands on his jeans and then attacking his covers until they lay smoothly on the bed. He then lifted a handful of dirty clothes and shoved them beneath the springs.

"Coffee's strong." He moved a gold pan to the counter and placed a steaming cup in the empty spot between pans.

She sat, stifling a groan. Exhaustion made her very bones ache.

"So you and Cole are retrieving your people?"

She nodded. The aroma of coffee tempted her, but she feared it would keep her awake and all she wanted to do was rest her head on the table and sleep.

"He knows the mountain, sure enough. I'm one of the ones he walked out. He tell you that?"

She straightened, her fatigue suddenly gone. He had been there and knew things, private things about Cole. She told herself she only cared because it better prepared her to travel with him. But it was a lie. She longed to know the secrets he kept.

"He came back for you."

He shook his head. "I was one of the Forlorn Hope, that's what we called ourselves. Sorry bunch we were, too. Hired hands, mostly, and servants with no food or livestock of our own." He looked off out the window, his expression sour. "When we got stuck, the masters looked to their own first and no mistaking. Left us little choice, really. Only Mr. and Mrs. Devlin had a wagon, but they lost their cattle in the storm and thought their best chance to reach the valley was with us. Turned out they were wrong."

Bridget swallowed hard and she forced herself not to ask why.

"What happened to Cole's daughter?"

Sam scratched his sunburned neck. "Lee-lee. She was bright as a new penny, that one. They left her with the Broadners. Delirium took her before Cole ever made it back."

Bridget tried to picture Lee-lee but saw Chloe instead. The tears welled in her eyes. Was she sick with fever? Her heart ached as if clenched in some giant fist. *Oh, God, protect her.*

Sam had his back to her now and did not see Bridget's tears. He pulled out flour and soda and added a dipper full of water, mixing biscuits in an empty gold pan.

"Broke his heart, her passing."

Bridget wiped her eyes. Yes, she understood that.

"Never seen a man mourn so. Stopped eating, 'course—"

"Pickett!"

Sam wheeled around to find Cole filling the door frame, scowling like a tyrant.

Sam flushed, looking guilty as a boy with his hand in the pickle jar. "I didn't."

"What did you tell her?"

"Nothing. Just about Lee-lee."

"What else?"

"Nothing, I swear."

Cole glared daggers at the man. Sam lifted his flour-coated hands, waving him off.

"I didn't."

Cole motioned with his head, beckoning, and then disappeared. Sam moved to follow, pausing as he remembered Bridget.

"Ah, help yourself to the coffee." He trotted out.

Bridget crept to the door and saw no sign of either man. She stole along the outside cabin wall and peered around the corner. She spotted Cole pacing along the corral while Sam loped along to keep up with him.

"I didn't tell her. I didn't. I swore I never would."

Cole paused to grasp two fistfuls of Sam's shirt, bringing them nose-to-nose. The miner lifted not a finger to defend himself. "You nearly did."

"She's been there."

"Not for two months. She left before the food ran out."

Sam offered his chin, closing one eye. "Slug me if you want. She asked about Lee-lee and I told her."

Cole released Sam, who staggered a step before regaining his equilibrium.

"How can you go back?" he asked. "We swore we'd never set foot there again."

"She tricked me."

Sam scoffed, making Bridget bristle. Obviously he thought her incapable of making Cole Ellis do anything he did not want to do.

Cole headed back her way and Bridget ducked behind the cabin, listening as his footsteps halted and he spoke again.

"I promised to go, that's all."

His friend's voice rang with desperation.

"I got money. *We* got money. Wait'll you see the vein. It's just like a dream, shining through sugary-white quartz as pretty as you please. Rich and wide. No telling how far back she goes and I put aside half, just like we agreed. We could back a rescue—get other men to go."

Bridget peeked around the cabin, seeing them both in profile.

Cole shook his head.

The miner stilled. His haunted expression made Bridget wonder again about the secrets they swore to keep. What had happened in the past that it still made Sam tremble and the muscle on Cole's jaw tick like a tiny heartbeat?

Cole drew off his hat and slapped it idly against his thigh. "The food won't last."

Sam fell back a step. Clearly, he knew exactly what that meant. He had been there without food, and desperation had driven him out.

"And there's a posse behind me," said Cole.

"You seen them?"

"Not yet."

Sam scratched beneath his chin. "I thought you said she got you out?"

Cole gave him an impatient look.

"Oh." Sam said, comprehending. "They know you're headed this way? I can hold them off."

"No, you can't and I don't want you to try." He blew out his breath in frustration. "Know who's mayor of Sacramento now?"

Sam nodded.

"Then you know why they'll come." Cole glanced toward the cabin and Bridget darted out of sight. Had he seen her?

He came around the corner at a speed that nearly stopped her heart, grasping her wrist as he dragged her out into the yard. The next thing she knew he had her crushed against his chest with both her hands seized behind her back.

"You make a poor spy," he whispered.

He was so near she could see each bristly whisker on his strong jaw. But it was his full mouth that she focused on, recalling the tingling thrill of his kiss. He leaned forward as if to kiss her now, but instead he pressed his lips beside her ear, speaking to her alone.

"I should teach you a lesson." His lips lingered there, nuzzling her ear until she was dizzy with anticipation. He pressed her to arm's length, still holding her wrists. "Can you make biscuits?" he asked.

Her brow wrinkled, wondering if it was a trick question. She had expected him to storm and possibly strike her and instead she received a sensual assault that rattled her down to her new boots and an inquiry that confused her. Her skin grew hot as her pulse beat in her face and belly all at once. Words failed her, so she nodded.

"Then do it."

His grip relaxed. She turned tail and fled to the cabin, with Sam's laugh ringing in her ears.

The men returned a few minutes later. She already had a full griddle of golden biscuits. She flipped them onto a pie tin, having found no plates, and then added bacon to the pan.

Sam took the spatula from her, so she sat across from Cole. The look he gave her made her feel like one of those strips of bacon, frying in their own grease.

"Get an earful?" he asked, reaching for a biscuit.

She flushed and dropped her gaze. "I only meant to understand you better."

"No, you meant to stick your nose where it doesn't belong."

"I've a right to know. I'm the one heading up the mountain with you."

His smile turned cold. "It doesn't give you claim to my secrets, little lamb. Trust is something you cannot steal. It must be earned. Besides, some things are best not to know."

In that moment, he seemed solitary as the mountain, but unlike the Cascades, he had a heart. Perhaps one day he would tell her what plagued him. Until then, she was glad he had Sam to share some of his burden.

She turned to the hearty meal, enjoying Sam's chatter about how he and Cole met in Independence when Sam had run afoul of a couple of toughs. "They didn't like the odds so much when Cole showed up."

As soon as she had finished her portion, her vitality quite deserted her, and to her embarrassment she nodded off at the table.

Cole laid a gentle hand on her shoulder and she startled awake. "Rest on the bed, Bridget."

He guided her and stooped to remove her boots as if she were his child. With his head bowed over her foot, she saw him in a new light. This dark imposing man had a tender streak. Was this how he had cared for his daughter? The thought of it made her heart ache all over again.

"Lie down now," he said.

"Where will you sleep?"

"Beside you."

Her eyes widened in shock, but instead of the protest she knew she should make, she found she could only imagine his long hard body, pressed close to her. She slid nearer to the wall to make room for him.

Cole's eyes glittered with desire. "On the floor, Bridget. I'll rest beside you on the floor."

His friend cleared his throat. She recalled Sam now and her face burned with shame. What must he think— must they both think—of her?

Cole turned to his friend. "You'll keep watch?"

"Will do." Sam grabbed his shotgun and stepped out into the cool evening air.

Cole's heated gaze mesmerized her. "We'll give you some privacy. But don't come sneaking out to eavesdrop."

He left her then, following Sam into the yard, but his thoughts stayed behind. That look she'd given him had been a look of pure anticipation. It made him harder than cordwood. What had started as teasing had become deadly serious ever since that damned kiss. If not for Sam, he would likely have taken her up on her offer. What the hell was she doing staring at him and licking her lips as if he were a peppermint stick?

Sam matched his strides as they crossed the yard, checking the horses once more, breaking the silence.

"Been snowing like a bastard up on the peaks. Maybe twenty feet already. You can take my mule up a ways.

The jenny is fresh and surefooted. Just turn her loose at the snow line and she'll find her own way home all right."

"I appreciate it. Sam? If they come, just tell them you found the horses, saw the brands and were planning on bringing them in on your next trip."

"You won't reconsider? I could sure use you, partner."

"I can't, Sam."

"Thinking of selling shares, starting a company. Wanted your opinion first. Come up and take a look."

"I need sleep. Been up all night. But if you want to sell shares, have at it. I trust you." He laid a hand on his friend's muscular shoulder. "Trust you with my life, Sam."

"What about your share?"

"If I don't come back, use the money to close that damn pass. I don't want anyone else to have to go through this."

"How?"

Cole thumped him on the shoulder. "You're the one with all the ideas, Sam. You'll think of something."

"Did you think about going over to the other side? The posse can't follow you there."

"Got to reach her family first."

"That alone will take a miracle." The two stared toward the mountains, both silent in contemplation.

"Don't know how you can face it again," muttered Sam. "I sure as hell wouldn't."

"They've got a baby up there. Sam. Not yet one year old."

Sam pressed his hand to his mouth and then slowly dragged it away. "God protect them."

Chapter Nine

Bridget slipped beneath the blanket as Cole stretched out beside her on the floor, wrapped in a moth-eaten bearskin. It seemed only an instant later that Sam was shouting.

Bridget swung her legs off the bed and stepped on Cole's chest as she scrambled by.

"They're coming!" Sam yelled. "Saw them from my lookout."

"The supplies," said Cole, now on his feet.

Bridget slid into her boots and then tugged on her coat, before dragging the lavender shawl over her head. Sam grasped her by the arm, hauling her along after Cole, who charged out the door.

Bridget stumbled blindly across the dark yard, guided only by Sam's sure hold.

Outside the corral, she saw a white mule bridled and tied.

"I packed my jenny," he said to Cole. "All your gear. Now scat. Can't lie about not seeing you with you standing here."

Cole checked the ropes on the packsaddle, while Sam tightened the girth.

"Run! They're close, but if those clouds stay put, they might not see you."

Cole glanced up at the wispy clouds darting over the moon, now in three-quarters, and knew the heavens were against them.

He returned his attention to the terrestrial, staring at his old friend. The men exchanged a rough embrace before Cole accepted the lead line. Bridget's breathing came in frightened gasps.

"Thank you, Sam," she said.

"You can thank me by not dying on that damned mountain. Now get."

Cole was already jogging up the trail behind the corral. She turned to follow, running like a rabbit. She passed the mule and then him. Her legs pumped hard as her mind harkened back to another desperate flight.

Run, Bridget. Run!

They'd not catch her this time.

The pines seemed impossibly far up the rough trail. Patches of silvery light danced along the path as the clouds raced past the moon.

Cole tugged on the lead, urging the rugged little mule to trot. He did not look back. They would make it or not. He hoped they would make it. Deep inside him, he noted the difference. Somewhere over the last two days, he had had a change of heart. He wanted to climb the mountains, wanted to rescue Bridget's family and save the child.

Bridget dashed along before him, fleet-footed as a deer. The eyelets of her new boots flashed in the moonlight as she darted into the high sagebrush that lined the steep incline. The mule would be easy to spot, with its hide white as a bleached bedsheet. Cole lowered his chin and pushed himself for greater speed.

As the trees closed in around them, he slowed the punishing pace. The mule's sides heaved under the heavy load. Bridget came to stand beside him, gazing back the way they had come.

"Did they see us?"

"Don't know." He had not heard any rifle fire. Likely Sam had them trapped in his yard, staring down the wrong end of his shotgun. He nearly smiled at the image. "We'll know soon enough."

From somewhere below them came the bray of Sam's other mule. The jenny drew a breath. Both Cole and Bridget dove, grasping her muzzle and holding it down, for if their mule responded to the lonely cry, they were done.

Instead, they caught the nicker of several horses. The posse had arrived.

"Come on." Cole lifted the line and tugged the mule back into motion. They stole farther into the pines, like moving shadows.

"What if they follow us?" asked Bridget.

"Then it will be a short trip." He grinned but saw her expression frozen in fright. His smile faded and he gave her the hope she craved. "Sam will keep them busy even if he has to hamstring their horses."

"Oh, dear."

"They'll not follow past the snow. We've got to get up this trail."

"How far?"

"Three miles, maybe. On this grade, take us over an hour."

"They're riding and we're on foot."

"Life's not altogether fair, Bridget Callahan."

This time she did smile, and it surprised and delighted him.

She didn't chatter or fret, but fell in beside him, keeping up as he marched along. The pace was punishing. Bridget's cheeks puffed and sweat beaded her brow, but she did not complain and she did not fall behind. He admired her, this little titan. She was more than she appeared, with a heart like the mountain, deep and strong. Watching her determined stride gave him hope. A gift, he thought, that she did not even know she had given.

They might actually succeed.

He heard no sound of pursuit. All that reached him was the steady blow of their breath and the rhythmic clip-clop of the mule's hoofbeats on the animal trail. Ice filled the center of the path, reaching down the mountain like an extended finger. From beneath its frosty appendage, water ran steadily, sending a frigid runoff down to feed Sam's stream.

Above them, the line of snow hugged the mountain.

"Half a mile and we're safe." He laughed.

"What?" she asked.

He shook his head in dismay. "The world's gone crazy."

She nodded in understanding. If ever there was a woman who could understand, it was this one.

"I never thought I'd be heading up this trail again. Lord, I'll be glad to come back down again with my family."

It was still a long shot, but he hated to wipe that pretty smile off her face. Let her hope. He'd do nothing to destroy it. The mountains, however, had a way of crushing the life out of you. Cold, uncaring and deadly, that was the Cascades, the last damn hurdle in the race to California.

He continued up onto the snow, pulling the reluctant mule along, determined to have the creature carry their load as long as possible.

The trail was well-packed from the sun melting and the nights freezing the ice, so they scrambled up the steep icy slope pushing another half mile before the snow grew too deep and the mule floundered.

"We've come nearly four miles since the cabin. A good start."

"But it will get harder from here," said Bridget.

It would—much.

Cole unloaded the mule in the morning light, stacking their gear on the ground. The lower elevation and warmer temperatures made the packed snow icy enough to bear their weight, so he did not untie the snowshoes. Once he had the packs ready, he helped Bridget into hers. Her eyes shone with determination as she shouldered her load.

He admired her more with each passing hour, this tough little Irish thief.

Cole turned the mule toward home, slapping her flank to encourage her descent, hoping Sam would not suffer for his generosity. The two men had shared a desperate journey down this very trail and it had forged a bond, making them closer than brothers. When they discovered gold in these accursed mountains, Sam had talked him in to staking a claim. Partners, that's what they were. Cole had bought the claim, but Sam did all the work, leaving Cole time to drink himself near to death. He should have stayed on the claim. Sam deserved better.

With a sign of resignation, he turned toward the task at hand, lifting his heavy pack.

The gentle slope belied the difficulty ahead, allowing them to climb side by side. With his feet on the same trail, his mind fell naturally back to the last time he'd come this way. He'd done as his wife had asked, leading the rescue party to the survivors. The sight still gave him nightmares. He thought his party had suffered, but their deaths were quick because the walking burned up their strength like a log in a bonfire and the sleet made short work of them. They did not linger for months as the food disappeared. For most, the struggle lasted only days.

Lee-lee would not have survived the trip—he knew it—but neither did she survive the camp. She was doomed the minute they entered the Cascades so late in the fall. He had killed his child as surely as the mountains.

Bridget broke in to his brooding silence. "I was so glad to see the yellow grass here in the valley. It was the moment I knew I had survived. That stream from the glacier was the first water I'd drunk in two days. So cold it numbed my teeth." She brushed a strand of hair from her eyes. "I hoped to leave the rescue to others."

"The world is full of cowards."

"Well, I know it, for I'm one of them."

"You? You're the bravest woman I've ever met."

She flushed at that, making her look more beautiful. His palms began to sweat, but not from exertion. It was this damned attractive female. She stirred him like a hot poker in the coals.

She gave him a bashful smile that set his heart to tripping.

"I'm here because I am afraid, right down to my toes. Make no mistake about that now. But if I don't go, they'll die. Them dying frightens me more than anything in this world, even more than, than…"

He waited, but she had her jaw clamped tighter than a live oyster. What frightened her more than their death? Her own, or something else?

"Than?" No answer. "Bridget, I'll not betray your confidence."

She cast him an impatient look, as if it was ridiculous to even suggest he could keep a secret. But he could and did. Even had his own share of things that shamed him.

She wrinkled her chin. "Well, you know already, don't you?" She flapped her arms at her sides. "Prison is what. Darkest time of my life. I can't go back there. And now I've gone and broken the law and they'll find out. But I had to, don't you see, for Mary and Chloe."

"They don't know about that."

She gave him a steely look, as if taking his measure and finding him lacking. "You know."

He understood her thinking now and he scowled. "You implying I'd give you up?"

"Under the right conditions, I'd say so."

"Conditions like saving my own skin?"

"You said it, not I." Her chin gained a superior lift.

He fought the urge to grab her by the shoulders to make her look at him. "Perhaps you've forgotten why I was in prison in the first place." He had wanted to die, wanted it with all his heart. Longed for it as he longed for his wife. But this irritating woman marching beside him had made him reconsider. She'd given him a reason to put one foot before the next. A reason to fight on. Somehow she'd made her mission, his mission.

Now he wanted to snatch three more lives from this mountain—wanted her niece to have the chance that he could not give his own daughter. It wasn't Lee-lee up there. He knew it, and yet, it was a little girl just like *his* little girl.

"I've forgotten nothing. But I know something of men."

"Whoever it was that hurt you, Bridget Callahan, it's not my fault. I'll not turn you over, you have my word."

She blew through her teeth. The sound told him exactly what she thought of his word.

"Suspicious little thing," he muttered.

"You tried to back out of your last promise, and here you are offering another."

He did stop then and she followed his example. Her eyes flashed a warning, which he ignored. Now her fists were knotted at her sides. The woman was screaming for a fight. Well, so be it then.

"I only wanted to protect you from this." He motioned to the path before them.

Her eyes grew round.

His words were less than honest, a half truth. He

filled his lungs with cold air and told her the rest of it. "And I didn't want to face this happening again."

All the fight drained out of her. Bridget's chin began to tremble, but she held on to her control. "My family is starving up in that pass."

She met his gaze a long while and then looked up the mountain pass at the clouds that covered the peaks. "It's snowing again."

"Better than sleet."

She shuddered as if shaking off the cold. Here in the sunlight, it was warm enough. It was only her memories that chilled her. Had she had sleet as well?

Their eyes met again.

"The ice saved me and nearly killed me," she said.

They started off again, walking side by side, her words falling into rhythm with their steps.

"The first day I made it only as far as the slope on the opposite side of the lake. Mary could see me still. I waved before sunset, thinking I'd likely freeze that night. I was sorry I couldn't at least make it out of her sight before dying. When the sleet came, it soaked me through. It was freeze or move, so I started off in the darkness, clawing up the pass. Snow clumped on my shoes and I waded along as if my boots were filled with sand." She rubbed her nose with her index finger. "Then something happened. The temperature dropped fast. My skirts froze and the ground froze. The crust of ice on the surface was thick enough to bear my weight. Like a miracle and a curse."

"That's how you did it."

"What?"

"How you walked out with no snowshoes. It's usually impossible without them. But the ice supported you."

"Ice and walking all night. I didn't stop until well into the morning, but I'd cleared the pass. By afternoon, I hung my skirt and coat to dry in the wind and huddled in my shawl tucked in a pocket I carved below the ice."

"Out of the wind."

"That's true enough."

"You are a smart little fox, Bridget."

She cast him a glance as if trying to determine whether he mocked her. He meant it as a compliment. The girl kept her wits and made good choices. He could not help but nod his approval.

"Our group had more difficulty," he said. "The snow was powdery and deep. Only five of the fifteen had snowshoes. We beat the trail down as best we could, but those without shoes couldn't go far."

"How long?"

"Eleven days."

Bridget absorbed the magnitude of that. His trip had taken longer than her horrible ordeal had. She could not think what to say.

"We had women, young mothers," he said by way of explanation.

"They slowed you down."

He nodded. "The mothers, they all had young ones. They knew their children would be first to perish when the food was gone. So they left them, saving the rations for those behind, and trying for the valley."

Hadn't she done just the same? He had taken the

same gamble, only he had lost. The outcome of Bridget's choice was still in doubt.

"Why were you on that train?" she asked.

"Mule driver. Had a team of eight on Broadners' main wagon. My wife came as their cook. Working our way across. We missed our chance at the pass by one day." His fingers clenched the straps of his pack. "It was like the skies opened and snow fell faster than you'd dream possible. We barely had time to make shelters. Then the animals wandered away from camp. We lost most in the snow."

Bridget nodded. "We had only the one ox and that was lame. It's why we fell behind. We butchered it, but it was easy to see it would not last. We'd seen deer and elk, but they all vanished with the snows. I shot a fox, but that was all."

"We caught a few foxes, too. Also an elk. You've never seen an elk disappear so fast. The Broadners used their wagon for shelter with no room for us."

"George cut logs for a little cabin. Only eight-by-eight, with canvas for a roof."

"I had only a bush shed with a rawhide cover." He'd seen what was to come. Soon they'd want the skin back. He had planned to be gone before it came to that.

Could she see why he left?

"The wind howled right through the bush. The Broadners agreed to take Lee-lee and let us use the oxbows to fashion showshoes, thinking we might have a chance. It was a struggle. The travel stole Angela's strength."

He stopped there, not planning to tell her any more. He didn't talk of this to anyone. Sam knew, of course, and that meant he didn't need to speak of it. No one else would understand—except perhaps this woman. He glanced at her. Bridget's cheeks glowed pink in the chilly air and her face was impassive. Would she judge him? He drew a ragged breath.

"For a time I thought we'd make it. But most of the party was without snowshoes, so we made only a mile or two a day—less as the days passed." Cole scowled at the mountains. "I hate this place. I hate the snow and the ice and the death."

Bridget wiped at the tears that coursed down her cheeks. He looked at her wet cheeks, thinking he should stop. She was trying to rescue her kin and hearing how he had failed would not bolster her. But the words kept coming, like water from a leaky pump.

"We ran out of food." He broke off, pressing his lips tight. He'd not say what happened next. Some secrets were too dark to reveal to anyone. "She lasted only three days."

"I'm sorry."

"I promised I would get help and save Lee-lee." He bowed his head. "I failed."

He felt hollow inside, like the shell of a gourd. This mountain had taken away his world and left him with nothing but grief and fury to sustain him.

The trail grew steeper and Bridget fell into line behind him. Flurries swirled about them like powdered sugar. He trudged along, thinking back, moving forward.

"Cole?"

He turned to see Bridget twenty feet back, standing

in snow well past her knees. Only then did he notice that the ice had given way to soft powder. It clung like sand to his trousers, reaching halfway up his shin.

"Should we use the snowshoes?" she asked.

The answer was obvious to anyone who wasn't so deep in his own mired thoughts that he did not note his surroundings. He nodded, disgusted with himself for not realizing her struggles.

They dropped their packs and Cole helped Bridget lash on her shoes. He drew out the great mittens made of moose hide and lined with beaver, insisting it was time she wear them over the thin woolen gloves.

The going was slower now. Bridget stepped on her shoes often. Each time she tripped she fell into the powder. The snow clung to her skirts and coat, making her look as if she were carved in white marble.

"Owff!"

He turned to see her lying on her side again. He righted her once more. Her brow wrinkled as she scowled at her new footwear.

"I look like a pork cutlet ready for frying," she muttered, dusting off her skirts. "I think it is easier to wade through the snow."

"Soon it won't be. Spread your feet wider when you walk so you won't catch the other shoe."

"It's not the shoe. I keep stepping on my skirts."

He examined her hemline, now dragging on the snow. The shoes sunk in a good five inches with her passing. That and the incline combined to drag her hem under the rawhide laces.

He pointed at her legs. "What's under there?"

She settled one bulky mitten on her hip and gave him an incorrigible look that made him want to laugh out loud.

"You were married, Mr. Ellis. I should think you would know."

Now he did laugh. A great booming guffaw that echoed off the hills. He reached for her trailing hem. Her attempt to evade him was clumsy and caused her to totter sideways. He caught her in his arms and grasped her hem.

She slapped at him with her bundled hands. Ignoring her, he tugged at the pack strap that circled her waist and thrust the hem beneath it.

He stepped back, admiring his work. He now had a clear window to her quilted bloomers, thick socks and boots.

"That'll do."

She sputtered, her lovely face flushed with high color. She seemed about to protest. But instead she squared her shoulders and adjusted her pack.

He admired her practicality. The woman would walk naked through the snow if she thought it would help her reach her family.

She strode past him with her chin high. "Have a good look, Mr. Ellis, for it is all you will get."

A wicked smile curled his lips. He did love a challenge.

Chapter Ten

Cole called a halt well before dark. He chose a ridge of pines as a windbreak and set up the two sheets of tin. One he rested on the ground, the other he thrust into the snow at right angles to shield his fire from the wind and reflect its heat.

Bridget did not sit idle as he worked to build a fire, but unpacked the blankets, canvas and buffalo hide.

"What food do you want out?"

"Oats, jerky and raisins."

She was suspicious of the combination, but did as he bid. Soon he had his pot full of granular snow tucked between the fire and the reflectors. Next he dug down into the snow, with the sawed-off shovel Sam had donated, until he had a pit three feet deep and roughly six by three feet in dimension.

"Pine boughs," he said to her.

They set to the task, gathering armfuls and laying them in the pit. Next came the buffalo hide and then the blankets. They sat side by side in their nest, while Cole tended his melting snow, carefully testing the temperature of the water with his little finger. Satisfied, he offered the pot to Bridget.

"Drink all you can."

She held the pot with her gloved hands, the heat radiating through the black wool and into her numb fingers. Gradually they came back to life.

"What about you?"

He motioned to the snowy hillside. "Plenty more."

She brought the pot to her lips and drank down the warm water. Instantly, the liquid heated her throat and belly. Who knew that warm water could taste so wonderful? She finished more than half before returning the container.

He slipped it back between the reflector and fire, adding more snow. Cole had not thought it necessary to bring cups or plates. He carried one pot and two spoons. Efficient, she thought, wondering what meal he planned.

After he had had his drink, she watched with growing uncertainty as he broke the jerked elk into small pieces and tossed them into the water, turning the liquid brown. Next, he added raisins that plumped like ticks on a hound. Finally, he cast in a handful of pine nuts and a generous helping of oats. The resulting mush was the oddest thing Bridget had ever seen.

At last he set the meal between them, and they dug in with their spoons.

The pot was empty before Bridget felt full and she glanced up hopefully, but Cole had put the foodstuffs away, so she scoured the container with the grainy ice.

The job made her hands numb once more, but her belly was nearly full and she felt warm inside.

Cole proceeded to fill the pot with snow once more. A few minutes later, he poured warm water into the wide mouth of a skin sack. Bridget expected the water to run right out again, but the vessel held, bulging like a full bladder.

"For our feet?" asked Bridget.

"If you like. It's our drinking water for tomorrow."

"It will freeze and split," she warned, having seen ice crack glass.

"Not if you keep it inside your coat."

Understanding struck. "Clever."

He eyed her boots. "Feet cold?"

She nodded. Before she knew what was happening, he had her laces untied and her socks stripped away. She tried to draw back, but he had captured her heel in his large palm.

"They're fine, just cold as a block of ice." His thumbs began a delving journey over her tired arches. He might just as well have thrown her onto the fire for the heat generated by his touch. A tingling thrill spiraled through her body until it centered like hot lead in her belly. Her breasts ached and she had the urge to grasp the lapels of his coat and drag him to her for a kiss.

Instead, she bit her lower lip as his powerful hands massaged the sole of her foot. He kneaded her heels and arches and the balls of her feet, causing a groan of pure animal pleasure to escape her. Their eyes met and he seemed to realize that his ministrations were not having the intended effect. This new insight brought that devilish smile to his lips.

He pressed her frigid toes between his hands, allowing his heat to warm them. All the while he grinned, capturing her with the glittering promise in his eyes.

He lifted her feet, forcing her to fall back onto her extended arms. Still he lifted, until her pink toes were inches from his mouth. Hot breath fanned them. She gasped with pleasure, telling herself to draw back but longing for him to continue.

He pressed her feet to his chest with one hand and dipped a rag into the pot of water with the other, using the cloth to wash her feet. The hot water and cool air raised a sensation unlike anything she'd ever experienced.

At last, he lowered one foot to the blanket, and she thought his primal seduction had ended, until he lifted the other to his mouth and sucked on her toes.

She jumped and struggled at this new delicious assault, but he held fast, his tongue darting between her toes.

Bridget lay on her back, panting, aching for this man to free her or to take her. Instead, he lowered one foot and took up the next.

She tried to hold her breath, but it was no good. The moan issuing from her lips left no doubt as to the effect he had upon her. He had her panting for his ministrations. It took every ounce of the fraying control she had to keep from writhing before him. He stole her dignity and broke her restraint with only the touch of his lips to the most unlikely of places.

He was at her arch now. Oh, sweet mercy, if he could bring her to near madness by kissing her instep, how much more would she feel should he move his lips to other locales?

He lowered her foot, but still captured her ankles in his powerful hands.

"Warmed up now?"

She could only look at him in horror. She had given him the knowledge of what his touch did to her and by doing so, she had lost all power to him. He knew that no matter what she said, she felt something completely to the contrary. How could she have done this again?

"You're a dreadful man."

His stirring laugh kept her nerves jangling. Why didn't he release her? She tugged, but he only tightened his grip, telling her without a word that she would have her liberty only when it suited him.

"I used to rub Angela's feet. But I never got that reaction."

She wanted to ask if he had used his tongue, but did not dare.

His frown told her that he recalled his wife now. His grip loosened and she drew back, scrambling for her socks.

"Dry socks," he said, still frowning. "Dry socks every night. Keep the wet ones inside your coat until they are dry as well."

"How do you know so much about this?"

"Winter hunting in Vermont. The snow is not so deep, but the cold can be worse."

He removed his own socks now, showing her his wide flat feet with neatly trimmed nails. She examined his long big toe, lightly dusted with dark hair, and wondered what he would do if she sucked on his toes.

He shoved his socks into his coat.

"Put your pack there." He motioned to the edge of the hide, suddenly all business. Whatever he had been feeling before was now locked behind an inscrutable mask.

She did as he asked and he placed his belongings on the opposite side, hemming them in.

"We'll sleep now, so if you need some privacy, take it."

She dragged on her boots and snowshoes. Her feet still tingled with delight as she walked the path he had broken to the trees. After a few minutes she returned. Twilight made the fire bright, but he did not build it high for the evening, as she had done when she had traveled this trail alone.

She saw that in her absence he had thrust his snow-shoes into the snow at the head of the sleeping pit and tied the oiled canvas to them. He gazed up at her, his face now that cold, condescending mask that she so hated.

"Lie down, Bridget. It's time to rest."

She had no fear for her person, for one look told her that the man now resented her as if his little game had somehow been her idea.

She removed her boots and tucked them tight between her pack and her body. She rolled her shawl to make a pillow for their heads and he drew the blankets over them. On her last journey, this shawl had been her only covering. But now she had the blankets and his body to warm her.

Finally, he dragged the canvas over them, anchoring it to the tops of her snowshoes. It hung only inches over their bodies, but completed the wind-break begun by his pit.

She inched closer to him and he rolled away, giving

her his back. Bridget pressed her lips together, scowling. He made her feel cheap, using her and then tossing her away. It was small wonder, for he knew her already as a thief. She vowed to do nothing more to lower his opinion of her.

She peered through the darkness at his back as if her glare might somehow bore a hole in him. The man was infuriating. She huffed and rolled to face her pack. Their backs pressed together, generating warmth, but the silence stretching between them lingered crisp and cold as any frost.

She dozed in this position, but woke when her shoulder throbbed from the uneven bedding. Her discomfort overcame her pride and sometime in the night she rolled to her back. He did as well, pinning her half-beneath him for a moment before he grunted and moved off. He did not rouse or stiffen, so she edged closer, pressing her thigh and leg against the warmth of his.

When she next woke, the wind whistled above them, blowing beneath the canvas. Gray light stole into their nest, but she was warm beside Cole. He had rolled toward her, his irritation forgotten in slumber, and lay with his chin resting on the top of her head and his warm, heavy arm thrown carelessly across her waist. One bent knee pressed over her thigh, holding her close. She sighed at the comfort he brought her. He might resent her, but at least she was not alone. For so long she'd felt alone, even with Mary. She knew she'd imposed on the newlyweds, but with no other option, she had taken what they'd offered.

Cole Ellis made her think crazy thoughts, like how

precious it was to wake next to a man and how two bodies pressed together could bring solace to feed the soul.

But he didn't want her. She knew it, knew he wanted to be rid of her as soon as his promise was fulfilled. Any ties beyond that were just silly reveries, and she was too old and too battered to believe in fairy tales.

She pushed at his arm and he growled. Bridget turned her face toward his, their noses nearly touching. One of his eyes opened and he peered at her.

"Morning?" he asked, his voice gravelly and deeper than usual.

She nodded, not trusting her words. There was a compelling quality in his voice that made her quicken. She felt her heart speed up and her skin flush. He'd used his magic on her again, rousing her with just one word until her skin tingled as if she'd jumped in cold water.

He sighed. Was he reluctant to leave her embrace or only to leave this cozy nest he had built them?

His other eye opened and he seemed to recall their surroundings and situation simultaneously, for he drew back.

Stretching took her mind off the loss of his tender touch. Never in her life had she felt so cherished as when she slept in his arms.

Fairy tales, again.

He didn't cherish her, only kept her close as a man would do with a favorite hound on a cold night. Beside her, he yawned. His face showed a three-day growth of dark whiskers. She envied him that. Soon he'd have a fur coat on his face and she'd have only her shawl.

He scratched his neck. "No fire in the mornings. We'll eat jerked beef and dried fruit here then, set off."

She tried not to let her disappointment show. The sooner they departed, the sooner they would reach Chloe, she reminded herself.

"Wear the boys' trousers today. They'll cover you from hip to ankle."

"I have quilted bloomers and woolens."

"I've seen them. Wear the trousers."

She nodded, then fumbled in her pack for the attire he suggested, sliding them under the blankets and over her bloomers and stockings. Next she struggled with her boots. It was a difficult task, since she had to dress lying down or sit up and face the wind. Finally, she had them on, but not laced.

"Ready?" he asked, his hand on the edge of the canvas.

"Yes."

He released the lashing and the sheet flew up and over them. A blast of cold air took her breath away. Cole stifled a groan as he rose to his feet.

"Roll the canvas and blankets." He laced on his snowshoes and headed toward the pines.

Her full bladder told her she'd soon have to do the same, but now she would have to wrestle with skirts, bloomers *and* trousers. She'd be lucky not to stain her skirts. Blast the man.

She had the blankets, canvas and buffalo hide rolled and tied onto their packs by the time he returned. He ignored her as he turned to rummage through his pack.

She drew back her foot and kicked snow at him. It struck the side of his face squarely and then slid down his temple and cheek. A clump filled his ear. He shot her a look of dumbfounded astonishment.

"I did not ask you to rub my feet!" she shouted.

Then she strapped on her snowshoes and stomped away, very glad that she did not fall and spoil her dignified retreat.

She was gone long enough for her temper to cool and to wonder what awaited her return. She found him sitting in the pit, dividing jerky and dried fruit into two leather sacks.

He did not scowl or pretend she did not exist, but looked directly at her as she approached. She found his impenetrable expression more troubling than his resentment, for she could not judge his mood.

She paused on the edge of the pit, waiting.

"I felt guilty," he said without preamble.

She nodded.

"I feel things with you, Bridget. Things I did not even feel with my wife. How can that be?" His eyes reflected remorse and confusion and something else. Could it be longing?

Her stomach gave a twitch in response. She had no answer for his words or the pain in his crystal-blue eyes.

"She's been gone three years," she said. "It's a long time for a man to be alone."

He scowled. "I've not been alone, though it shames me to say it. I've sought out willing women on occasion."

Willing women. Did he count her in that lot? Surely he must, for he treated her without respect. Her mind understood this, but her body longed for what he offered. He raised an ache in her, making it difficult to recall that his intentions were not honorable. "Perhaps we'd best start?"

"I'm sorry, Bridget. You stir me and mystify me like no woman I've ever met. Sometimes I'd as soon strangle you as kiss you. I can't believe that on this frozen mountain, you'd kick snow in my ear."

"There were no rocks at hand."

He blinked at this for a moment and then roared with laughter. It was a merry sound and she found herself smiling at his mirth. The tension broke between them, but not in the pit of her stomach.

His words vibrated through her. *I feel things with you, Bridget. Things I did not even feel with my wife.* Did he speak of longing or lust?

It would be easy if she felt nothing for him, but it was not so. He appealed to her. His touch made her throb and ache. But she did not trust his words. Sean had given her pretty words and then cast her aside like rubbish. But this man before her understood grief and anger and passion. Didn't he? His words echoed all the feelings that swirled in her.

His admission and her longings made him dangerous, and climbing the pass was deadly enough.

Had he really said he felt things for her that he did not feel with his wife?

Chapter Eleven

George stared toward the west. "Bridget might be in Sacramento by now."

Mary's spirits plunged and she held her placid expression only with great effort, trying not to let her husband read the truth. She'd been out in the deep snow on many occasions and knew the impossibility of traveling such a distance. She had watched Bridget all that long, dreadful first day. If her sister had made two miles, it would have been a miracle. As darkness fell, Bridget's hunched figure had disappeared, and then had come the freezing rain. All night it had poured down, leaving a thick crust of ice on the snow.

Without a fire or shelter, what chance did her sister have?

George counted on his fingers. "At five miles a day, she'd have reached Sacramento over a week past."

Mary had pretended not to know of Bridget's earlier efforts to break a trail. Hunting, Bridget called it, coming back wet and exhausted. Before she ever made her attempt both she and Bridget had known she had no chance. That was why Bridget had slipped back the rations and Mary had looked the other way.

Bridget had gone to give them a better chance to survive until spring.

Now Mary saw it was no chance. It was the first of December and the meat was gone. She had sighted no game since the heavy snows. Not even a weasel track broke the endless sea of white. They were buried as surely as if they lay in their graves.

"How long do you reckon it will take her to muster a rescue party?" asked George, still staring at the mountain peaks.

When Mary did not answer, George gave his best accounting.

"I'd say a week, and then they have to cross the pass. The winds are bad, but there's less snow. Still, it will take some time."

"Yes," Mary agreed. "We have to be patient."

Cole made sure Bridget's water sack was strung across one shoulder and nestled safe beneath her coat. Then he tucked a pouch of frozen jerky and dried fruit inside the gap above her pack belt around her hips. She buttoned her coat knowing soon her body would soften the frosty meal.

Each time they stopped that morning, he drew out his water and the pouch, and she did the same.

They had made fair progress yesterday, managing about eight miles since Sam's cabin by his reckoning. The summit lay twenty-two miles from the snow line and the lake, where her sister floundered, three miles down the steepest, meanest descent on the entire California trail.

He hoped for six miles this day, but it was not to be. He had expected the incline as they climbed one of the taller ridges, but the wind blew in their faces and the snow commenced, laying two feet of fresh powder before them.

He broke trail all morning and they did not even make two miles. His legs ached from lifting his snow shoes, laden with soft powder that then sifted through them like flour.

Still he struggled on, racing to cross the ridge before nightfall. Here, the winds scoured the snow clean off the bare gray granite in many places. He kept to the snow when possible, but made an error in one ascent, reaching a dead end against a cliff of stone.

"Damn."

He glanced behind him to see Bridget struggling along in his tracks, head bowed and shawl wrapped around her head so nothing showed of her face.

"Stop," he called.

She glanced up and her shoulders sank as the realization that they must go back struck her.

For three hundred long yards they retraced their steps, until he found a better route. They crossed the ridge at twilight, with winds roaring over the rock like a hurricane, lifting Bridget's skirts and showing the trousers he'd insisted she wear. She clutched her shawl, wrestling in her thick leather mittens to keep the gale from tearing it from her.

Why had he agreed to bring her? He knew the futility of the trip, even if she did not. They'd freeze if he did not get them off this rock.

He couldn't feel his feet and was certain Bridget fared no better. Walking no longer warmed him and he shivered as they pressed slowly onward. The woolen union suit beneath his flannel shirt was soaking wet, adding to his misery.

He could go no faster, for Bridget was already falling behind. Each time he stopped to wait for her, the wind stole into his clothing and robbed him of more heat.

The descent was steep and he had trouble finding a safe route in the growing darkness. Huge boulders and misshapen pines, bent by the relentless wind, loomed like gorgons.

The night closed in and he realized then that they would not make it off the ridge this night. Their only chance was to get out of the wind and hope they did not freeze in the night.

He searched for a safe place, finding it in a large boulder, split down the center and tipping to the left, which offered a slight overhang and a solid mass to block the wind. It was twenty feet at the base and the snow was not so deep on the leeward side.

He dropped his pack and then his snowshoes, using one as a shovel to carve out a hollow in the snow. He looked back for Bridget but did not see her.

He threw a blanket into the rabbit hole he had created, a pit four feet deep and three feet wide. The snow fell heavily, as if it were trying to fill the burrow.

He refastened his shoes and wrapped a rope about

the great rock, tying the canvas down to form a lean-to. He retraced his steps now, finding Bridget down on all fours and struggling to crawl along the trail. He crouched before her, wanting to shout at her. *Do you see? Do you understand why no one would come? I tried to keep you from this.*

Instead, he removed her pack, slipping it onto one shoulder. With the weight removed, she managed to stagger to her feet. He scooped her into his weary arms and turned toward their rough shelter.

He laid her on the blanket and added more covering on top of her, then tucked their packs against the stone and crawled in beside her. The laces of her boots were frozen and he could not release them with his numb fingers. At last he gave up and threw the buffalo robe over their heads, drawing Bridget close to his chest and belly. They huddled there, beneath the heavy shroud, shivering uncontrollably.

How long they nestled together, he did not know, but gradually his teeth no longer clicked and she no longer shook like an old man with palsy. He tried again to remove their boots and, this time, succeeded, placing the boots between them, so they would not freeze. He found her dry socks inside her coat, with what remained of her water. He moved by touch, feeling her feet. There were no blisters, but the temperature of her toes frightened him. In a few moments they both had on dry woolens. He drew her feet up and held them to his belly until she began to whimper. The feeling was back and with it the pain. He did not release her until she ceased to struggle and her toes were once more the temperature of his skin.

Her anguish at the warming told him without words that she had not lost them to frostbite, but she would be more susceptible to it from here forward.

When he finished, she did the same for him, grasping his ankles and holding his feet to her bare skin. She gasped at the first touch but said nothing. He knew her skin must be soft but could not feel her. It was as if his feet were no longer a part of him. Gradually, the sensation began, as if a thousand pins pricked his skin. It grew to a burning, as if she poured hot lead upon him. He fought the urge to draw back, knowing it was necessary. Finally, only a throbbing ache remained and he drew away.

"Thank you," he said, gathering her again and cradling her close.

"I thought you'd left me," she said.

He felt a physical pain at her low opinion of him and wondered about the men in her past. Who had made her always expect the worst from him?

"I could not find a place to stop. The ridge is deadly. We're barely across the top. It's a bad place to rest."

She nestled closer to him.

"I'll never abandon you, Bridget. I'll keep to my vow." *To my last breath*, he thought, but did not speak that aloud.

She sighed, though whether in relief or contentment he could only guess.

"I've been cast off before. The wagon train left us when our ox went lame."

"Our entire party was stopped by the snows."

"My parents abandoned me, as well. If not for Mary taking me in, I'd have not a soul in this world to care for me."

He stiffened, wondering why her parents had cast her out. The most obvious possibility hit him first.

"A man?"

She nodded. "I believed him when he told me he loved me. I'm wiser now."

He wanted to ask the fellow's name, wanted to hunt him down like the dog he was. Instead, he gritted out the words, "Not all men are scoundrels."

"No?"

He drew her closer.

"What happened?"

"He told me he'd take me away. There was nothing for me in Kentucky, save to be a miner's wife. You see? The mines for the men and babes for the women, until a cave-in takes your man or he dies of the black lung. It's a hard life. So when he said he'd take me, well, didn't he only say what I longed to hear?"

"Your parents found out?"

"There was no hiding it. I didn't try because I believed his lying tongue. Here I was packing my things and he was already up and gone." She shivered, but he thought it was not from cold this time. He lifted his hand to test his theory and found her cheeks wet.

He felt the burning desire to kill the man for what he'd done to her.

"What was his name?"

"What does that matter?"

"I'd know it."

"You'll not. Besides, didn't you think I was a woman of easy virtue when we met? Thought I'd use my wiles to gain your freedom? You admitted as much."

He couldn't deny it and now it shamed him. The silence stretched on. She gave a little disapproving sniff, as if he had just confirmed her low opinion of him.

"Nothing but Irish rubbish, same as he thought." She moved a few inches away. "Well, I don't care what you think. I'll not let a man beneath my skirts again. Do you understand, Cole Ellis?"

Is that what she thought?

Remorse settled over him like a heavy cloak as he realized he had misjudged her, when she deceived the jailer and lured him away. Her confidence and her sensuality all pointed to a woman well aware of the effect she had on men. But now he knew her better. The self-assurance seemed bravado and the deception grew from desperation.

But the sensuality?

He took in the sweet scent of her hair and skin. That was just her nature. She could not cease to glow any more than a firefly. Today, dressed in trousers and snowshoes, she still lured him. Even now, when she was draped beneath a buffalo robe, so he could not even see her face and form, his body still pounded in response to her.

Finding her irresistible, he'd followed his instincts, but he hadn't thought of her as a soiled dove since their first meeting. Rather, she was a lioness. But she believed he thought the worst, and that pained him.

"I don't think you're a light skirt, Bridget. It's only that you make me want things I have no right to."

"No," she agreed. "You don't."

He stretched toward her, nuzzling her ear.

She trembled.

He breathed in the sweet scent of her neck. "You feel it, too."

She drew away. "Whether I do or not, does not change the fact that I'll not be deceived by a man again. There's a reason a woman needs a ring before she'll lift her skirts. Men have a habit of forgetting the promises they whisper in the dark."

He stiffened at her implication. As if he could marry again. As if he'd ever again accept a woman into his heart and open himself up to that kind of loss.

Her man might have abandoned her, but what had happened to him was worse. He had loved Angela, but she gave up and in so doing, left him as surely as Bridget's·unnamed man. That was what he felt in the secret places he would not ever speak of. He had learned his lesson. If he loved another woman—this woman, any woman—the very same thing could happen again.

A gust of wind ripped past the canvas, causing it to flap madly. He stiffened to listen. The wind was strong enough to tear it from the rivets. He wondered if he should take it down.

"What is it?"

"I'm worried about the canvas."

"If you remove it, the snow will bury us alive."

"It might in any case." He extended an arm from beneath the hide and knocked his fist against the oiled cloth. The base was covered already. He'd need to mind the opening through the night to ensure they had fresh air.

"Where's your water?" he asked.

"Here." She extended the empty container.

He wiggled out of their nest to fill both skins with

ice, packing it into the opening until his fingers went numb. Once it melted he would add more. He rummaged in his pack for the sack of dried apricots. They were as hard as peach pits. He tucked them beneath his coat. A packet of jerked buffalo followed.

They sat side by side, with the hide over their heads and the darkness so thick he had to rely on touch. But their breath did not freeze and they no longer quivered from the cold.

He'd save them. But how long would the storm blow? It could be days before it let up. They'd never last that long, up on the ridge. They needed to get down where he could make a fire.

"You're worried," she said.

How did she know? "Why do you say so?"

"You grind your teeth so they squeak."

She had him there.

"The storm's pinned us."

"We'll dig out tomorrow."

Her optimism did not soothe him, for he'd been in such a spot before. The storm had raged for nine days and dropped fourteen feet of snow on his party.

He checked the food and found it had thawed enough to eat. They had their poor cold meal, crouched beneath the hide. Afterward he added more snow to their water skins. Then he rose to knock the snow clear from around their shelter. Here on the lee side the snow was already eighteen inches deep. The wind had died somewhat and so it no longer aided in removing the accumulation.

He crawled back beneath the hide and Bridget brought him close, wrapping her warm body around his.

"How far did we come today?" she asked.

"Five, maybe," he lied.

"Since the ridge?"

"Oh, say ten."

"Nearly halfway, then." She sighed.

By miles, they were less than halfway, with the steepest, meanest slopes yet to climb and a storm descending. Still, she found reason to hope.

They sat together in the burrow. When sleep took him, he sat upright, cradling her against his chest. Sometime later he awoke to someone tugging at him. Bridget gripped his arm, shaking him as insistently as a terrier.

"Do you hear that?" she asked.

He listened. The world had gone silent as a tomb.

"The wind stopped," he said.

He tried to throw back the hide, but the canvas bowed under the load of snow above it. Darkness pervaded, though he could not tell if it was still night or if the deep accumulation blocked the light.

He used his snowshoes in an unsuccessful attempt to punch a hole. Finally, he put them on and burrowed upward, breaking free of the four feet of accumulation. His head popped to the surface, like a gopher's, to find a gray morning and heavy wet snow falling hard. The air felt mild, compared to yesterday's icy blast.

"What do you hear?" called Bridget from within their rabbit hole.

"What?" He cleared the opening. "Hand up the packs."

She did and he laid them aside before crawling out onto the fresh snow. He returned to get her snowshoes, the blankets and the hide and finally to drag Bridget up to the surface by her extended hands. She stood on his snowshoes until she finished hurriedly strapping on her own. Next she scrambled into her pack. What was wrong with her this morning? She was as jittery as a fox before a hound.

He grabbed the canvas, rolled it and tied it below his pack.

"Ready?" he asked.

She nodded, but she did not move to follow.

He paused, frustrated. They had to get off the ridge and back to the tree line. Down the ridge was the surest route.

"This way," he said, pointing and took several more steps.

Bridget craned her neck, looking around her. "I heard something, like a boom."

He scowled as apprehension pressed in upon him. There should be nothing like that here. He listened intently until he could hear the wet snow landing all about them.

Silence. Eerie, ghostly silence.

Then he did hear it—a crack, like a gunshot only louder. It reminded him of the sound the ice made during the spring breakup on Lake Champlain.

"There," she said in a low whisper.

The low vibration reached him next, followed by a rumble like a distant locomotive.

He looked back to see Bridget standing on the barren slope, facing the ridge. He glanced about at the field of huge boulders, scattered like marbles along the slope. Cold terror washed through him as realization dawned. His head swiveled frantically until he found the line of trees to the right. If they could just reach them, he thought, they might be saved.

But it was so far and the roaring now filled his ears and shook the earth. Bridget shouted, but he could not hear her above the din.

He ran back to Bridget, tossing her over his shoulders, pack and all.

Then he turned and ran diagonally across the slope. Chunks of ice the size of pianos bounced past him.

Avalanche!

Cole ran, tearing toward the trees, to the rock ridge that jutted out above the pines.

The shaking of the earth made him unsteady. He went down on his hip and could not rise.

"Put me down!" howled Bridget, thumping on his back with both hands.

He released her and she scrambled to her feet, tugging at his arm until he was up and running behind her. Bridget ran past the rocks and into the trees, without stopping.

Where was safe ground?

He glanced back to see the rock he had thought was part of the ridge line, the one he had chosen for the windbreak. It fell against the onslaught of the mountain, tumbling away with the boulders of stone and ice.

They had taken shelter in a saddle, a dip between adjoining ridges. The absence of trees should have warned him, or the large boulders strewn along the slope. But he had not seen them in the dark.

Instead, he had placed them on this avalanche plane. Bridget returned to his side. She stood as solemn and silent as if she stood beside a grave. Together they watched the ice cascade past like a white-water river.

In a few moments the rumbling ceased. The snow halted its liquid flow, solidifying into a deathly grip with speeds that chilled his racing heart.

Cole regarded the place where they had slept and knew that Bridget had saved his life.

He draped an arm about her, never taking his eyes off the devastation before them.

"How did you know?" he asked.

"I sleep light, ever since…" Her voice trailed off.

"Dublin?" he asked.

She gave a quick nod.

He squeezed her shoulder. "If you had never gone there, you might not have awakened and we'd both be buried in about forty feet of ice." He gazed down at her. "You saved both our lives."

Her smile was sweet and he longed to kiss her, but he recalled her words of last night. He had hurt her enough with his jibes and advances. Well, no more.

Damned if he'd be the next man to let her down.

His arm slipped away. "Come on."

He took the lead, zigzagging through the pines until they reached the valley between the two peaks.

The deep wet snow packed down easily as he passed and they made good progress. By midday, they were climbing the trail on the opposite side. He elected to keep to the wagon trail here, because the grade was gentler, though there were many switchbacks.

They stopped at a spring, refilling their water and breaking for lunch.

They gnawed on the jerky as Cole chewed on his thoughts. The icy water numbed his lips and chilled him. Stopping always brought the cold to his bones. He noticed Bridget wrapping her shawl over her head and face. It was time to move on.

He rummaged in his pack, drawing out a sack of foodstuffs. He cached it in the pines, storing it high enough that the wolves could not retrieve it.

They'd need that on the return, assuming they could reach her family. They'd come only four miles since their narrow escape. He estimated they had better than eleven hard miles to go before they reached the lake.

It didn't seem that far until you took into account that the final five miles were straight up and the last three straight down. It was the pass once called Tuckee and now forever known as Broadner, a dubious honor given to the doomed wagon train.

He shouldered his pack and glanced at Bridget, finding her ready to go. They set off, up the trail. He was determined to stop before sundown this night. They would have a fire and hot food and a proper shelter, out of the wind and out of harm's way.

He glanced at the sky. The night came early in the winter, early and fast. He judged they had only three more hours of light. In that time he meant to climb another thousand feet.

As he plodded methodically along, he thought of Bridget's words. She did not trust men and seemed to have good cause. Her father and the man she would not name had both treated her shoddily. He did not like being painted with the same broad brush and wondered if he might be able to change her opinion of his gender. But to what purpose? She didn't trust him and he didn't trust himself, although he did admire her. If he didn't watch out, his lust might grow into something more perilous. He could think of nothing worse than to care for a woman who did not trust him—except, perhaps, to love one who left him behind.

Even if Bridget did trust him, which she did not, and even if he were willing to take another reckless chance with his heart, which he was not, he had nothing to offer.

He had chosen his fate long before he had ever met Bridget and had done exactly what the mayor had hoped he would do, intentionally playing in to his hands. At the time, he had thumbed his nose at Mayor Barnnell and at death.

But no longer. He glanced back to find Bridget trailing him with steady steps. He'd found a reason to live, but not the means to escape his death.

Chapter Twelve

$\mathcal{B}$ridget followed as he led her up the steep slope along the wagon trail that now lay buried beneath twenty feet of snow. Today she could feel her feet and hands. The walking warmed her and soon she traveled with her coat unbuttoned.

She glanced behind her at the pale white glow of the sun through the clouds. A few hours and night would fall. The prickling anticipation in her belly began again.

Why couldn't she control it? She told him she was not some plaything, yet here it was only midafternoon and all she could think of was the night. He'd hold her and breathe warm air against her neck. No one had ever held her like that. With just a little imagining, she could pretend she was his beloved wife cradled safe to his body.

Had Angela appreciated what she had? She must have loved him. And Bridget understood why. Sometimes he was as thick as a chunk of wood. His words were not always gentle. But when she had fallen behind, he had come back for her. This, more than anything he might say, convinced her he had a good heart. He had suffered greatly, but he had not lost his humanity. He had not sunk to the point where he could no longer see the needs of others. Now he was risking his life to rescue her family. That only added to his allure.

With Sean, she had mistaken this rising beat of desire for love. She was wiser now, and knew what she and Cole shared was attraction, nothing more. Only it was so strong, heightened by her growing respect for him, that it now verged on painful, tearing at her with sharp claws and giving her no rest. She craved him as she craved fresh water.

That was why resisting him was so hard. Her longing made her weak. She feared she might surrender to it if she did not keep constantly vigilant. He was a man, and so not above taking what she offered, even when his heart belonged to his wife.

Angela had been kind. She had no doubt come to him a virgin and had no dark secrets or black deeds to her name. Bridget's head hung in shame as she marched on, following in his footsteps.

She did not delude herself. Cole only wanted what Sean had wanted—to bed her. Cole would tell her what she longed to hear. Men did. It was only afterward that a woman learned the truth, and then it was too late.

What was wrong with her that no man wanted her for his own?

She was not good enough for marrying. The truth chilled her worse than this frozen landscape.

Knowing all that, how could she even be thinking of

lying with this man? She understood exactly what came from such dalliances. Her parents had found her sins unforgivable. Only Mary would have her in her shameful condition.

That's what she should be thinking on—Mary and Chloe and George. Had they come to boiling hides yet? She calculated the days and the supplies. Likely the beef had gone. She lowered her chin and pressed on.

They cleared the second ridge an hour later. He paused there and she came to a stop beside him. She hated the breaks because her legs grew stiff and her toes went numb. The only way to stay warm was to keep moving, but it was hard to drink while walking. She felt her energy draining away. The first journey had stolen her stamina and it had not returned. But she would not tell him how weak she felt, how her legs trembled and how sometimes she could not tell the snow from the spots swimming before her eyes. It was just fatigue. After a rest, she would feel better.

He drew out his food bag and she followed his example. His eyes stayed pinned on the high mountains before them. There was a deep cut between the peaks. Snow filled the gap like a frozen river between the jagged granite teeth.

Broadner Pass.

"That's it," he said, lifting his stubbly chin in the direction of their travel.

Mary was just over the ridge.

"How long until we get there?"

He shook his head. "We'll make it partway down this trail today. Tomorrow we'll cross that valley and the river. There's a cabin halfway up the ridge there. Made by somebody on one of the trains to cache their goods."

She kept him focused on the journey. "Will we reach the cabin tomorrow?"

"Easily.

He recapped his water and grabbed another hank of jerky. "Where's yours?" he asked.

When she hesitated, he scowled. There was no telling him that she had no appetite. Instead, she drew out a portion. He waited until she took a bite before starting down the trail.

She stored her food bag back inside her garments and gripped the jerky as she followed. It was frozen before she finished and then it rolled in her stomach as if rancid. She felt the urge to bring it back up, but resisted. She began to sweat. Beads erupted from her skin like droplets of dew.

Soon her mouth watered as her stomach cramped. There would be no stopping it, so she did her best to cover her illness. She did not want him to slow his pace, coddling her meant delays. Despite her efforts to be silent, he stopped, turning just after she emptied the contents of her stomach.

From the scowl on his face, you would think she had vomited on his boots. She smiled at him, feeling remarkably better after eliminating the cause of her discomfort.

"You're ill?"

She grinned. "Some of the jerky is bad."

His glower turned to suspicion. "There is nothing wrong with the meat."

He tramped back to her and drew off his glove, pressing his broad hand to her forehead. "You have a fever."

"And how would you know that, with your hands like blocks of ice?" She batted his arm away. "I'm fine."

He grasped her head between his hands and drew her to him. For an instant her heart thrilled as his lips descended, but he pressed them to her forehead, not her mouth. He held her there a few moments and then drew back.

"You feel warm."

"I've been walking."

Cole looked unconvinced. He glanced about the trail. "We'll stop here."

She flapped her arms in frustration. "We've an hour of light left."

"But tonight I want to see where we camp, and I need time to build a shelter."

The wisdom of that was self-evident. She nodded her reluctant consent.

He moved back along the trail, his head swiveling from side to side as he searched for a resting place. A quarter hour passed before he found what he sought.

He crushed out an area beneath the pines and went to work lighting a fire on the tin. Once he was certain the flame would take, he left Bridget to the tending while he gathered more wood. His last task was tearing green boughs from the pines and setting them against the trunk of a large cedar.

She fed the flame and watched the tin slowly sink as the snow beneath it melted away. By the time he had the conical structure ringing the tree, the fire had melted four inches down.

He nudged her aside. "Lay out the canvas on the branches. I'll put out the blankets."

She rose wearily, stifling a groan at the icy stiffness in her joints. He watched her with the penetrating gaze of an eagle, so she made no sound as she trudged off to do his bidding.

She returned to find the water heating.

"How many miles today?" she asked, sitting beside him on the frozen log.

"Nearly three. But we climbed down a thousand feet and then back up again."

Bridget looked at the gray sky. "If we were birds, we could fly from peak to peak."

"If we were birds, why would we want to? There's nothing living here. The place is as dead as any desert, only good for killing things."

"Aren't you a little bundle of hope this evening?"

He grunted, turning his attention to stirring rolled oats into the boiling water. Soon he had a thick mixture that looked more like lumpy plaster than food. He set the pot between them like a challenge.

She accepted the spoon he offered. Her stomach heaved.

When she looked up she found him glaring at her, his face radiating undisclosed fury.

She dipped her spoon and lifted it to her mouth. It took great effort to swallow. Only then did he begin, eating in angry, silent strokes. He seemed to have drawn an invisible line across the portion, for he ate exactly half in very short order, making it apparent that she had no appetite.

"You're not sick, but you can't eat."

"I am eating." But there was no hiding the obvious.

"Would you drink tea?"

"You have some?" Tea did sound good.

He ate the remaining oatmeal and scoured the pot, setting the snow to melting as he retrieved a small bag of tiny dried flowers from his pack.

"I thought you said we could not bring extra weight."

"This is light enough. It's chamomile."

What a strange thing for a man to carry. Then a notion struck and would not let go.

"Angela drank it."

He nodded. "We had none toward the end."

A suspicion niggled in her mind. It explained his fury. "Did *she* stop eating?"

He showed her a startled expression for just an instant, and she knew she had guessed correctly. He swallowed hard, as if forcing down a lump. Then he gave a great sigh.

"We all stopped. The food was gone. Sam wanted to boil the laces of the snowshoes, but I wouldn't let him." He met her gaze and she saw that his eyes brimmed with tears. "Do you know how it starts? First you will eat anything—bark, pine needles, the leather of your shoe. Then you can't eat. Your stomach shrinks and you're dizzy from lack of nourishment."

Bridget hoped the terror did not show in her eyes. She must eat, she knew it, but her stomach would not listen to reason. She had starved on the journey out. But this was different. There was food. She just had no appetite.

He pushed the tea forward, offering it to her. She lifted the pot, holding it in her lap.

"I'm not dying," she said, though whether to convince him or herself, she did not know.

Soon the tea cooled enough to drink. It tasted like summertime. Her stomach accepted the offering without complaint. She smiled.

"See?" she asked.

He returned her smile, but the worry remained in his eyes. They sat beside the fire until the darkness settled and the wind made the flames leap and then sputter.

"Bed," Cole said, and they crawled into the shelter he had made.

The pine boughs and canvas broke the wind, but it was colder inside than out. They nestled under the blankets and Cole drew the heavy buffalo robe over them.

She laid her head on the pillow of his arm and pressed her back to the warmth of his chest and belly. His breath fanned her cheek. She began to relax, then twisted with that strange falling sensation that sometimes took her into sleep.

The last thing she heard was his low whisper.

"Don't you die on me, too."

Chapter Thirteen

During the night the snow fell so heavily that Cole got up twice to clear the drifts from the entrance of their shelter. Each time he returned to Bridget she welcomed him, curling about him like ivy around an oak. The comfort of her body increased the aching worry. He no longer saw this mission as hopeless. They were tantalizingly close to reaching her family.

If they reached the river by today and could cross it, they might get to the little supply cabin before dark. There they could rest and Bridget could regain her strength.

But if they could not cross, if the river ice would not bear them, they would be trapped below the pass. Bridget grew weaker and slower each day. Now she had a fever. He knew she was giving her all, but he also saw the pallor of her skin and the heaviness of her tread. It was pure stubbornness that drove her, but it would not drive her forever. Her body was failing her.

At first, he only wanted to keep her alive so as not to

have another death on his conscience. But now, the thought of losing her frightened him to near panic.

How could he go through this again?

He would not. That was why he would not love her. To do so was to make himself vulnerable to that pain again. Bridget's spirit called to him, but he would not love this woman or any woman—never again.

Besides, she did not know him, not really. If she knew what he was capable of, she would not be snuggling in his embrace. If she knew what he would do to survive, that look of faith would die. He didn't deserve his miserable life. It came at too high a cost.

Bridget's mission and her unflagging belief in him had made him forget that—made him think himself worthy of her trust. But he was as he had always been.

Yes, he was a survivor, and for that he was damned.

Reluctantly, he left her again and saw the gray morning stealing into his cedar grove. The silhouettes of the trees were black against a gray sky. Dawn was coming, though it was hard to note it past the heavy snow.

He used a snowshoe to clear the entrance and relieved himself in the snow. Normally he would not take the time to light a fire in the morning, but Bridget's weakness and lack of appetite had shaken him badly. He drew out the tins, making them into a pyramid to deflect the snow. Beneath that he laid green cedar bows, then dry bark and finally small branches. Then he poured gunpowder onto the shavings and used steel and flint to send a spark into the midst of his waiting powder. It flared brilliant white. He blew, encouraging the powder to catch the bark. A tiny flame emerged and smoke rose into the air. After a half hour the fire was hot enough to remove the cover and support the pot filled with snow.

He brought her tea in the shelter. She sat half beneath the buffalo robe shivering as she held the offering. Gradually the tea warmed her.

"Oatmeal?" he asked.

She gave a tentative nod. He withdrew. Before he had heated the next batch of water, she emerged from the shelter. Her color was still bad, but she did not shiver. She strapped on her snowshoes and disappeared behind the shelter for a few minutes, then joined him by the fire.

"This is a treat," she said.

He stirred in the oats and waited for his porridge to thicken. She ate less than he had hoped, but it stayed with her. He finished the rest and then kicked snow on the fire.

They set off, continuing down the steep embankment, zigzagging back and forth to reduce the angle of descent.

The snow collected on his hat and shoulders. It stuck to Bridget's long eyelashes and piled two inches high on her lavender shawl.

He stopped to brush it away and she did the same for him. All morning she kept up with him and that made him hopeful. His optimism irritated him. He didn't like to be disappointed and the tide was still against them. Chances were slim that they would reach her sister's camp and nearly zero that they would ever see Sacramento again.

As they continued downward, Cole caught glimpses

of the river through the trees. It was frozen over in places, but in others the flow rushed between the icy banks.

This was bad: The elevation gave him a clear perspective of how dire their situation was. The ice bridges were thin. If they fell through, they could be swept under by the swift-running river. Even if they didn't drown, soaking their clothing was a sure way to kill them both.

Getting a fire started before they froze would be a race. But he saw no other way to ford the river.

He had not realized that he had stopped until Bridget came up beside him.

"How will we cross that?"

"How did you?"

She examined the water below them. "On the ice."

He continued, breaking a trail through the light, deep snow. The air was warmer during the snowstorms, but the going was slower. It took the entire morning to reach the river.

They stood on the bank, well back from the unstable ice, contemplating the challenge.

"Do you think this is the best place? It's wide," she said.

"Wide places are shallow. The ice forms here first."

Bridget studied the snow, as if trying to gauge the ice buried beneath. "Shall I go first?"

"Not yet."

He walked back to the pines, searching for two stout branches, returning with them and offering one to her.

She held it like a staff. "What is this?"

"For the ice. If it breaks, it will keep you from falling through."

She hefted the pole and then nodded, turning to the river.

"Wait."

She paused and he removed her pack, spinning in a half circle and then throwing it across the river. It landed and disappeared in the snow.

Bridget cocked an eyebrow.

"Less weight." He threw his over as well. It did not clear the river, but skidded, coming to rest against the far bank.

He did not like to let her go first, but it made sense. She was lighter and had crossed before. She trod cautiously, gripping the pole like a tightrope walker as she moved steadily on, the wide surface of the snowshoes spreading her weight across the dangerous surface.

He listened for sounds of the ice cracking, but heard nothing but the hissing of the snowflakes falling heavily all about them.

She gained the bank and turned back, waiting, her body rigid with worry. He braced himself and stepped out onto the ice. He went carefully, but quickly, trying to beat the weak spots to reach the bank. There was no warning, no cracking or shifting. One moment he was standing on ice and the next his left leg punched a hole. He pushed off his right, trying to extract his leg, but only succeeded in breaking a larger hole. He fell to his waist in freezing water, stopping only when the pole hit the ice. He gasped, past the knife blade of pain of the frigid water. The agony washing his skin nearly caused him to lose his grip on the pole. Below the ice, the river ran swiftly, tugging at him in an effort to drag him under.

"Cole!" Bridget was on the ice, returning for him.

"Stop!" he shouted.

She did, seeming only then to realize her peril.

"Get your pole," he gasped. The pain squeezed him, tearing away his breath.

Bridget headed back onto the ice. Did she not understand that she might break through as well?

"On your belly!"

She did as he ordered her, dropping onto all fours and then crawling forward.

"Your pole." It was hard to breathe now.

She pushed it out before her. Thank God his hands had not been in the glacial water. He could still grip. But how could she pull him out?

It came to him then, the entire picture of what would happen. She could not lift him out and she would not leave him. She would stay until his strength left him and then watch him slip below the ice.

The pain was going, already replaced by a strange warmth that he knew was a trick of his brain.

The longer they delayed, the more impossible the task. He would get himself out or die.

"Hold on," he cried.

She did, flattening to the ice and spreading her legs wide.

He kicked awkwardly with his frozen legs, heavily laden with the wet boots and snowshoes. At the same time he climbed, hand over hand up the pole. But she could not hold him and as he inched out of the hole, he dragged her closer to it.

He let go with one hand, prepared to sink to his death rather than take her along with him.

"Don't you dare, Cole Ellis! Don't you leave me out here in this frozen hell."

He paused, stunned by her order. He had been prepared to give up, just like his wife. Instead, he clasped the pole with both hands.

"Come on, damn you. You're nearly clear."

He wasn't, but he did as she bid, heaving himself up until he could lift one shoe back to the opposite side of the hole and push off. The other snowshoe now cleared the gap and he kicked against the rim, escaping the river. He was inches from her now. She reached a bare hand to him.

"Get back to the bank."

She crawled away. He tried to follow, but his legs moved clumsily.

"Come on!" she called, motioning him on.

He gained his knees and finally stood to scramble up the bank. But it was no good. His legs were frozen. He could feel nothing below his thighs.

"B-Brr-idget." His teeth chattered like an organ grinder's monkey. "Fire."

She understood. She retrieved his pack, hefting it and dashing toward the pines. He watched her go and then scooped up her pack and followed. He brought it to her at a run and then turned and ran back the way he had come. It was the only way he knew to stay warm, to run and run. At each turn he noted her progress.

Why hadn't he taught her how to set a proper fire?

She laid down the tins, and then gathered bark and dead needles. She laid out tiny sticks, but forgot the punk. Without the decayed cedar, the sparks had no chance of catching, no matter how hard she tried.

He felt his movements growing more awkward. Soon he would not be able to run. He would fall and he would freeze. Bridget struggled with flint and steel.

"Use my t-tinder pouch, gunpowder."

She reset the fire with the crumpling, decaying dry wood at the center. He saw her open a pouch of gunpowder and then he was off on his way to the river again. On his return he glimpsed a fine stream of gray smoke. The kindling burned and the smallest of sticks caught. On his next pass she had branches the size of his thumb in the fire. On his next trip the buffalo robe was out. He made one more loop and could run no more. He dove, hoping to reach the hide and terrified he would fall into the fire and put it out.

Bridget grappled with the icy binding of his snowshoes and then the frozen laces of his boots. His socks were stiff, as if they had been dipped in wax. At last she reached his feet.

They were white as codfish. The ghostly sight caused them to exchange looks of grave concern. Tears ran down Bridget's face as she rubbed his feet, bringing them toward the fire.

"C-careful not to burn them."

"Yes, yes, you already said that."

Had he? Her hands rubbed, but he felt nothing. It was as if he watched her rub two blocks of wood.

"Your trousers. We have to get them off."

He unfastened his belt and slipped the heavy wool down his thighs. She took over from there, dragging them away and then draping them over her pack near the fire.

She stripped him out of his coat, shirts and at last the

woolen union suit before wrapping him in two blankets. She left his feet clear so she could rub them.

"Shall I set the canvas over us, to keep off the snow?"

He glanced up at the sky. The flakes clumped together and fell in heavy wet blobs. It was coming faster, several inches an hour and no sign of letting up.

"No. We can't camp here. The snow is deepest in the valleys. We have to get out, to high ground." That is, as soon as he could feel his legs again.

He bent them, gritting his teeth as his joints ached in protest. It felt like someone held both knees in a vise, turning the handle and increasing the cramping pain. He slapped his thighs and felt only a dull pressure.

Bridget continued to feed the fire and rub his legs. She stayed beside him, using her bare hand to gauge the heat of the flames.

She had not panicked when he had fallen and she had done exactly as he said. Now she worked frantically to save him, building the fire and setting a rough camp, even in these conditions. Snow was piled two inches deep on her back, but she kept her head bent over her task.

"How do they look?" he asked.

She made a clucking sound with her tongue that reminded him of a hen with wet feathers.

"The soles are still yellow. I've never seen such an unnatural color." She rubbed the soles of his feet again. "Your legs are pink again. That's good, I'm thinking."

"You saved me," he said, knowing it was true.

She shot him an impatient glance, as if it was his head that had gone in the river instead of his legs.

The prickling started in his heel and moved rapidly

toward his toes. It grew, roaring to life, the sensation exactly as if she poured scalding water on his bare skin. He pulled his feet from her grip.

"They're burning!"

She checked the fire's heat with her hand once more. "They're not."

He pounded the ground with his fists to keep from crying out. Sensation had returned and the agony of it had him writhing on the hide. He panted and growled like a dog with a broken toenail.

Bridget sat motionless on her heels, snow melting on her head and sticking to her eyelashes as she watched him with worried eyes.

"Give me my socks."

She rummaged in his pack, coming up with a dry pair. His wool trousers and his boots steamed. She wrung out the water from the cuffs and then turned them, busying herself while he gnashed his teeth. Finally the burning dulled to a hammering ache. He wiped his watering eyes.

Bridget checked his woolens. "It will take a bit·for them to dry."

"Best eat while we wait."

Bridget melted snow and they drank the hot water and ate jerked elk and dried fruit. He was pleased to see her appetite had returned. The snow continued to fall so heavily that the trees only thirty feet away became nothing but shadowy shapes against the gray sky.

"Cole?"

He looked at her.

"You'll be all right now?"

He tried not to take her outward concern to heart. To

her, losing him meant losing any hope of reaching her family. Any notion that her worry stemmed from deeper emotion was just an illusion, a trick born from his yearning and his need.

"I am. Thanks to you."

She breathed a sigh and shook the snow from her lavender shawl. She knotted it beneath her chin and gave him a smile.

If not for the cold and the mountains, she'd have left him to rot on the *Stafford*. True, she'd worked desperately to save him, and at night she curled up beside him and kept him warm. True, in the dark, she nestled against him like a lover, but it was necessity, not love, that brought her to him. Regret bit into him with the force of freezing water. His hold on her was transient.

And that was how he wanted it. Then why did he feel this ache in his belly? For just a moment, he allowed himself to pretend that her anxiety over his welfare was not mercenary and that she cared for him just a little.

He pushed back the silly notion. He didn't want her fussing about him. Hadn't he told her he had no place for a woman in his life?

But this was not just any woman. She was special, formidable. He could not think of anyone who would have acted so coolly in such a crisis. Even his friend Sam was known to panic in a pinch. But not Bridget. She was as steely as a sharpshooter. He gawked at her in utter amazement as she put away the cooking pot.

He should be thankful that she needed him. But what would happen when she no longer did?

Chapter Fourteen

The day had been wasted waiting for his gear to dry. By the time they cleared the valley, the afternoon was creeping toward evening.

The snow fell heavily, making it hard to break the trail. That, added to the elevation they climbed, hampered their progress.

Cole began to fear he had erred. They were up high on this rocky ridge with no trees to break the wind or to offer cover from the snow. This was no place to make camp and it looked doubtful that they would reach the cabin before dark.

To reach the cabin, they had to clear this ridge and gain the plateau at the base of the pass. A glance up the trail did not tell him how much farther they had to climb.

His legs trembled with the exertion.

The damned snow lowered visibility to nearly nothing. He would not know when the sun set, but he felt it coming. The time ticked in his mind as he struggled up the steep trail. Only one place would be steeper than this ridge and that was the descent between the summit of Boreal Ridge, through Broadner Pass, to the lake. Three terrible miles that his party had not been able to climb.

The snow and the ice had been insurmountable. Wagons slipped off the trail and oxen floundered, forcing retreat. Had they known that there would be no second chance, they would have slaughtered the oxen and crossed that pass on foot, or died trying.

But there was no way to know, just like there was no way to know if he had made a terrible mistake by not setting the canvas in the valley in favor of pushing for the cabin.

He feared the low places. Snow came so fast there. He'd seen five feet fall in just one night. Seen animals buried alive. Most they never found, even after searching for days.

How much farther?

He glanced back, noting that Bridget had fallen farther behind. He paused, waiting.

She got no rest, for as soon as she drew even with him, he set off again. He could see the exhaustion in her face, read the effort it took to lift one snowshoe and then the next. But he did not pause at the plea in her eyes. She needed rest, but more than that she needed shelter.

They *had* to reach the cabin. It was their only chance.

He beat down the snow, clearing a path for her, easing her way in the only way he could.

Lead her to safety. Get her to the cabin.

Better to dig out from under twelve feet than to sleep exposed on this damn ridge. Why had he not stopped where Bridget had set the fire?

Because the fire had been sinking by the minute. Before his boots were dry, it had melted down two feet. The snow had been too light to support it.

"Cole!"

She was counting on him and he had led her away from the fire to this.

"Cole!"

He halted, looking back. She staggered along like a drover on payday. Cole trudged back until he reached her. She had reached the end of her endurance. He recognized the look in her eye, for he had seen it once before. She was giving up—just like Angela.

"Where is it?" she gasped.

He knew she meant the cabin, but he did not have the heart to tell her they would not make it by dark.

"Over this ridge."

Her breathing was heavy and the words came with great effort. "We *are* over the ridge."

How near she was to exhaustion. It sent a shaft of trepidation through him.

"What?"

"Look." Bridget pointed back up the trail.

For the first time, he really looked. Visibility was still poor, but he noted the level path. Had he veered off the route? Perhaps tramped diagonally across the ridge? He turned back and saw his trail disappearing downward.

Hope sparked in him. They were close. A glance at the sky told him nothing.

"Nearly there, Bridget."

Her shoulders slumped. "Are you saying so to lure me, or because it is true?"

He met her gaze and smiled. "I'll show you."

Her expression changed. She seemed to be gauging something. As she scrutinized him, the determined glint reappeared. She returned his smile and nodded. He had her back again—fighting.

As they crept onward, he began to worry that he had missed it or, heaven forbid, the cabin was buried in the drifts.

But it was where it should be, beside the tall pines that were used in its construction. He did not know what immigrants had built the cabin. Had they realized that they had crossed the highest point of their journey?

He found the pines first and just walked along the ridge until he spotted the chimney sticking up unnaturally from the snow-covered roof. The door was half-buried.

He set to digging as Bridget reached him.

"This is it?"

He did not remove his shoes, but used them like plows to lift and toss the snow away.

"Inside that door there is a western fireplace and dry wood." Or there had been. "Did you stop here?"

"I did not know it was here."

He paused to look at her, trying to fathom how she had missed it. "Easy to see from the pass and on the descent."

Her troubled gaze settled upon him and her expression turned bleak. "Not easy, if you cross at night."

He stilled. She had climbed the pass in the darkness, without snowshoes, alone. A new respect for her blossomed in him. He wished again for just one-tenth of her courage.

"Don't look at me like that."

"Like what?"

"As if you expected me to change your water to wine. I had no choice. Desperation drove me, not daring, and if I had seen this cabin, I'd likely still be inside."

He didn't believe that—not for a minute.

He worked down to the door frame, then halted. There, he held his breath and pushed the door inward. Was the firewood still stacked shoulder high along the sidewall? He stepped into the darkness, lowered his pack to the dirt floor and searched blindly for his ammunition bag. Behind him, Bridget climbed down the snowbank and into the single room. The light from the open door did not reach to the opposite wall where the fireplace stood. He threw his heavy mittens aside, poured a small pile of gunpowder on the floor and set cedar curls upon it. Then he retrieved a stub of a candle from his pack. Ready, at last, he drew a breath and offered a silent prayer.

One strike of the steel to flint and a shower of sparks struck the powder, catching the tinder. In an instant he had the wick lit and the delicate flame sheltered in his cupped hand. On the floor, the powder and shavings sputtered and died.

Bridget broke the silence. "Saints be praised."

She closed the door, leaving them in the warm glow of the single candle, and came forward, drawn by the light. He glanced about, familiarizing himself again with the room. The interior was a box only eight-by-eight, but there was a bed, a fireplace and, yes, a good supply of wood.

He heaved a sigh of relief.

Bridget followed him to the hearth, still wearing her snowshoes. He released his and set them aside. The room was colder than the air outside and his breath came in vaporous puffs, like the steam from a locomotive. He laid a gentle hand on the hearth, giving it a caress, as happy to see it as any old friend. The fireplace had been shaped from logs and then coated with a thick layer of clay. This crust protected the wood from the fire. He dropped to a knee and hastily set the makings for their survival.

The kindling was dry and the flames ate greedily at the fuel. He sat back on his heels to admire the fire that danced with delight. The snow on his coat began to melt.

He smiled.

They had made it to the cabin. He had never expected to come so far. Her family was only five miles from this spot. But it was a terrible five miles. In between here and there was the toughest, most unforgiving pass in the entire Cascade Range.

Her kin were not rescued, but it did seem possible.

Bridget drew off her moose-hide mittens and then her gloves, extending her hands to the fire. She stood still as the ice upon her coat and shawl slowly dissolved, leaving her covered with tiny beads of water. Her shawl dropped back and the snow on her head melted, dripping down her wavy hair to land on the dirt floor.

He unfastened her snowshoes and helped her step out of them, drawing up a bench for them to sit upon.

It was the first time they had been indoors since they had left Sam's cabin.

They sat in silence before the warm fire. Was she as astounded as he was to have survived this long?

After many minutes, the fire chased the chill from the room. His face felt overly warm and he noted that Bridget had unbuttoned her coat.

"I never thought I'd feel warm again," she confessed.

"I'm as surprised as you are."

"But you seemed so sure we could make it."

He shook his head. "I was only sure we would die if we didn't."

Her eyes rounded at this and she shuddered. After a moment, she slid out of her boots next and extended her stocking feet to the fire. After a moment she seemed to recall something, and she knelt before him, untying the laces of his boots.

"You frightened me back there, Bridget."

She glanced at him and held his gaze. He could find none of the weakness he'd glimpsed earlier. But it was there, like the rotten core of an outwardly healthy oak. The inner flaw that brought the tree down in a heavy wind.

"Did I?"

"I thought you'd given up."

She pressed her lips together, but did not deny it as he had hoped.

"I didn't." Her tone did nothing to convince him. "Not really. I wanted to keep going, but I could not convince my body."

"It amounts to the same thing." He could not keep the disappointment from his voice.

She glared.

The warm air did not cut through the ice that now settled between them.

"Bridget, I—"

She lifted a hand. "I'm thinking you were about to do the same, when you were trapped in the river."

He stiffened with indignation. "I didn't want to pull you under."

"Oh, so you do see a time for giving up."

"I wasn't giving up."

She raised her chin in disdain. "You know best."

He shifted uncomfortably. The woman had not fallen behind. She had reached the cabin under her own steam and he had insulted her.

"I'm sorry, Bridget. Just don't want you quitting on me, too."

All the starch went out of her spine at this and she stared at him with wide eyes. "Is that what you think she did?"

He looked away, knowing he would never say it aloud. Not to anyone. "Of course not."

He could feel her stare boring like a beetle into soft earth, but he kept his gaze fixed on the fire.

"Yes, you do. You think because she could not go on that she chose dying over staying to fight. That she abandoned you."

How could she know that?

"I've been abandoned, too," she said.

He did look up then, could not have kept himself from it even if he had tried.

"By who?"

Now she looked at the flames. Her shoulders shrugged.

"By that man?" he asked.

"Yes, by him as well."

As well? He began to wonder if Bridget's tough exterior was like a scar, protecting an unhealed wound.

Understanding seeped into his mind like tea into hot water. "Your family then. They left you to rot in prison."

Her expression turned sullen and her chin dropped to her chest. His arm went about her and he drew her up beside him, gripping her tight.

"There must be something wrong with me, for people keep leaving me."

That was exactly how he felt, how he still felt. Only she had said aloud what he kept locked in his heart. That if he had been a better husband to Angela, she would not have died.

"There's nothing wrong with you."

"You said yourself that I'm no better than a thief and a liar and worse. And it's true. All of it." Her voice broke at the last words.

He wrapped her in his arms, wishing he could fix what lay broken within them. But what could mend such a tear?

And she, this strong, fearless little fighter, was actually full of fear. Was that the fuel that drove her?

"I won't leave you. Not until the job is done. I swear to you."

Instead of brightening her dark mood, his words caused her to weep. She clutched his coat and buried her face in it, as if shamed to let him see her frailty. What had he said wrong?

He rubbed her back, as he had done with his wife. Bridget felt natural in his arms and he mentally blocked the images that formed in his mind. Here she was crying and he was picturing her…well, he'd best put his thoughts to other matters.

She did not cry long. Soon she had herself back in

check, the vulnerability tucked safely away. When she lifted her head, her nose was a pretty pink and her mouth was pressed tight. She scowled at him as if waiting for him to mock her. Instead, he brushed the hair from her face. She drew a deep breath as if putting this behind her.

"We need to see if your feet are still frostbitten."

She had him stripped to the skin in no time and she studied his feet by the warm glow of their fire.

"They seem fine. Not even a blister."

"It was your quick work starting the fire."

She cast him a mournful look. "I've never been so frightened."

Because she knew she could not reach her family without him?

She kneeled at his feet. He kept his hands on his knees, resisting the urge to stroke her soft cheek.

The gravity of this settled over him. They were safe, dry and warm. She continued to watch him, her delicate fingers running up the back of his legs and then coming about the front, climbing toward his hands until she had captured them in her own.

He cleared his throat. "I best unpack."

She hesitated, as if about to protest, but then her warm hands slipped away and she rose to her feet.

He turned to his gear, anything to keep busy. "We should take everything out and see what needs drying or repair."

The packs were quickly emptied and their few possessions neatly organized on the bed and little table. Cole strung a line and Bridget hung their clothes, blankets and canvas up to air and dry.

Cole divided their rations carefully. He needed to bring enough to feed four adults for as long as it took to return to this cabin, but not so much as to leave them short for the descent.

He made his mental calculations, checked them again and put the foodstuffs on the shelf.

"You're not leaving that, too," said Bridget, a note of alarm in her voice.

"Less weight."

"What if they need it?"

"That is all we can spare."

"But they're starving!"

He watched her, wanting to be certain she understood. "We will be as well if we eat all our food."

"But what if we can't cross back immediately?"

He did not lie to her or try to hide the truth, as he had done with Angela. Bridget was strong enough to hear it. "If we cannot make it back here, we all die. The same will happen if we bring the food and consume it. It's a race, Bridget. Do you understand? From this moment onward, it's a race to get them out of these cursed mountains before the stores run dry."

"We should go tomorrow."

She was too weak for the pass. He felt it as surely as he felt the fire's warmth. "We'll see."

He found a second pan, and so they had the luxury of heating water in one and cooking their porridge in the other. They ate in silence, sipping their hot tea from two tin cups.

"What a treat," she said, looping her fingers through the handle and admiring the battered vessel. "To drink from a cup and sit out of the snow and ice. I feel almost human again."

Her smile flickered and died. He knew what she was thinking.

"You being safe and dry does not increase their suffering. We are doing everything possible to reach them. We have to rest before the pass."

"I need to see her. I need to know she is alive."

He nodded. "If your sister is anything like you, she will last until we reach her."

Bridget gave him a confused look, opened her mouth to speak and then clamped it shut again. What had she been about to say?

"Bridget?"

She dropped her gaze, staring at her half-empty cup.

"I am sure you are right."

Something was amiss. He sensed it, but also perceived she did not want to share it with him. He frowned, waiting, hoping she might release the tight hold she kept on her secrets. He would keep them, if only she would trust him.

"Bridget?"

She looked up.

"You can tell me."

The look of longing she cast him was bleak.

He reached out and stroked her cheek. "What have they done to you that the truth frightens you so?"

He received no answer.

Cole needed her to open her heart. Everything depended upon it. He and his wife had had no secrets and the intimacy they had shared had been the most wonderful part of their love. He wanted to share that with Bridget. But she was so different from his wife. Angela had been mild and loving, devout and submissive, while Bridget was suspicious, fierce and passionate. From the moment he'd met this woman, their relationship had been as volatile as a thunderdome. This crazy up and down emotion exhausted him, but also invigorated him.

He tried to imagine what kind of life he would have with such a woman. Surely he would never be bored.

"Bridget?"

She turned to meet his gaze in silence.

"I wish I'd never stolen that damned horse."

Chapter Fifteen

Mary used the axe to split the long bones of the ox, retrieving the precious marrow. With each swing, she wondered if the effort of extraction would be worth the end result.

Her shriveled stomach had long ago ceased to growl. Now it only ached like a thumb struck with a hammer.

Again she lifted the axe above her head, aiming for the chip she had started with the last blow. She strained against the throbbing ache of her swollen joints. Biting down caused her teeth to shift unnaturally. They now rocked in their sockets like rusty nails in rotting wood. She ran her tongue over her teeth, tasting blood.

Her family needed the marrow.

She struck with all her might and felt the frozen bone crack. Mary checked the smooth surface, boiled clean days ago. Yes, there it was, a tiny, almost imperceptible fissure running down the length.

She struck again and the top third split away. She

smiled in satisfaction, gathering up her prize and returning the other bones to the hide.

Funny that the exertion of hauling the bones up into the trees should cost her so much. It seemed heavier now than when it was full of meat. But it was her stamina, not the load, that had changed.

She tromped along her trail, back to the wretched camp, past the snow now shoulder-high. George rested with Chloe beneath the quilts. They lay so still that her heart began to pound.

"George!"

He pulled back the covers from their faces. They watched her with sunken, hopeless eyes, their attention shifting immediately to the shattered bone beneath her arm.

George struggled to sit. "Is that all that's left now, bones?"

Neither of them moved unless they had to. Their life drained away like the meal from a torn feed sack.

"There's marrow here. My mother used to make a fine pudding from this." She grew weary of sounding hopeful and found she did not quite manage it this time. She thought of her mother's kitchen in Dublin. It had been empty on more than one occasion, but never so empty as Mary's larder now.

She recalled a pot resting on a warm stove. Her mother pouring in milk and adding eggs. She had let Mary grind the cinnamon stick and nutmeg, sprinkling the fragrant brown dust into the pudding. Mother added the marrow from two bones, as Bridget stood ready with the cup of raisins, not stealing a one, but waiting for the signal from mother to add them to the mix.

George stared morosely at the leg bone. "We'll be boiling hides next."

Why did Cole regret stealing that horse? Bridget knew he no longer wished to die, but his remorse was something new.

She allowed herself to hope he had feelings for her. The bright light of promise lasted for only an instant before reality snuffed it like a blazing candle. They had no future as long as he was a wanted man.

No future and no past—they had only this moment. They might only ever have this moment. Her heart gave a flutter as an irrational desire gripped her.

Below them, men clamored to recapture Cole. Above, Broadner Pass dared them to cross. But somehow they had found a tiny oasis from their troubles here in this little shack.

Bridget stiffened her spine and prepared to take a chance.

She laced her fingers through his. "We're safe here tonight."

Bridget sat beside Cole on the little bench, tucked up snug and tight to the warm fire. She wanted to stop time and stay here with him. Here the posse could not reach them and the winds did not bite through her coat.

She thought back and could not recall a time in her life when she had ever felt more content.

"You're smiling," he said.

"Am I?" She met his gaze and held it. "It's nice here."

"A sanctuary." He clasped her hand.

She thought of Mary and her smile vanished like the summer dew. "But it can't last."

His grip tightened as if trying to hold the moment. "The trip is taking a toll on you."

She lifted her chin, defying the bone-weariness that gripped her. "It's not."

He knew from the circles under Bridget's lovely eyes that she was past exhaustion. He was about to argue at her stubborn refusal to admit the obvious when he remembered the cost of delays. Heading west, his party had rested in the lowlands to let the cattle graze. Just one day, but it had been crucial and the pass had closed before them. Later, when he returned to the trapped party, he found his daughter had died five days earlier.

He felt the now familiar shot of regret and aching helplessness.

"What is it?" she asked.

"I was recalling my last visit here."

"Would you tell me?"

He didn't want to. It was a terrible tale. She had her hope and he did not want to douse the very flame that sustained her.

She rested a gentle hand over their clasped ones. "Please."

He nodded, tired already just thinking of the emotional effort this required. He drew a deep breath in preparation for the ordeal of the telling.

"We tried three times to cross that infernal pass. The animals could not climb through the ice and the deep snow. So we led them back down to the lake and to their death. Better if we had slaughtered them right there, but we did not know.

"We were exhausted from the attempt. It was dark when we reached the lake. We huddled in our wagons, with plans to butcher the stock in the morning. I've never seen it snow like that before or since."

Bridget held his gaze and he knew from her haunted look that she had seen it as well.

"The next morning, we found the stock had wandered off. They never did that once on the trip, but there's something about those snows. They went to ground. Spent days searching for them with hooks fixed to poles. Found thirteen carcasses up against the trees, frozen solid. It was obvious to all that we would die. The party broke up into families, leaving us to make our own shelter."

"Did you have supplies?"

He shook his head. "It made the decision to go an easy one. As soon as we had fashioned snowshoes from the oxbows, we made our way out. We had fifteen in all. That's what we started with, anyway."

Bridget shifted as if suddenly uncomfortable on the bench. She knew what was to come. Everyone in the country had heard the tale. But she did not stop him, only braced herself, gripping the plank in preparation for what came next.

"The first of our party to go was Kathleen Rouche. She left two children back at the camp, knowing they'd die without aid. She begged us to reach Fort Sutter and send help. We buried her under a pile of rock right here on this ridge."

He set the pot of water on to heat. "We lost three

more in the next two days. Charlie O'Dell, his wife, Virginia, and the mule skinner, Gordon Learner. They had no snowshoes and could not manage. We didn't even pause to bury those poor souls."

He sprinkled the dried chamomile blossoms into the steaming water. His jaw worked hard, as if grinding a root between his teeth. It seemed to help him summon the courage to tell her the next part.

"Angela took a fever." He pinned Bridget with an accusing gaze as he tried to beat back the panic her warm brow had caused him earlier in their journey. He lifted his hands in a gesture of hopelessness. "No food, no water. When she fell, I was too weak to carry her, so we sat in the snow. The others went on. She never got up again."

Bridget poured the tea and offered him a cup. He clasped the warm tin in his hands to mask the shaking. This was why he didn't speak of that time.

"I begged her not to leave me, but she died on that second ridge."

He set the tea aside and pressed the pads of his fingers into his eye sockets as if to rub away the memories. He wouldn't tell her the next part.

She stroked his arm, silently encouraging him, and he found the words tumbling out.

"Sam came back to warn me. He said he didn't trust Devlin, who was acting crazy and had a gun. Sam helped me cover Angela, but wouldn't let me wrap her in the blanket. Insisted we needed it and for that I struck him. He never lifted a hand to defend himself."

"You were grieved."

"The others came back." He balled his hands into

fists and heard his knuckles crack. "Not all, just Devlin and his wife, Amelia, with their two grown sons, Peter and Jake." He pressed his fists to his knees as memories flashed like lightning across his mind.

"Cole, what is it? You've gone pale."

He glanced up, recalling his surroundings.

"Have you heard of them? Charles Devlin and his wife, Amelia Barnnell Devlin?"

It was obvious from her round-eyed expression that she recognized the name.

He nodded. "Yes, that Barnnell. She was the mayor's sister. They never made it out."

"It's why he hates you."

He smiled. That sentiment was mutual. He was very like his sister—greedy, entitled and powerful.

"As I said, they came back, but not for me."

She fidgeted absently with her thumbnail, tearing off a tiny sliver as she peered up at him. He thought to have pity on her, spare her this, but some part of him needed her to know.

"For Sam?" she asked. He read the uncertainty in her voice. She was not willing to entertain the other possibility.

He shook his head and watched her go white as flour.

He merely confirmed the prospect that was too terrible to voice. "Yes. They wanted Angela. Amelia made a pretty speech. Speeches are all the Barnnells are good at. Said Angela's death would be noble, for it would save us all. They wanted me to hand her over like a side of beef…insisted."

She held her breath. He did not make her wait.

"I said I'd be damned first.

"Devlin ordered me off, like he was still the boss and I was still just a mule driver…the bastard.

"I said I'd kill the first man who touched her. Devlin called off his wife and sons. Made a great show of going, as he pulled his pocket pistol. Piss-ant little double derringer, thirty-two caliber with an ivory handle." Cole turned up his empty palm as he recalled the gun used by gamblers and whores. "A coward's gun."

He cast her a glance and found Bridget stared without blinking, her attention unwavering.

"He missed. I didn't."

"You killed him."

"Shot him in the forehead and told his widow that if she was hungry she could eat that."

Bridget muffled a cry by pressing her hand to her mouth, but said nothing else.

"Sam stayed with me. Stood watch in case they came back."

"Did they leave? I mean to say, did they leave Mr. Devlin?"

"His sons dragged him off. Found him the next day. They didn't drag him far before stripping the meat off him."

Bridget gagged. Then she stiffened.

"That's why you said that. About who was with me. You though— You thought…" She shook her head in denial. "Cole, did you…"

She couldn't finish. He read the horror in her face and thought he deserved that and more.

"I didn't, Bridget. I left him as I found him, poor bastard." Did she believe him? He could not tell.

She held his gaze. "Sam?"

He looked away.

"Sam kept me moving. He's the reason I survived. I wanted to stay with my wife." He lost control then, pressing his hand across his eyes, trying to stem the tears. His voice broke but he kept on. There was no stopping him now. "But he kept telling me that Lee-lee needed me and saying I promised Angela. So I went."

Bridget said nothing as she wrapped an arm around his waist and held him.

He wiped his face, accepting the truth. "But I failed her again. It was my job to protect them, to keep them safe."

"You did all you could."

"I didn't. Because I'm here and they're gone."

"Perhaps Angela died to give you a better chance."

He stiffened in her arms.

"What?"

"Perhaps she knew she slowed you down, reducing your chances. If she felt a burden…"

"I loved her."

"Of course, but for her child. She needed you to rescue her daughter."

The truth of Bridget's words hit him like a clap of thunder and he recognized she was right.

"She told me to save Lee-lee." The guilt hit him again like a falling tree. He'd failed even in that. "But I didn't."

"Angela was trying to save you both. She did the only thing she could to help you. She died."

He turned to her. "How can you possibly know? What makes you so sure what she did and why she did it?"

Bridget looked at the fire. It was as if she could not

meet his eyes. Suddenly, he understood it all, his wife and Bridget and the choices they had made.

"You know because you did the same thing," he said. "You didn't walk off to save them. You walked off to die."

She nodded. "It was all I could do to give them a chance."

His mind reeled. He had blamed his wife for dying, secretly in the places he never revealed even to himself. He saw her death as weakness, as the unwillingness to stay with him through the hard realities. Now he saw things differently. In that instant of comprehension, he understood that the actions he thought were frailty actually grew from a core of strength mightier than these mountains.

His wife had been braver than he ever imagined. He had been so close to death himself. If she had not died, what chance would he have had?

The answer came to him with certainty. No chance.

He regarded Bridget through new eyes, seeing his wife's sacrifice and her desperate gamble.

"She saved my life."

"Yes."

Chapter Sixteen

They sat side by side before the fire. It was hard for Bridget not to delve into his mind and pry into his thoughts. But she waited until he spoke. It was a long wait.

"I thought she gave up, so I did the same. But now, I think I'll try living again." He turned and gave her a weary smile. "Because of you."

She looked at him in wonder. "What do you mean?"

"I had nothing before. I'd lost everything and everyone. Most of all, I lost my purpose. You gave me a new one."

Had she really done that? Had she and her family afforded him the will to go on? Her pride made her puff up like a nesting hen. For a moment, it chased away her worry, making her feel she had done something worthwhile.

"You've brought me back to life. You believe we will reach them, so I believe." He turned her to face him, staring earnestly into her eyes. "If I can save them, Bridget, it will make my life worthwhile."

She tried to understand. Had he stayed alive only for their mission? His willingness to help her should have been enough, but somehow she had hoped that his will to live came from his need to stay with her. She bit back her disappointment. It seemed men never stayed with her.

He grasped her shoulders. "I need to reach them as much as you do. Don't you see?"

She didn't.

"I could not keep Angela from slipping away, and I am years too late to save my child. But I might save *your* family. I might restore them to you. It would be my gift to you for giving purpose to a life that was meaningless for so long."

Did he really credit her with this transformation? If it was true, then she had given him a second chance, a reason to keep on breathing, and it was a tribute to her.

They shared a smile.

She did not recognize the exact moment when the comfortable silence ended. His smile was gone, melting slowly away like an icicle in March as her stomach tightened in anticipation. Some unseen force squeezed her, making it hard to breathe. She watched his pupils expand until they were dark circles ringed with ice blue. His nostrils flared as if he labored along on his snow-shoes.

He seemed to feel it, too, this unseen force drawing them together as surely as two magnets. He moved closer and she stiffened, knowing she must move off now or send the wrong message. Still, she stayed like the possum she had frightened in the grape arbor. Any moment now she'd faint dead away, just as it had.

He leaned forward, gathering her trembling hand. He planted a feathery kiss upon the sensitive skin of her inner wrist. Could he feel her pulse pound beneath his lips?

His thumb stroked the blue veins, brushing away the moisture he left a moment ago. It was the simplest of movements, like the sweep of a bird's wing, yet it roused a pounding desire low in her belly and, lower still, she felt herself grow moist with wanting.

Their eyes met. She knew they might never cross that pass, that the winds and the snow might drive them back. He knew it, too. She read it in his gleaming eyes, made bright by the understanding of their frailty.

She swore she'd never again take a man who did not have the decency to make an honorable proposal. But what proposal could he make, this wanted man? Any future they had would be a gift, for time and the mountain were against them.

She hesitated. He held her gaze and she knew she would take Cole and all he offered with those sparkling blue eyes.

She stood, drawing back, and saw the uncertainty in his expression. She made him wait, made him want. Then her lips curled in a smile that offered…everything.

He sprang to his feet and drew her into his arms. His kiss drove all misgiving from her mind. She wanted this man she could never have, wanted him enough to forget the cost, to forget that he would leave her to deal with the consequences alone, just like the last time.

Her head dropped back and her mouth opened to his. He crushed her against his body, smothering her with his desire. Her fingers found the gap at his shirttails and slid beneath.

"Bridget."

He did not beg, as Sean had done, except with his eyes. She read the yearning there, strong and quick as her own.

His breathing told her how tenuously he gripped his shredding control.

"It isn't wise," he said.

She knew that without him saying so. She drew closer, resting her head upon his chest. The sound of his heart's rapid beat thundered beneath her ear.

"Will you have me?" he whispered.

She stilled, astonished. He did not cajole or threaten to leave her, like a child trying to get his way. Instead, he left the choice to her. She glanced up at him, seeing his grave expression. She relished the hunger she read in his eyes, the urgency in the tightly coiled muscles of his arms.

She waited, as if considering what was already decided between them. But he did not know that she was as hungry for him as he was for her and had even less will to stop this madness.

"Bridget?"

She'd never seen a more desperate man and the sight thrilled her. She wondered if anything on earth was powerful enough to smother this fire roaring between them.

She inclined her head, consenting. "I will."

He gasped in relief as he drew her to the bed. In a moment, he had the blankets and the buffalo skin draped. Then he drew back. When he turned to her, she had already removed her shawl and coat.

The fire in the hearth heated the air and she felt warm down to her toes.

She sat on the bed to remove her boots and then turned to the fastenings of her dress. It was then that she recalled the time she'd seen him, cast in the golden light of the setting sun as he stood in her hotel room, naked to the waist. Anticipation made her blood race as she realized she would see him once more.

She glanced up. He already had his outer clothing and boots off. He stood barefoot in his union suit. She stood to release the buttons at his chest to slowly reveal inch upon inch of muscular torso. She slid the fabric over his strong shoulders, gliding her fingertips over the hot, velvety flesh of his back. Her nails raked his skin and he gasped.

The fire crackled, giving the room a cheery glow. If she did not think too hard, she could almost imagine this was home and he was hers for more than just one night.

Don't think of that now.

She kissed the warm naked flesh of his chest. His groan made her hot with anticipation. He lifted his hands to her ribs and then moved slowly upward to cup her breasts. Now she stifled a groan, but it came deep and low in the back of her throat. How wonderful it felt to have his hands upon her, pressing, caressing.

His nimble fingers flicked over the buds of her nipples, beading them to tight aching pinpoints. Their eyes met. He seemed to relish watching her face as he aroused her with his touch.

He released the narrow row of hooks and eyelets at the front of her dress as if he were racing down a hill on skis. Sean had been clumsy, tearing the delicate fastenings from their anchors. But not Cole. He worked like a master. How did he know so much about a woman's clothing?

His wife.

The realization threatened to destroy her desire.

But there were benefits as well. *Yes, think on that now.* He would know his way about. This was no green boy without knowledge of such things

That thought thrilled her, giving her a little tremor of delight, until another thought struck her.

He would have had two women now and he would compare them. Bridget felt instantly lacking. For one thing, he had offered to make Angela his wife.

She stayed his hand.

He cast her a questioning gaze. She turned her back and lifted her skirts, releasing her boys' trousers and dragging them away. It gave her a moment to think, to consider what she was doing.

But the instant she straightened, he had his hands upon her again, those knowing, devilish hands. They clasped her shoulders and drew her back against him, letting her feel the hardness of his chest and belly as he molded her to him. She sighed. Her thoughts fragmented at the coaxing stroke of his fingers upon her bare neck. He brushed her hair back and trailed hot kisses over her heated flesh.

He stroked her belly, opening her dress. His fingers danced over her chemise, stimulating her as he drew her sleeves down and away. The dress slid from her shoulders and fell at her feet.

He slid a finger beneath the chemise at her shoulder,

drawing it down her arm. The chemise sagged low. She stood in her quilted petticoat, wool stockings and bloomers. He stepped before her and his gaze raked her as if seeing her for the first time.

"You're beautiful."

She felt her cheeks and neck heat. The blush bloomed over the skin revealed by the drooping chemise, glowing with high color. He reached for the white ribbon closure and drew back, releasing the knot. His fingers and mouth worked together releasing shell buttons and wetting her skin. His kisses traveled downward as he drew the top away. He reached her breast and suckled one erect nipple. She gasped at the thrill of it. Never in her life had she felt such a tightening pleasure. It came near to pain, but was simultaneously pure delight. She bit her lip to keep from crying out, for she did not want him to stop. Could he know what he did to her?

Her underskirts fell about her. His eager fingers now rolled her stockings down below her knee. He grasped her hips and sat her on the bed as he worked each stocking over her ankle and foot. His clever mouth followed, laying sweet, hot kisses on the tender flesh between her bloomers and woolens. His lips and the sensual scratch of his growing beard drove her mad.

She watched him and thought she had never seen a more erotic sight than Cole kneeling there, his dark head between her knees. Wicked and wonderful, she realized as a shot of desire flared from the point his mouth touched her heated flesh to the very core of her. Who could have guessed that the inside of her knee was so sensitive to touch and so intimately connected to that place at the junction of her legs? His touch made her grow wet there as her body prepared for him. The yearning grew more insistent and she struggled against the unnatural desire to grasp his dark hair and pull him still closer.

He had her stockings off, leaving only her chemise and bloomers. He stood and drew back the covers, making a place for them, and then scooped her up in his arms and laid her down in his bed.

He did not fall upon her as she feared, but moved to sit on the base of the bed, lifting one of her feet in his big, strong hands. He massaged the ball and her head fell back on the pillow at the captivating pleasure of his touch. He worked up her ankle and calf, following along with tiny kisses.

Cole reached for the cord to her bloomers and she grasped his wrist. He stopped, waiting again for her to tell him yes or no.

Her eyes darted nervously. He tried for a reassuring smile. It was difficult when it was all he could do not to tear the clothing from her perfect body. Who could have imagined that her nipples would be as big and pink as the inside of a cockleshell?

"I'll never hurt you," he assured her.

She drew her hand away and he pulled the cord, releasing the knot. She lifted her hips for him as he drew her bloomers down her slim legs. She was smooth and soft with a narrow waist and flaring hips. Her belly was sunken from the hardship she had endured. He grimaced, knowing she was too light for her height. Had she ever had enough to eat?

He paused to look at her lovely breasts. At his hesitancy, she reached to cover herself, clasping her hands across her generous bosom. He quelled the urge to grasp her wrist and draw back her hands. Instead, he met her cautious gaze. He knew she thought of that other man and Cole felt his rage seethe within him like a pack of rabid dogs. He drew a breath to calm himself. He must not frighten her. He could not bear that.

He held her gaze as he spoke in a low voice. "Let me look at you, Bridget. I've done nothing but imagine this since I first saw you. Let me, please."

She paused and then slowly drew her hands away, opening herself to him. His gaze devoured her.

His voice came low, hushed, as if he spoke in a church, for in truth he had come to worship her as only a man can worship a woman. "Ah, you take my breath away. Beautiful as a blooming rose," he whispered.

"My middle name is Rose."

He laughed. "Of course it is."

Cole lay beside her, clasping her cheek in his palm and kissing her deeply. When they drew apart, she was breathless and her cheeks flushed pink.

"Will you love me, Bridget Rose?"

In answer, she pushed his undergarments down his legs. She was bold, even in this, he thought and smiled his approval. True, her hands did tremble and her eyes were wide, but she went bravely forward, just as she had done since he had first met her. He admired her willingness to try, even when afraid. It was, in his estimation, the truest measure of courage.

He slid between her legs, waiting for her to accept

him. She rested her hands on his shoulders and parted her thighs. He moved against her, poising himself, and found her wet and ready. It took all his will not to drive forward and thrust himself deep into her welcoming heat. But he could feel her comparing him to her first experience, and he aimed to show her what a man could give his woman.

He kissed her deeply as he entered her, thrusting with measured slowness until she accepted all he had. Their hips met and he closed his eyes to savor the sweetness of this first joining. He expected her to lie still as he rocked against her, as Angela had always done, but she did not.

Instead, she lifted her hips and brought him farther inside. He gasped at the unexpected rush of pleasure. Then she did something he didn't know possible. She squeezed him, down there. Deep within herself, she grasped him tight. He startled at the exotic ache of her grip. It felt as if she held him in her hands and kneaded him.

He glanced up at her in utter astonishment and met the desire flashing in her eyes. Her smile was lush, erotic and full of promise. He knew at that moment there would be no slow taking of pleasure, no savoring, no delay. As if emphasizing her need she rocked sharply against him. He inhaled in a last-ditch effort to control the urge to take her swiftly and lost the battle.

He rose up on his arms and she tipped toward him, opening herself, even as she wrapped her legs possessively about his hips.

He thrust and she met him, lifting to take each stroke. Her head flung back as her strong legs gripped him, bringing him down with even greater force. She seemed to thrive on this violent merging of their passions and he could not stop himself from the madness she roused in him.

Bridget grasped his hips with her hands, digging her nails into his buttocks as she demanded he move faster. He did, driving deeply.

She coiled about him and then screamed, falling back to the bed as her body trembled about him. The sight of her writhing in her release and the feel of his body moving with hers were his undoing.

He thrust once more, crying out in bliss as his seed poured from him in a rush. His arms failed him and he collapsed upon her, unable to move except to draw breath.

His heartbeat pounded in his ears. She looped one arm about his neck as the other fell lifeless to the mattress.

They lay there with no sound but their breathing and the crackle of the logs burning in the hearth.

What had she done to him? He'd become some kind of crazed animal. Never in all his married life had he felt this depth of passion or allowed himself free rein to give and take with such abandon.

Surely he had hurt her. A woman was a delicate creature, not made to be used as some kind of vessel for his lust. Regret and shame mingled. He squeezed his eyes shut, summoning the will to face her.

She lifted her hand and brushed the hair from his face. He opened his eyes, but instead of seeing Bridget's condemnation, he saw her gaze glowing with satisfaction, a tired smile curling her lovely lips. She kissed the tip of his nose and yawned.

"That was wonderful," she said.

He was shocked speechless and she laughed at him, the sound musical as tiny chimes.

"I—I thought I hurt you."

She shook her head and blushed.

"But I was too rough," he insisted.

Her smile was wise, making her look much older all of a sudden. Her nimble fingers stroked his back and then his buttocks, finding the crescent marks her nails left in his flanks.

"You, at least, left no mark."

He hadn't hurt her. The relief was sweet.

He sank down beside her in bed. The cool air raised gooseflesh on her arms, so he drew the covers, cocooning them away together.

Sated and relaxed, he pulled Bridget close and wrapped her in his arms. She sighed and snuggled tight against him, pressing her round bottom to his haunches, and he thought this the most perfect moment of his life.

One eye opened. How could he think that? How could he betray his wife's memory with such a notion?

Betrayal or not, it was true. He had never been so taken away, never enjoyed bed sport more. Bridget's passion was like a prairie storm, wild and fierce. He felt lucky to have survived it and now longed to taste that maelstrom again.

He woke sometime later to find the fire ebbing. He slipped from the bed, shivering as he hurried to add more wood. When he returned he found Bridget on her side, facing him, her eyes closed. He lifted the covers and slipped in beside her, pressing his back against her and letting her warm flesh drive back the chill.

She made a little humming sound and reached out for him. Her fingers splayed down his belly, possessively, as if taking measure of something that was now hers.

The stroke changed instantly, the possession turning to a demand. Her fingers did not comfort or love, but roused him to her insistence. Up and down the distance from his navel to his groin her caresses traveled, hardening him in an instant. Her fingers slipped around him, measuring his length from stem to head, pausing there to explore with the tips of her fingers, before returning to a torturous, slow stroke. It was all he could do not to cry out.

He gripped her hand, preparing to move over her, but she batted him away. He retreated, wondering what to do. His wife had never batted at him, but neither had she reached out to stroke his privates as if they were her pet cat. What kind of game was this, to bring a man to attention and then slap at him?

He did not have long to wait for the answer, Bridget moved next. Instead of opening her legs and welcoming him, as he hoped, she rolled him to his back and mounted him. He could see her, as the firelight gilded her skin. Fiery red hair cascaded down her body in wild curls. She looked like an ancient Celtic warrior-queen, about to do battle.

She had already conquered him.

He could not quite squash his shock as she grasped him, positioning him to accept her body as she slid over him until she had impaled herself. She sat full on his hips, head thrown back as she savored the merging of their bodies. He reached up and touched her breasts and she leaned heavily on him, pressing her full round orbs to his eager hands. He stroked her taut nipples and she groaned, deep and low in her throat like a contented lioness.

She rocked forward, taking her weight on her arms and lifting her hips until she almost released him. Then she thrust down hard again.

How could he have reached the age of twenty and six and not have known a woman capable of this? She rocked and arched and curled, milking him until he could no longer lie still. He grasped her hips and tossed her to her back, driving deeply into her, again and again. Her cry of pleasure triggered his own and he shook with his release. The woman would kill him, surely.

He smiled.

She blinked up at him, spread out beneath him like a banquet. He leaned down to kiss her breasts and then moved upward until his lips met hers.

"You are a wonder, Bridget Rose," he whispered.

He drew her against him and wrapped them in the covers.

She dozed, and he pressed his lips to her ear. "I thought you said you couldn't ride."

Her tinkling laugh made him smile.

Bridget's gentle breathing told him she slept. His body ached from the exertion of the climb and the lusty bed sport they had shared. He longed to follow her into slumber. But his conscience kept him awake.

He had never taken advantage of a woman before. But that was what he had just done. He could not even make it right by offering to marry her—not with the mayor longing to stretch his neck.

Barnnell would not rest until Cole was dead. The stolen horse had only been the excuse he'd needed to come at him with everything he had.

Cole stroked the riotous waves of Bridget's hair. He was not free to claim her, but that had not stopped him in his mad rush to begin something he would not live to finish.

Chapter Seventeen

Bridget woke in the narrow bed with one bare leg flung over Cole's naked hips, his arm clasped her to his side. The dreamy lethargy of last night leaked away like water through a sieve and harsh reality intruded.

The fire had burned to ash, leaving the room dark and the air cold. The chill seeped into her heart. Her breathing caught as implications rushed into her mind. She forced herself to relax. If she stiffened, she might wake him, and she needed a moment to think.

When she had lain with Sean, she had been awkward and embarrassed. She had changed her mind as he tried to enter her, but he would have none of it, calling her a tease and taking what she no longer wanted to give. It had hurt and there had been blood.

But she had had none of that with Cole. Suddenly, she understood why men and women chose to do something that seemed so awkward and uncomfortable. It wasn't unnatural at all—not with the right man. They fit together like the sections of an orange, and the blending was just as sweet. Had it not been for Cole, she might have lived her whole life long and never have known such nectar. He had roused her body, preparing her to experience something that she had not even known existed. Now she did, and already she ached with remorse for the ecstasy that she had tasted but could never keep.

They had no future, for, one way or another, he would leave her, with only the memory of this night to warm her.

What future? He only asked you to share his bed, not his life.

Her breath caught. It was true. She had given herself to him, just as she had done once before. But Cole was different, wasn't he? He wouldn't abandon her if she needed him. He came back for her in the avalanche. The memory gave her hope. Then she recalled another man.

Sean had told her he'd not have a woman who lifted her skirt to any man. That cut still bled, for the truth was she had lifted her skirts only for him...until now.

How quickly she had been ruined. When her father had learned of her shame, he would not have her under his roof.

She listened to Cole's steady breathing. What would he do if he knew her secret?

The truth gripped her. Icy fingers seemed to squeeze her throat until Bridget could hardly draw a breath. What if it happened again? No, it couldn't.

Dread settled over her.

He knew of Sean, of course, but that was only the start of her shame.

Cole's talk of honesty was a trick. If he knew it all,

he'd toss her out like a blighted potato. Just as her father had done. Any man would, wouldn't he?

How she longed to confide in him. But she couldn't, ever.

She drew away from the comfort of his arms, slipping out from beneath the covers.

His voice was sleepy and as warm as his body.

"Where are you going?"

"To rake the fire."

"Mmm," he said and dropped his head back to the pillow.

She made her way cautiously along, but still stubbed her toe on the bench. She roused a flame from the hot coals and laid on more wood. When she returned, he lifted the covers for her and she slipped back beside him.

What would happen in the morning? Would he still cherish her or would he cast her out?

He dragged her pliant body to his and his warm wet mouth was on her neck again. She should stop him, but she found his caresses irresistible. She'd have him once more, for resisting now was foolish.

She wanted to feel the fire again, the wild passion that only this man ignited within her.

"Ah, Bridget Rose, I can never get enough of you."

Such pretty lies he told. She sighed and turned her head, offering her exposed neck. He rolled her and then slipped his hips between her thighs. She wrapped her legs about his lean, muscular haunches.

For the first time in her life she had a sense of belonging, as if she were home at last.

Afterward, she slept in his arms. How long she rested she did not know, but she became aware of Cole, his arm wrapped around her shoulders as she lay with her head upon his chest. He coiled one of her curls around his finger, stroked the lock between his thumb and forefinger.

Her breath caught and his hand stilled.

"Did I wake you?" he whispered and kissed her forehead.

She did not answer, could not answer. The night's secrets rushed back and she felt a sense of rising doom. What must he think of her, spread shamelessly across him? His wife must have worn a proper sleeping gown at night, every night. Of course she had. She would never have straddled her husband's lean hips and…

She groaned.

"Bridget, you're trembling."

Fear made her twitch like a nervous horse, dancing at the end of the lead line.

"Cold?" he asked, making a logical guess.

She nodded. She was cold, right through to her aching heart.

He drew up the blankets to cover her shoulders and cuddled her close. She ached with longing for this man and for the future they could not share.

"Let me get the fire going again. I'd say it's morning."

She did not ask how he knew. With no windows, the cabin was dark as a crypt. But if he was right, their moment of safety and comfort had dissolved like a dream.

Cole moved over her. She had to stifle the urge to

cling in some desperate foolish attempt to keep the morning from taking him from her, for with the morning came all the worries of the world.

She lay motionless as he slipped from the bed and drew on his socks, union suit and trousers. He easily set the fire to blazing. The cheery glow made her grateful again for this temporary oasis. Here, they were safe and they were together, for the moment.

But the mountain loomed. She felt it, pressing down upon her, waiting, just beyond these walls. Did she have the strength to cross that pass yet again?

He turned to find her huddled in the covers and his smile faded. Reality seemed to have dawned. He picked up her scattered clothes and handed them to her, then turned his back. She dressed quickly, now embarrassed by her nudity. He did not face her until she stood beside the bed, fully dressed.

"I hope you have no regrets," he said.

How was that possible? She was nothing but regrets. She regretted that she'd started something she'd likely finish alone and that her longing had destroyed any respect he might have held for her. She regretted that they had no future and that he still loved his wife and that she'd never share such a moment with him again.

"Last night…" he began and then stopped as if to gather his courage. "Last night was like nothing I've ever experienced in my life."

He must have seen doubt in her eyes, for his chin tilted downward and his penetrating gaze seemed to take in everything.

"But your wife," she said. "You still love her."

That made him straighten. "Of course. I'll always love her. But it doesn't change how I feel for you."

Doubt wiggled in her belly like a worm on a hot stove. "And how is that now?"

He gazed at her with patient eyes. "You must feel this attraction. I'm dizzy with it. Never in my life have I wanted a woman so much."

She could not believe it. "Never?"

He shook his head. "Not like this. It's like a living thing. You're all I can think of."

She turned away. "You're speaking of lust."

He grasped her upper arms and drew her back until she rested against his chest.

"No. I'm talking of passion."

Hope filled her for one bright moment, then she recognized that it did not matter—love, lust or passion. It was over and would not come again.

"We have to get ready." She tried to pull away, but he held her.

"I'm sorry for the circumstances, but not for last night."

She turned to the clothesline, plucking down the dry canvas tarp and roughly folding it for the journey.

"What are you doing?" he asked.

"Packing."

"You need more rest."

She glared. "Is that what you call it, tumbling in a warm bed, while my family is freezing in the cold?"

He looked as if she had struck him and she realized that she had, not with her fists, but with her words. Still, she could not take them back.

Cole looked away. When he returned his gaze to her, he had assumed a stern look she had seen her parents use on more than one occasion.

"You had a fever. You barely made the cabin."

"We're going."

"No."

She pounded the canvas to flatten it and then roughly tied the cord. "If you were so concerned about my rest, you should have let me be last night."

He stepped back. The shattered look had returned, but she did not relent.

"Bridget, I thought you wanted…" He wiped his hand over his mouth as if holding back his words by sheer physical force. "If we leave now, you won't make it."

"You don't know how long they have left. I'll not rest knowing they might die this very night."

"It's suicide."

She gritted her teeth. "And you'd know all about that now, wouldn't you, stealing that horse?"

He glowered at her.

"You're no different, walking away from camp alone. If that's not suicide, what is?" he asked.

"I left to try and save my…my family. Not because I couldn't handle life's disappointments." She had nearly said "daughter." In her anger, she had almost told him the secret she had vowed never to tell.

"Disappointments? Have you lost your other half, lost a child? Can you even imagine?"

"Yes, I can."

He scoffed. "How? How can you, when you've never been in love? Never taken the chance and lost everything? Never held your child in your arms and then had her ripped away from you forever?"

His raw pain thrashed inside him. Bridget felt it like a living thing and was ashamed to have spoken so rashly. When would she ever learn to hold her tongue?

She cast her gaze down to the hard-packed floor, seeing the bits of charcoal ground in amongst the earth.

"I'm sorry, Cole. I had no right to challenge you." She glanced up to see him nod his acceptance of her apology. "I don't know the pain of losing my family, nor do I want to. That is why we must go today."

He tried to capture her hand, but she drew it behind her back. He sighed.

"You'll not help them if you are too weak to walk back out. You need more rest."

George's cough now came from deep within. Mary watched his chest rise and fall in rapid, shallow breaths as he sat motionless within the shelter.

How much longer could this go on?

Carefully, Mary scraped the hair off the piece of hide until the top was as clean as tanned leather. The bottom still held small bits of sinew and fat. She was glad they had done such a rough job skinning their ox. Every bit of fat and grizzle was welcome now. She set the raw hide on the plank floor and used her knife to slice the leather into thin strips, adding each to the boiling water.

All morning she listened to George's cough as she fed the fire and stirred the glutinous gray liquid. Her wooden spoon caused the bones at the bottom of her cooking pot to rattle against the copper sides like rocks tumbling in a stream. She had cooked them more times than she would count, hoping to glean some little morsel. Now she kept them always in the kettle even knowing that any nourishment they had once held was gone long ago.

At last, she set the gelatin aside. When it had cooled, she fed Chloe first. The child wrinkled her nose and avoided the offered spoon. Mary grew cross.

"Chloe Frances. You will eat!"

Chloe's lip quivered and then stuck out.

Mary did not relent. She had promised Bridget they would hold out as long as possible and she meant to do her best.

"Eat, I say!"

Chloe did, gagging at first and then settling into a mechanical rhythm.

Satisfied, Mary split the remaining portion with George, scraping the pot clean of all but the bones.

When she looked up she found George's melancholy gaze upon her.

"She didn't make it," he said.

Mary's heart grew heavy. She could not bear it if he gave up. It would kill her as surely as the hunger. "We don't know that."

"The others in the wagon train, they should have reported us missing long ago."

"I'm certain they did."

George's gaze wandered toward the cursed pass. "But they can't cross it. Not in winter. No one can."

Chapter Eighteen

Cole knew it was best for Bridget to delay departure and give her a chance to rest. But he also knew she was correct. One more day meant they'd consume another day's rations and her family would face another day of starvation and freezing cold. Eventually it would be too much.

He had learned through hard experience what one day's rest cost when his party had grazed the cattle, instead of harnessing their weary teams. This delay might bring the same disaster to her family.

He reached a rational decision.

"You'll rest here, while I try to reach them."

Her eyes rounded in shock as her mouth dropped open for an instant and then clamped shut. "And how will you carry my brother-in-law and Chloe over the pass?"

He had no answer, so he tried reason. "You're exhausted."

"But not starving in the cold. You need me and if you leave me, I'll follow."

He knew with certainty that she would. Cole briefly

considered stealing the snowshoes. He sighed. She'd follow without them.

Their eyes met.

"All right, then. We go together."

Before departure, Cole cleared the cabin's entrance, gathered more wood and carefully laid out a fire so that it only needed a spark to light it. He left most of the food behind, taking only the minimum to conserve on weight.

This time, Bridget did not argue.

The race was set. Delay would be costly. They must reach them and return before the food ran out and they all starved.

Bridget and Cole ate once more and then left the snug cabin. He wondered if they would see it again and what would transpire in the next few days. It would not take long to starve once the food was gone.

He set a rigorous pace. They must climb over the peak before dark or be trapped at the highest elevation, where the cold and the winds were a deadly combination.

Bridget did her best to keep up, but by late afternoon she was struggling to catch her breath. He decreased his pace for the third time and accepted that they might not clear the pass.

It was two miles up and three down. Five short miles, but the incline made the trip pure torture. Today the weather was clearer than he'd ever seen it. The air was crisp and cold and the sky a brilliant crystal blue. Despite the lack of clouds, snow dusted them, falling from a clear sky.

At last they neared the summit. He turned to see Bridget clutching her side and doubled at the waist.

He returned to her, finding her gasping for breath.

"I should have let you leave me. I thought I could make it."

"You'll make it."

"I'm slowing you down."

That was true. But it was equally true that he could not bring three people over this pass alone, especially if they could not walk. He wondered again if they had come this far only to fail.

He glanced at their surroundings and caught his breath at the majestic vista stretched out before him.

"Bridget, look."

She did. Slowly she straightened as she took in the scene. It seemed as if the whole world lay at their feet.

"Isn't it grand?" she whispered.

"There's the Sacramento and the American. Look." He pointed. "Those ribbons of silver."

"What are those mountains?" She motioned, seeming to forget her discomfort as she viewed the beauty below them.

"Those are the eastern foothills outside San Francisco. We can nearly see the Pacific from here."

"It's a gift from God."

Cole felt the familiar tick at his eye that came whenever God was mentioned. God had given him few blessings and taken most everything he had.

Standing here on this mountain, though, he could not deny that Bridget was right. He had her beside him, and the sunlight and the view. He took a moment to draw it all in, savoring it, then tucked it away, knowing he would remember this moment always.

He pulled out his water and offered it to her.

"No, I don't need it."

Cole shoved the bottle into her hands. "You do."

She accepted the skin and drank heavily. He drew out some jerky and she opened her mouth to refuse that as well.

"Bridget, you need strength to reach them. We have enough and you will eat your share."

"But…"

"Do you want me to have to carry you down as well?"

She accepted the jerky, taking tiny bites. He was patient and waited until she had eaten it all.

He took one last look at the view and then put away his water skin. The color returned to her cheeks and the sheen on her forehead receded in the cold dry air.

"Ready?" he asked.

She nodded and he was off again, breaking the trail. He calculated that the snow was not deep here, perhaps only five feet. How deep was it in the valley?

Cole trod on, up and over the high point. He could not see the lake yet, but soon he would. Bridget stayed close on his heels, like a hound on the scent.

They rounded the trail and caught the first view of the lake.

She peered over his shoulder.

"Where is the wagon?" she asked, her voice sharp with alarm.

"Buried, likely, or broken up for shelter."

The trees and lake stood in eerie silence. Cole repressed a shiver of dread as he scanned the area for smoke or a trail. He saw neither.

He felt his shoulders slump. They were dead, then.

Bridget broke from the packed trail to stand beside him. Her head swiveled as she searched the barren valley. Her hand shot out and she pointed.

"There!"

He followed the line of her arm to the grove of pines on the northern shore of the lake. The tiniest wisp of smoke lifted through the treetops, as ethereal as a sigh.

They lived.

"Hurry, we must hurry." She actually pushed him from behind, so desperate was she to cross the final three miles to her family.

He smiled. They were not safe by far. There was still the matter of seeing them out, but he knew her faith was justified. Somehow they had held out.

The snow crunched beneath his shoes as he made steady progress toward their goal. Bridget did not fall behind, but actually clipped the back of his snowshoes on two occasions in her haste to descend.

The sun crossed behind them, casting the pass in shadow. If they did not reach the valley before dark, they might not be able to find them until morning.

That would be torture. He pushed himself for greater speed, hurrying along just short of a trot.

As they grew closer to the valley floor, he realized how deep the snow had fallen. He examined the trees, half-buried, calculating their height. Here in the interior, the snow was at least forty feet deep, deeper even than when he had returned for his stranded party.

They would have had to move their shelter higher and higher, or dig out from deep within the drifts. Either way, the struggle to survive would have cost energy—vital, precious energy that stole the strength and wasted the muscle.

He calculated that Mary would have suffered the most, because her man would have been unable to gather wood or prepare the food. Had she been wise and eaten more than the others, or had she been selfless?

She was Bridget's older sister. He prepared himself for the worst.

In his party, it was the men who died first, from breaking trail or chopping wood, leaving the women to struggle on.

"I'll break the trail," Bridget said. "I know the way from here."

He wasn't going to let her, but she was already past him and churning forward through the snow. She reminded him of a locomotive chugging along, finding the new reserve of energy that comes when hope and fear lock in fierce battle.

Bridget's heart pounded in her chest until she thought it might burst, but she did not slow down. She pushed her aching legs and trotted through the powdery snow until the ground leveled. She thought to call out to Mary, but did not have the wind.

The pine trees surrounded her now and she struggled to keep her bearings in the maze of tall trunks.

She saw the path to the trees first and the lower branches broken close to the trunks, showing the pale gray dead wood. Mary had been this far to gather wood.

Cole caught her. She did not realize that her trot had slowed to no faster than his walk. He assumed the lead and she fell gratefully behind him, following on in his wake. The snow crunched beneath her snowshoes, but did not filter through the laces as it had when she took the lead. She recognized the effort he had made breaking the trail day after day with no respite or relief, and was grateful down to the center of her being. If only they arrived in time.

They walked now, parallel to the deep trough that Mary had made, as she tried through the impossibly deep snow, without the benefit of the wide shoes that kept Bridget aloft.

With Cole ahead, she soon found her wind once more. She could see the smoke drifting up through the trees, but no shelter.

What had happened to the little cabin they had fashioned? Could they be living in that bundle of sticks hugging the tall pine tree?

"Mary!"

She forged on.

"Mary, Chloe, George!"

She saw movement and then a flash of scarlet wool as someone emerged from the snow. Bridget recognized the shawl of her older sister, dirty and shabby though it was.

"Mary!" Bridget cried.

Her sister turned and her arms shot in the air as she recognized Bridget. Bridget gaped at the gaunt woman wearing Mary's overlarge clothes. It could not be Mary.

The woman staggered forward. "Bridget!"

It was her sister's voice. Tears welled in Bridget's eyes as the truth struck her. It was Mary, more dead than alive. But what of little Chloe?

Bridget reached her sister, worry and relief making the tears come so fast she could barely see past the blur.

They fell into each other's arms, sobbing. Talking simultaneously.

"I thought you were dead," said Mary.

"You're alive," said Bridget. Through the coat, Bridget recognized that Mary was as insubstantial as a bird. She feared she might snap her sister's arm, just by hugging her. Bridget drew back, wincing at the changes that time and suffering had wrought.

Deep brown circles ringed Mary's eyes, and her hair fell thin and limp about her painfully angular face. Her cheekbones jutted out like the granite ridge line of the mountains; her flesh had wasted from beneath her skin, melting away like snow in the springtime.

The joy remained twinkling in Mary's eyes. "I never thought to see you again. Oh, thank God! Thank God."

She fell to her knees, clutching her hands together in gratitude.

"Where are the rest?" asked Cole, voicing what Bridget was afraid to ask.

"Inside," said Mary, not even asking who this man might be or why he had come.

He was her salvation. That much was plain to them all.

The shelter was so small that Bridget could do no more than get her head inside. She noticed the stench first. It smelled of unwashed bodies and sickness. From the gloom came a wet cough.

George.

"Ge-ge!"

Bridget extended her hands and felt her daughter's

warm body. She snatched her up and hugged her, carrying her outside the shelter.

"Oh, my darling!"

Mary crawled inside the shelter on all fours like the animal she had become.

Bridget clutched her child, unable to even speak past the elation. She rocked Chloe at her breast, looking down at the tiny girl. She seemed to have withered like an apple left too long on the ground. Her skin was papery and pale, and her head seemed overly large for her tiny body. But, oh, she was alive.

"George," Mary said from inside. "They've come. Bridget has come."

The cough came again. It made Bridget tense. It sounded as if he were drowning in his own fluids.

"Bridget?" His voice was hoarse. "How many others?"

"Just two." Mary's head appeared. "Where are the others?"

Bridget met Mary's eyes, trying unsuccessfully to stifle the anger that still burned within her.

"They would not come. This is Cole Ellis. He was the only man who would help."

Mary looked at him for the first time.

"You are an angel sent from heaven, Mr. Ellis. Bless you."

Cole looked at his boots but said nothing.

Bridget filled the awkward silence. "We need a fire."

Cole dropped his pack and set to work before the shelter.

Mary and Bridget managed to wrap George in the buffalo robe. At first Bridget thought his color was a trick of the fading light. But when she realized that his lips were actually purple and his skin a frightening gray, she glanced at Mary.

"His lungs are bad, since the fire."

"Fire?" Bridget examined George, noting for the first time the scabs on his ear and forehead. And, dear Lord, his hands. They were a mass of raw lesions and dirty bandages.

"We lost the shelter," said Mary. "But you are here now!"

The happiness rang in her voice like the call of a chickadee in springtime.

By the time Cole had the fire going, twilight had turned to night. The clear sky darkened and the stars appeared. The cloudless night made the air bitter cold. Bridget wrapped a blanket around Mary and one around Chloe. Her daughter nestled down in the warm wool, safe in her mother's arms.

Cole melted snow in his pot and made a soupy oatmeal, adding no raisins or jerky as he usually did for her.

Mary licked her lips and studied his progress with ravenous eyes.

"What about the meat?" asked Bridget.

"See if they can keep this down first."

What did he mean? They had had nothing but salted ox for six weeks. She thought their first meal should be something more. But instead of questioning him, she hesitated, deferring to him. It felt uncomfortable to do so, but he had done this before. He knew things she did not.

She trusted him.

That realization made her eyebrows lift in surprise.

Cole smiled at her. "Their stomachs have shrunken. We have to go slow at first."

Bridget fed Chloe as Mary fed George. A second batch was made for Mary and then a third for Cole and Bridget. Cole had been right. Though Mary had eaten her fill, she did not eat much—far less than either Cole or Bridget.

Bridget imagined her sister's shriveled stomach now swollen with grain and felt a pang of apprehension. She glanced at Cole for reassurance and he gave it without a word, nodding his head slightly.

He staked their canvas, back from the fire, and laid out pine boughs for them to rest upon. Soon they had Mary, Chloe and George tucked beneath the blankets and the great heavy buffalo robe. Bridget and Cole flanked the little family.

George's cough continued. Cole made him hot tea, and the vapors from the pot and the warm liquid eased his suffering greatly.

"How much food do you have left?" asked Bridget.

Mary said nothing and Bridget felt a stabbing pain in her belly as the dire circumstances hit her like a stone.

"I've been breaking the bones to get at the marrow, but there's none left now. We've had only the hide for eight days."

They had nearly died, so nearly it chilled Bridget's flesh like a dip in ice water.

She squeezed her sister's hand. "We have plenty now."

But it was a lie. They had little and needed to get them clear of this cursed lake with all haste.

George and Mary were very weak and Bridget had barely made it this far. With a sinking feeling, she realized that this was only the halfway point on the journey.

Chapter Nineteen

In the morning, all her family appeared in better health. Just the little food she had eaten seemed to have restored the color to Mary's face. It still hurt Bridget to look at her, with her sunken eyes and her hollow cheeks, but soon they would make that right.

Cole added dried fruit to the porridge and gave them as much as they could eat. She noted that he did not eat much and she followed his example. He glared at her and seemed prepared to reprimand her, but must have recognized that he was guilty of the same crime, and so said nothing.

She went with Cole to gather wood, insisting that Mary rest and prepare for the journey over the pass.

"They are very weak," said Bridget.

They moved easily over the snow to collect branches that Mary had not been able to reach. Cole effortlessly snapped off a limb the diameter of her arm.

"I'll make a sled for George. It will be slow going. Might take two days just to climb the pass."

He did not say the rest. They would have to sleep on the pass, exposed to the elements. Bridget thought of Chloe and shivered.

"Do you think Mary can walk?" he asked.

"She has to." Bridget wondered if her sister could. Doubt ate at her stomach with tiny stabbing bites. *Mary has to.* She wouldn't come this far only to lose them now.

But what if Mary could not keep up? Would she stay with her, as Cole had done with his wife, or leave her to save Chloe?

Please, God, don't make me face that devil's choice.

"We'll go tomorrow. Today, Mary must learn to use the shoes."

That afternoon Bridget taught Mary to walk on snowshoes. Mary often stepped on her hem and then the opposite shoe before she got the hang of walking with her legs slightly apart. Bridget worried at how quickly Mary tired from the slight exertion of walking on the level ground of the lake and wondered again how she would manage the pass.

Only five miles separated them from the cabin and their first food cache. How would they ever reach it?

They returned to camp, Mary puffing steam and flushed from the effort. Cole watched her with concern, which was reflected in his mood. Bridget prepared to defend Mary, but he turned away, working with his hatchet to split wood for the sled. Bridget recalled him buying the runners all those days ago. How she had resented the coin. Now she saw the wisdom of the purchase. There was no way to bring George over the pass without them. Still, it would cost great effort. Did

Cole have that much strength? Bridget wondered if she would have to break trail and the fear returned, leaping onto her back like an attacker. Try as she might, she could not shake it loose.

George's coughing had settled since the arrival of the chamomile tea, but he labored with his breathing. Bridget and Cole exchanged worried looks.

"Mary has the knack of the shoes," said Bridget, her voice light with false optimism.

"We'll go tomorrow before first light." Cole looked at Mary. "Gather what you'd bring, but don't bring more than you can carry."

Mary and Bridget crept into the shelter to sort through the family's belongings. In the end, Mary left everything behind—all but the clothing on their backs and the small silver embroidery scissors that George had given her as a wedding gift. The handles featured tiny rosebuds and the blades curved slightly so as not to nick the fabric when cutting the thread. They were her most prized possession.

"I still have all your things," Mary told Bridget. "What will you bring?"

Bridget chose her most precious belonging. "Chloe."

Mary smiled.

"Thank you for keeping her safe." Bridget's eyes filled with tears.

Mary hugged her. "Thank you for not dying and for coming back for us."

They sat side by side in the little hut Mary had made, clasping each other's hands, with their heads touching.

Mary drew a ragged breath. "I watched you all that first day. I called out for you to come back."

"I heard you."

"But you didn't come."

Bridget said nothing.

"I saw you at the base of the mountain. When the sleet started, I lost you in the dark." Mary sniffled. "I listened to the sleet all night, thinking of you out there. There was two inches of ice on the canvas when I crawled out before dawn. I stood there waiting for the light so I could find you again, but you were gone."

"The ice made it possible to climb the pass."

"I thought it buried you."

"It takes more than that to kill a Callahan," said Bridget, repeating the words her father liked to spout.

Mary's laugh sounded more like a strangled sob. She hugged her sister. "Do you think we still have a chance?"

Bridget pulled back so she could look Mary in the eye. "We will get out of this, you and I. We'll reach the valley and live past one hundred. Wait until you see it, Mary. It's grand, grander even than our imagining. So green. The land is rich and the cattle fat. There are oranges just growing on the trees, and figs and apricots. It's like Eden."

Mary's eyes got a far-off look.

"We'll see it together." Bridget squeezed her sister's hand.

Mary studied her in the gloom. "I want to see it all."

Her sister looked around the hut. Finding nothing else she needed, she settled her gaze on her sister.

"Who is he?"

Bridget thought to lie to Mary, to spare her the truth, but she did not keep secrets from her older sister. Mary was the only person in the world she trusted completely.

She told her the circumstances of her meeting with Cole and the bargain. Mary's mouth dropped open, but there was no stopping her now. Words poured out of her in a flood. She told her sister about the man she had hit with the firewood, and the posse that nearly caught them, and finally about their night in the cabin.

By the time Bridget had related it all, Mary had both her hands pressed to her mouth.

"You lay with him?" she asked.

Of all she had told her, this is what Mary had latched on to, and she held on as stubbornly as a terrier gripping a rat.

Bridget felt her insides wash cold, but she lifted her chin in defiance.

"I did."

"You'd think you would be wiser," she admonished her.

Bridget lowered her eyes in shame and then spoke the words she had not said to anyone. "I love him."

Mary made a disapproving sound. "So you said the last time."

Bridget met her gaze and held it. "I love him, Mary. I'd gladly trade my life for his."

"And leave your little girl?"

Bridget felt her heart torn in two pieces.

"Have you told him?"

Bridget shook her head.

"Well, you can't choose who is to steal your heart. What better man to do that than a thief."

"He's not a thief."

Mary said nothing. Bridget told her the rest—how Cole had wanted to die and for a time she thought she'd changed his mind, but here he was marching willingly to his death.

"Thief or no, you've no future with the man. You said yourself they want to hang him. The mayor holds a grudge against him, you say, so what business do you have hitching your fortune to his?"

Bridget knew this, all of it, and still she could not keep herself from bedding him. Her cheeks felt hot as her shame burned within.

"Are they following?"

"Not here. Cole thinks they are waiting down below."

Mary considered this for a moment. "He mustn't go back."

"What else can he do?"

"He could walk over the mountains eastward and escape."

He could indeed, but to do so he would have to leave them all to die. Bridget knew she and Mary could not drag George over that pass without him.

Mary read the truth in her eyes. "You can't hold him to that promise. You must release him from it."

Bridget balked at this suggestion. She had only just discovered how much she loved him, and now Mary wanted her to give him up.

"I don't want to lose him."

"Lose him? They're waiting down below to tie a rope around his neck. I'd say you'll lose him either way."

Bridget sat back as the truth of this coiled around her, squeezing the life from her. Still she fought against logic and reason, as belligerent as a spoiled child. "But—but I need him. We need him."

"We are not his responsibility."

"We can't make it without him."

Mary glared at her. "You say you love him, but you don't. Fancy him, perhaps, but no more."

Bridget drew herself up to argue and then stopped.

Mary was right. She didn't love him. If she did, she would do whatever it took to save him. Just like Angela had done.

"You're right," she whispered.

Mary clasped Bridget's hand. "You do love him."

Mary knew the truth of it. Bridget loved him and now God had given her the devil's choice after all. She could save her family or Cole, but not both.

Chapter Twenty

"Are you mad?" asked Cole.

Bridget laid down the pile of wood she carried and grasped his arm. "Then bring us to the cabin. We might last there until rescue comes. Then you can escape."

"We don't have enough food and you know it."

"We have the buffalo hide. I could boil it."

"Bridget, it's a death sentence. I won't do it."

"I'm releasing you from your vow. You don't have to do this. Please." She could not bear for him to die.

"What about the child?"

Her heart was bleeding, leaking sorrow like a spring maple leaks sap. What should she do?

"It is not your choice. It's mine," he said. "I'm going to bring you out, all of you. I don't care what happens to me after that."

"I care!"

He smiled at her and stroked her cheek. "You got me out once. Maybe you can do it again, my little thief."

This time, when he called her that, it was like a caress.

He gathered her close and kissed her hard. She opened her mouth and tasted the sweet pleasure of him once more.

At last she drew away. "I don't want you to die."

He tucked her under his chin, resting his jaw against the top of her head.

"If I can save the child, it's enough."

It was nearly dark when they returned to the sad little camp. Mary's gaze flicked between Cole and Bridget. Bridget could not force a reassuring smile past the heartache.

"We'll go before first light," said Cole to George.

George nodded and looked to his wife. Mary's shoulders sagged in relief.

That night, Bridget slept beside Mary, with Chloe tucked between them. The sound of heavy breathing told her that the men were asleep. Mary nudged her and she turned toward her sister.

"He loves you," she said.

"What?"

"Cole. He loves you. Only a man in love would give his life for us."

Bridget couldn't tell Mary that it wasn't for her that he made this sacrifice, but for the child he could not save. Would he still make this decision if he knew the circumstances of Chloe's birth? She had not told him and the guilt of that tore at her. She was not capable of selfless love for him. She was not, because she was a mother with an innocent babe who depended upon her. She squeezed Chloe close and rocked back and forth in sorrow.

She loved him, but he did not love her. He could not, because she was too afraid to let him see her as she truly was. Until he knew all that, she deceived herself as well as him.

Her father's words echoed in her mind. "No man will want another's leavings. You've ruined yourself."

But now that she had known Cole, could she return to the life she had lived before? She had always thought she would be satisfied as the spinster aunt of her own child. Happy and grateful to raise her child with her sister, by whose grace she was allowed to keep her baby and live free of the shame that should be hers.

But now—now she wanted so much more.

Go to sleep, Bridget, you've a mountain to climb. Save your strength. If you live, you'll have a lifetime to regret what you've lost.

She lay still, instead of tossing as she was wont to do, for Mary's sake and Chloe's. The moon glowed through the waxed canvas and she marked it as it crossed the sky. At last she fell into a restless slumber that seemed only the blinking of her eyes before she was roused by Cole's gentle voice.

"Bridget. It's time."

She got the fire going as Cole checked their packs. They shared the last hot meal they would have until after they crossed Broadner Pass. Finally, she melted snow and filled the water skins, realizing there was not near enough for four adults.

It took both of them to convince Mary to wear a pair of George's trousers. They gaped at her waist but were snug across her wide hips. Bridget tied a rope around her waist to keep them up. When she tried to hike Mary's skirts, there was a skirmish.

"I can't go traipsing about with my knickers showing."

Bridget grasped her hem with defiance and tucked it into her belt. Mary looked to Cole, who seemed preoccupied with the sled.

"I can't do that," insisted Mary, tugging down her hem.

Cole never looked up as he spoke. "You'll slow us down."

Mary hiked up her skirt.

They departed before sunup, as Cole had hoped. He pulled George and broke the trail. Next came Mary, unburdened, and then Bridget carrying Chloe and her pack. The going was difficult, even on the flat.

When Cole reached the incline, the grade rose so steeply he had to zigzag to keep them moving forward. The day was cloudy, but it did not begin to snow until midday. Even his slow pace seemed difficult for Mary, judging by the distance that steadily grew between them. She still tripped occasionally, falling into the deep snow. This would require Bridget to give George the baby, while she helped Mary to her feet. Cole was forced to watch because he could not let go of the sled for fear George would careen down the mountain.

The snow fell heavily in the afternoon, further hampering them. When the rocky spine of the mountain cut into the trail, he could do nothing but creep upward, one slow step at a time. With each step, his heart grew heavier. At this rate, they would never clear the pass by dark.

Then Bridget was there beside him. She clasped part of the rope.

"Where is the baby?" he asked.

"Tucked in safe with George." She pulled.

He stopped. "If you are going to do this, we need to change the rope."

Cole added a rope to the center of the one he had used for a handle and knotted it in several places. This allowed him to walk in front and break the trail as Bridget came behind. Mary trailed them all, struggling to keep up. As the snow fell heavily, she seemed merely a gray shadow in their wake.

Bridget called to George. "Do you see her?"

"Yes." Then a cough, from the effort of shouting.

"Watch her. Tell me if you can't see her."

Cole glanced back. "We could give her a line attached to the sled."

"Not yet."

George called out several times and at last they stopped to add a line to the sled so Mary would not fall so far behind that she lost her way in the storm. They tied the rope about her waist and then ventured on, dragging George and assisting Mary.

Twice the sled became unmovable and Bridget had to turn back to help Mary to her feet.

The weather grew worse as they neared the crest of Boreal Ridge. The last five hundred yards were among the most miserable of Cole's life. He heaved and strained just to keep the sled from cascading back down the mountain. Once he had the thing going again, Mary would tug the rope, making him feel like the loser in a hopeless game of tug-of-war. He longed to stop and rest, but to move the weight from a halt was more than he could endure. He raced to cross the pass before night took them. The light faded, but from the storm or twilight he could not tell.

He looked back and saw Bridget straining to drag her brother-in-law up the mountain. Her dogged determination to do the impossible shamed him. Each time he felt he must stop he looked back and found, in her, the strength to take another step.

It took a few moments for him to recognize the load was lighter. He thought perhaps he was light-headed from the strain. His wits were dull, from the cold, from exhaustion. Why was the sled moving so effortlessly?

Oh, God, Mary had come untied or George had fallen. The baby.

He stopped, turning into the wind.

Bridget halted as he came back to her. Her shawl was covered with snow, so he could no longer see what color it had been.

"He's fallen!" cried Cole.

"What?" The wind howled, making Bridget's voice a tiny thing.

"George!"

"He's there. Mary, too."

"Chloe?"

"All there."

She was wrong, addled from the work. He tried to move past her, but she grabbed him.

"We've crossed, Cole. We are on the downhill side."

Could it be true? Cole glanced about. He could not see ten feet in front of him. All about them the snow swirled. But the path before him sloped almost imperceptibly downward.

They had climbed the three miles up Broadner Pass. Soon the trail would fall away beneath them. The path was difficult enough, but the sled posed a new challenge. Two miles lay before them and the cabin at their feet, but they were two steep miles, with visibility near nothing. In the swirling snow and a gathering shroud of darkness, he might lead them straight off a cliff.

His smile faded. The day was spent. Sunset found them in the worst of all possible places—at the highest elevation along their route.

Bridget offered him her water and he drained the contents.

"We have to get out of this wind," she called.

Yes, they did, but he knew there was no cover for them. Instead, he picked up the rope and tugged. The sled resisted and then obeyed.

He trudged along, enjoying the short stretch of nearly even ground. The trail went on this way for two hundred yards, coiling slowly around before coming to the treacherous downgrade.

He had to reverse their position. He gave Bridget the baby for fear the child would tumble off the sled on the steep grade. She wrapped Chloe tight to her body and covered her with her shawl, and he checked on George.

"How are you doing?"

George gave a weak smile. His skin was the color of the snow except for his lips, which were a deep purple.

"I can't feel my feet."

"Not much farther now," he lied.

Mary stood beside him. She looked ready to drop. He could not bear the sight of them and so he set them in motion again.

George went first, in the sled, breaking the trail by

the force of gravity, as Cole leaned back against the rope to slow his momentum. The snow plowed up over the runners, covering George in an icy blanket.

Next came Mary, and finally Bridget with Chloe.

The wind was not so fierce on this side of the mountain. George had not moved all day. Likely his limbs were frozen and he needed warmth. Should they stop or keep on?

The answer came when Mary collapsed. Bridget roused her by patting her cheek with her wet glove, but Mary could go no farther.

Cole looked at the desolate place that fate had given them. He left them to tramp horizontally across the trail and found a rocky outcropping. This would be their camp.

The gray rock offered respite from the wind, but they would have no fire, for there were no trees at this elevation.

He brought his sorry party to the place he had chosen. Soon he had the tarp arranged as a ground cloth and lean-to. Bridget helped with the blankets as he filled their water skins with snow. With no fire there was but one way to melt the snow. He shuddered as he placed the skins against his belly, then helped George out of the sled and into the shelter.

"Bridget, you need to see to his feet. They will be frostbitten. You'll have to warm them on your stomach."

She hesitated only a moment before doing as he asked, while he helped Mary to the shelter and wrapped her in blankets. Mary held Chloe tight as the child's howl was carried away by the wind.

By the time Bridget had George's feet warmed, Cole had succeeded in melting enough water to soak some of the remaining oats. He gave them jerky to eat, but this would not do for the baby. When he checked the soaking oats he found them freezing in the pot. He returned the slush mix to one of the water skins and replaced it inside his coat.

They huddled together in the darkness. Mary had either fainted again or slept beside her husband, who cradled her as if she were his child.

"I'm sorry," said George. "Tomorrow, I think you should leave me."

Bridget cradled Chloe, who had cried herself to sleep. "We will not."

"I'm killing you," he said.

The darkness was so complete that Cole could not see the man, but he heard clearly the despair in his voice.

"You must," he said.

"George?" Cole rested a hand on the man's shoulder. "Down this mountain about a mile and three quarters is a cabin. There is fuel and a fireplace and food. You hang on now and make it through this night, and we'll get you there."

The next noise Cole heard sounded like a whine, but when he felt George's ragged breathing, he knew it was a cry. Mary's husband wept. It was several minutes before he could speak.

"You aren't lying?" George asked.

"No."

Bridget chimed in. "I've seen it, George, snug and tight, just down below."

"Thank God." He sighed. "So close to the lake. All this time and it was so close."

"Five miles without snowshoes and over the pass," said Cole. "You never could have made it."

The baby woke and accepted the water-soaked meal from the water skin that Cole had heated with the warmth of his body. For the adults it was a long, cold night, huddled beneath the hide.

During the night, Cole flipped back the hide and rose to punch a hole in the snow, allowing fresh air to enter the shelter. The snow fell so fast he feared it would smother them. Already, two feet blanketed the lean-to. The tarp helped keep them from the wind, making their burrow warmer, but it grew dangerous without the fresh air.

The night passed slowly. Bridget and Mary slept well, waking only when Chloe cried. George seemed awake each time Cole cleared the opening. His cough troubled him more at night and Cole wished he could make tea for the man.

Tomorrow, he promised himself.

After all his rising and fitful sleep, dawn caught him unawares.

Bridget rose and broke open the hole, filling the burrow with light. Cole blinked and dusted the frost from his beard. The party woke to find the snow still falling heavily, but the air mild and the wind not so fierce.

Once George was loaded onto the sled, he held the baby as the rest of them stowed away the bedding and readied the packs. Bridget reclaimed Chloe the instant the party was ready.

Something about the way she held the child, the way she gazed down at her, struck Cole as familiar.

The details of his recollection slipped into place like cogs in a wheel, and he remembered Angela holding her baby girl just after giving birth. She'd had that same misty elation, the same loving calm. He'd never seen Bridget more at peace than when she held Chloe, and that included after he'd loved her for all he was worth.

A nasty suspicion crept into his thoughts like a wasp crawling on a ripe apple. Mary seemed content to wait by George, fussing with the blankets and whispering encouragement. She did not look back once to check on her child.

Because the child was not hers.

It was Bridget's.

That was why Bridget had been so desperate to reach her kin. Why she understood his sorrow and grief over losing his Lee-lee. It had not been empathy. She was a mother and knew a mother's pain.

He felt taken in a second time. She had picked that lock and duped him once, making him a fool. Now she had done it again. He thought of how she had encouraged him. How when they reached the cabin, she had given herself to him. She'd let him fall in love with her, make love to her, pour out his heart and soul about his wife and his child to her. And she had shared nothing. A lie, everything she had said and done was a lie.

She did not tell him—did not trust him.

Had it all been an act to get him to bring her here? Had their lovemaking meant anything to her at all?

"Mr. Ellis?"

He found Mary's worried gaze upon him.

He nodded and took up the sled ropes, easing George back onto the trail and guiding his descent down the slope. His legs ached and burned from yesterday's exertions.

Not much farther to the cabin. You're just exhausted. You can't think straight.

But he could. For the first time in years, he saw with complete clarity. It was just like when he'd stood beside her on this mountaintop on that crystal clear day and could see everything in all directions.

He had been ready to die for her. How she must have laughed at his foolish love. How smug, how pleased she must be to have led him so cleverly to do her bidding.

Did she feel anything for him at all?

Chapter Twenty-One

Cole worked the sled down the pass to level ground before the morning had drawn to a close. Bridget followed behind Mary, who seemed buoyed by the knowledge that shelter lay near at hand.

Chloe did not share the party's enthusiasm. She was hungry and wet from her soiled diaper. Bridget clutched her and cooed, but the cries only grew higher in pitch and more pitiable.

At last, Bridget saw the cabin's chimney, still visible beneath the burden of fresh snow.

"There, Mary, there!" she shouted.

Mary's head swiveled as she tried to find the cabin but could not spot it among the pines.

It did not matter. She called to her husband, "Nearly there, George."

Cole said nothing as he trudged onward, unshakable, unstoppable. He had saved them.

Bridget knew she could never repay him for their lives.

The peak of the roof jutted out of the bank and Cole

had to dig down to reach the door. He dragged George inside, sled and all. She waited for him to call them in, but when he did not emerge, she grew concerned and entered after him, with Mary following in her wake.

He already had his gunpowder and flint out. The rhythmic knocking told her that sparks flew onto the dry tinder and he'd have a fire going in no time. Her eyes adjusted to the dim interior and the room came into view again. It felt like coming home. Her entire body ached with memories as she glanced at the bed. Chloe stilled in the cabin, sucking her thumb as she took in her new surroundings.

Mary entered behind her and Bridget passed Chloe to her sister. Bridget removed her snowshoes first and then set to work unpacking so she could make the bed. She helped George out of the sled and under the blankets, and then leaned out the door to gather snow into the pots.

She helped Mary out of her snowshoes and together they tended to Chloe.

The fire cheered her and the water revived them all. Soon she was cooking porridge. Cole tended the fire but did not help with the cooking.

Surely he was exhausted. She offered him the first bowl, but he waved it away.

"Give it to George."

She did, seeing everyone fed before again trying to feed him. He took the offering and set it aside.

"Are you ill?"

He gave her a look of such despair that it took the breath from her body.

"You must eat," she chided.

His smile was weak and never reached his eyes. "Still have a ways to go, don't we?"

She nodded, not liking his empty tone. What had happened?

Surely, the man must be exhausted. But that didn't explain the dead glaze to his eyes. Was it the shadow of the noose? Perhaps the posse would not be waiting, as he predicted. After all, the mayor's horse was not the only business he had to attend to, what with the squatters' riots and his reelection so close at hand.

Chloe's sob brought her about. She heated water, and together she and Mary bathed Chloe and changed her clothing. .

Dry and warm, her little girl dropped off to sleep as peacefully as an angel.

Mary made George tea and the party rested in the warmth and protection of the sturdy cabin. George tried to give up the bed, but Mary would not have it. The women made a place on the floor beside him and Cole sat by the fire, keeping his own counsel while wrapped in his great buffalo robe.

His unnatural quiet kept Bridget from sleep. Mary whispered to her.

"What is it?"

"He's troubled."

"Go to him, then," she muttered and turned over.

Bridget crept across the room and sat beside him on a stump, fashioned as a stool.

"Can you not sleep?" she asked.

He didn't look at her. "I was thinking of Angela."

Bridget fought a war with jealousy and lost. She could not battle a rival who was dead.

"She and I had no secrets." Cole glanced at her. "Did you know that?"

Bridget thought of the lies she had told him, lies of omission, and felt the sting of guilt as if she had swallowed nettles.

"Is there anything you want to tell me, Bridget?"

So many things it made her head spin. She wanted to confide in him, to speak of her daughter. But this lie did not just affect her, but her daughter and Mary, too. She and her sister had carefully worked through the story, designed to protect Chloe from shame. The lie would not work if she told.

Angela would have told him. Ah, Angela. She snorted. The saintly dead wife with no flaws and no secrets. Angela did not need to tell lies, for she had done nothing of which she felt ashamed.

And if Bridget did tell him? She took in his earnest, hopeful face and imagined his reaction. It struck her like the slap across her face that her father had given her. *Filthy little whore.* She felt the tiny white scar across the bridge of her nose, where he had split the skin open, but her gaze never left Cole.

He had forgiven her the thieving. But this? Her father never forgave her. Cole looked at her with steady blue eyes. Could she trust him with this?

How she wanted to unburden her heart, but in the end the fear kept her mute. She loved him, but still did not trust men.

"Bridget?" he coaxed. "Something on your mind?"

"I don't know what you mean."

He pressed his eyes shut and then looked back at the fire. She felt as if she had just made a dreadful mistake. But how could he know? She had been so careful.

"Cole, what is it? Please tell me."

"You want me to confide in you?"

She did not hesitate. "Yes."

His exhalation of breath was sharp, like a condemnation. "Go to bed, Bridget."

He had dismissed her, pinning his gaze on the flames. She regretted her choice, knowing she had failed some vital test. But how could she tell him the worst of her mistakes?

She slipped off to bed like a whipped dog.

They stayed in the cabin all the next day, resting. In the warm air, George was much recovered. He could walk about without coughing and the tea eased his breathing. It put color back in Mary's cheeks just to see him doing so well.

The food revitalized the party, but Cole drew Bridget aside. It was the first time he had spoken directly to her all day.

"We have to go tomorrow."

"But they are doing so well here and…" She was going to say they were safe from the men who chased him, but stopped herself.

"We will be out of food by tomorrow night. The next cache is over six miles from here. We have to reach it by tomorrow night or go hungry. Then we have to reach the valley before those stores run short. A race, Bridget. Remember?"

She nodded solemnly. To save her family, they must walk into the jaws of the lion. She would be with him only a few more days.

"Yes," she whispered and clasped his hand, pressing it to her cheek. "I do."

He did not draw her in as she hoped, but neither did he pull away. He simply waited for her to release him, staring down at her with sad eyes, and she died a little inside.

The next day, George insisted on walking. He hobbled along on the snowshoes, favoring his injured leg and slowing them down for much of the morning. The snow changed to light icy crystals. As the air grew colder, George's cough became worse.

Before noon, he conceded defeat and crawled back onto the sled. By midday, they had gone no more than two miles over the only level ground on the entire journey.

The party stopped by the river. Bridget and Cole exchanged looks, but said nothing. She recalled all too well that Cole had nearly died at this very spot. He was too heavy for the ice. She studied the flat expanse, knowing the deadly waters ran swiftly just below them. She had passed easily, because she weighed less. The snowshoes helped distribute their weight, but not enough. If only they had something larger.

She stilled as a thought struck her.

"Cole!"

He glanced at her, one eyebrow cocked in an unspoken question.

"The sled. We can use it to cross."

Now his brow knit in confusion.

"I can go across and pull you over one by one. Mary on one side and me on the other."

He thought over her words and a smile slowly erased his troubled expression. He looked at her with admiration glowing in his eyes.

"Might work."

The ropes were tied. Bridget crossed first, carrying her pole like a tightrope walker. She made the journey without mishap. Once safely on the far bank, she tugged at the forward rope and hauled George across. George sat in the snow as Cole drew the sled back across and then sat upon it. Together, she and George pulled and Cole slid safely to their side of the river. Mary tugged the sled back and she and Chloe made the final trip without incident.

Cole looked back at the way they had come, then met Bridget's eyes. "You are as cunning as a fox."

The compliment pleased her at first, and then, as they walked on, she started to wonder. He had not smiled at her, but rather seemed fascinated at her scheming, as one is fascinated by some dangerous zoo animal: happy to stare and happier still not to have to get too close.

Mary helped George back onto the sled and they were off again, heading for the ridge. Somewhere on the western slope lay a little spring and a cache of food.

Bridget wondered what they would do if some mink or marten had discovered their hoard. She shivered, bringing Chloe tighter beneath the blanket she wrapped about them. The possibility of losing their last reserve of food was too terrible to dwell on. Such musings only called attention to how desperate their battle now was.

They had left the safety of the cabin and succeeded in crossing the river. But the ridge line loomed and the afternoon ticked away. It was another reason no one had been willing to take up her cause. It was now mid-December. The days were cold and short, and the nights deadly long.

Why had they let George walk? She watched Cole, trudging along, hauling her brother-in-law behind him. Did he have the strength?

Did she?

Chapter Twenty-Two

Cole crossed the second ridge in twilight and somehow managed to get the party to the shelter of the pines before night took hold. But they did not reach the cache of food.

Chloe whined piteously. Bridget gave her water but could offer nothing more. It was not fair. Bridget raged at the fate that brought the darkness so soon.

Mary laid a hand on Bridget's shoulder. "We'll reach it tomorrow."

Bridget felt the tears leak from her eyes. "She's hungry now."

Mary only nodded. "Come by the fire."

She joined them there, rocking her child until she slept. The adults stayed up a long while, comforted by the fire. But at last their weary bodies won the battle. Cole set out the bedding and the next thing she knew he was rocking her shoulder and urging her to crawl beneath the buffalo robe.

They lay like cordwood, closely packed, sharing their warmth. Bridget dozed and woke often, checking the sky. At last she could see the outline of the trees against the gray morning. Frost covered the buffalo robe, but the canvas had kept off the snow.

They did not set a fire that morning.

"We'll stop when we reach the food," said Cole before lifting the rope for the sled and heaving it into motion.

Bridget tried not to think of the miles ahead but her mind crossed each obstacle—the next ridge, the avalanche plain and, most terrifying of all, the snow line.

Did the posse wait for them there?

The trail up the ridge was challenging, but the descent was more so. Cole controlled the sled's descent by a series of serpentine swings from one side of the trail to the other, increasing the distance they trod and the time it took, but decreasing the grade for the sled.

It was late in the day before they came to the place where Cole had cached the last of their food. Bridget was impressed at how he found this particular tree among a forest of pines that now surrounded them. All were glad to see the food stores untouched.

They neared the trail head. It had taken them five days to reach this place. How long would it take to reach the valley?

Cole set his fire on the tin and Bridget strung the lean-to rope between two trees. The party ate with good appetite and slept well with bellies full for the moment.

The next morning, Cole rose first and had the fire started before Bridget was even out of bed. She and her sister crawled out from beneath the robe, stifling groans.

"We'll reach the valley tomorrow or early the following day," said Cole.

Mary's face lit with joy, while Bridget sank deeper into despair.

She wanted a moment with Cole and so followed him when he went in to the trees to collect more wood, invading his privacy.

"Is there no other way down from these mountains?" she asked.

He stopped his gathering and shook his head.

"I don't want you to walk into their hands."

His expression revealed nothing. "Why?"

"Because I love you." There, she had said it. She held her breath, waiting for his reply. She died a little each moment he examined her with those impassive icy eyes.

"I'll bring them down safe, Bridget. I've agreed. There's no need for more lies."

She blinked at him. It was the one answer she had never expected. For him to say he loved her would have been sweet joy. For him to spurn her would have been agony. But to have him not believe her—it shocked her speechless.

He turned back to his work.

"But I do," she insisted.

He smiled. "How can I believe anything you say?"

"What are you on about?"

He dropped the wood—threw it, in fact.

"You won't tell me the truth. You have not been honest about your feelings, your purpose or your situation."

She gaped at him.

"My wife loved me and she kept no secrets."

Something inside her snapped. "I'm not your wife!"

He kept his tone civil. It rang with reluctant acceptance. "That's the truth of it."

Bridget battled her regret and the urge to tell him everything. She was angry and frightened all at once, like a cornered fox.

Cole waited, but when she said nothing, he spoke again.

"I told you everything. I told you about my wife and Lee-lee, about their deaths. I told you about the Devlins and about the mountains. You know I was a drunk and a thief. You know everything about me, Bridget. Everything. Yet I know of you only what I can surmise and what you've been forced to reveal. So don't tell a man you love him when you don't trust him. You can't have one without the other."

He scooped up the wood and left her there with her mouth hanging open like a trap.

Chapter Twenty-Three

Bridget still felt a frost in the air, but it came from Cole. He gave her no opportunity to be alone with him over the next three grueling days. The time blurred as they struggled up ridges and down slopes until they crept through the mighty boulders left by the avalanche and onto the grainy ice. Soon they were stumbling down the final slope, with yellow grass and exposed earth marking the place where ice and ground collided.

They reached the valley and George regained his feet, looking pale and drawn from his ordeal. Mary walked slowly at his side, bolstering him. Bridget trailed them, carrying Chloe, who lay weak and listless in her arms.

Cole discarded the heavy buffalo robe, sled and snowshoes to lighten the load, keeping only the blankets, rope and canvas in his pack. Bridget sighed in relief as he relieved her of her pack altogether, setting it aside before turning to lead them away.

He made for Sam's cabin, cutting across the draw and following the antelope trail through the low hills.

The yard was uncharacteristically silent. The two horses they'd left were gone, as were the mules. No smoke issued from the chimney. Bridget had the urge to run, but in truth she barely managed to stand. She had reached the end of her endurance long ago.

Bridget slowed as they entered the yard.

Someone shouted from the house. "That's far enough, Ellis!"

Two men stepped out, aiming rifles at Cole.

"Drop your weapons."

Bridget's heart hammered as she moved to step before him and then recalled Chloe in her arms.

He thrust her aside. "I have no weapons."

Bridget remembered the pistol he had taken from the man at the livery and for a moment feared he would use it to die in a gunfight instead of at the end of a rope. Chloe lifted a hand and tugged at Bridget's hair. Bridget backed away to protect her child.

The men conferred. "Drop your pack then."

He did. Mary and George stumbled into the yard. George fell to his knees, wheezing for breath.

"These folks need help," called Cole.

"Hands in the air," said the rangy one.

His partner had ears that stuck out beneath his hat like buttresses holding up the structure. He waved the muzzle of his gun.

"Do it."

Cole lifted his hands, still talking steadily. "They were stuck in the pass. They need seeing to."

"That's none of our concern," said the tall one.

"They can see to themselves," said Ears.

Bridget glared. "Where's Sam?"

"We run him off."

Wasn't that illegal?

"Down on the ground, Ellis, or so help me, I'll save the hangman the trouble."

Cole sank to his knees, hands still high.

"Hands down."

The man kept his rifle raised and his cheek resting against the stock as he crept forward. His partner secured a pair of shackles on Cole's wrists.

"But you can't," said Bridget. "He saved all our lives."

Mary left George to come to Cole's aid. "He's a hero."

"He's a damned horse thief. Now step back or I'll arrest you for interferin'."

Bridget fell to her knees, wrapping her one arm about him. "Cole, I'll get you out. You know I will."

He did not look at her as they dragged him up on a horse.

"You going to leave us here?" called George, disbelief in his voice.

The one with the jug handles for ears mounted up behind Cole. "We'll send help. There's beans and such, inside."

"You should be horsewhipped," said Mary. "Leaving defenseless women and a baby out here."

But the men were through talking and spurred their horses, leaving nothing but a cloud of dust in their wake.

Bridget clutched Chloe tight and ran after them, sobbing as she fell rapidly behind. Mary found her on the trail sometime later.

Bridget wanted to go after Cole, but Mary convinced

her to come back to the cabin. She needed food and rest before setting off.

Mary cooked a meal of biscuits and beans while Bridget told her everything about her conversation with Cole and how he said she couldn't love him if she didn't trust him and that she still hadn't told him about Chloe for fear she might lose him and now she'd lost him just the same.

Mary said they could all set off tomorrow for Sacramento. Exhaustion overtook Bridget and she slept hard on the floor beside the bed until sometime in the night when she rose and slipped into her boots, gathered her pistol, water skin and shawl before venturing out into the porch. She had not even wrapped her shawl around her head when Mary appeared.

"You're going?"

"Yes." She faced her sister. "Take care of her for me. I'll send help back."

Mary looked as if she wanted to argue, but how could she? They were safe here with food and shelter. She was too weary, and George too sick, to go on.

"Be careful." Mary handed her a cloth filled with the remaining biscuits, and they embraced.

Bridget set off by moonlight, following the silver ribbon that led to Sacramento. She had a terrible fear that the mayor would hang Cole before she could get him out, and that hurried her steps.

Thanks to a mule skinner and his team she did not have to walk the entire way to Sacramento. Upon arrival, she went to see Mr. Giles, her patron at the *Sacramento Transcript*. He sent riders back for her family and arranged lodging with board, in exchange for their stories. From him she discovered that Cole awaited hanging in the prison ship. His execution was set for just five days hence.

At the *Stafford,* a surly little jailor named Gibbs informed her that Cole was allowed no visitors.

She found Mr. Meredith on board, but now subordinate to Gibbs. Meredith would not permit a visit, either, but when bribed, suggested she return in the evening after Mr. Gibbs went home.

She returned after dark and held on to Mr. Meredith for support as she mounted the gangplank. Her thoughts raced as she stepped aboard once more. If she did this again, she would have to flee with Cole. She wondered if she would ever see her daughter again. She felt torn in two, wanting Cole and wanting Chloe. Oh, why did she have to choose?

Chloe would be safe and happy with Mary. But without her help, Cole would die. He might believe that love was about trust, but she knew it was about sacrifice. Hadn't she learned that over many a weary mile and many a hard choice?

Meredith held a lantern aloft to light her way. He assisted her down the stairs as she silently lifted his keys, still kept in the same right-hand pocket.

He seemed disinclined to leave her with Cole this time. She did not believe the dizzy trick would work twice and stood there racking her brain to think of some way to be rid of the odious man. Then, from down in the hold, came a steady banging followed by a howling that reminded Bridget of a baying hound.

"Meredith, come quick! He's killing me."

He swore as he shuffled off to see about the disturbance.

"Cole?" she whispered, but got no reply. "Cole, it's Bridget."

She slipped the key in the lock and turned it until she heard a click.

"Meredith is in the hold. We have to hurry."

She swung the door open to find a tall stranger aiming a cocked pistol at her middle.

The keys fell from her numb fingers, clattering on the floor.

Meredith trotted up the corridor. "I told you she done it. Didn't I say so?"

"So you did," he said, not looking at Meredith. "Miss Callahan? I'm Don Bates, the city marshal. You're under arrest. Step in, please."

She couldn't. The walls closed around her and she felt faint. Meredith shoved her from behind, sending her thudding into Bates. He righted her easily and held her as Meredith retrieved his keys and her pistol. His hands slipped from her trembling shoulders as he slid into the hall. She whirled in time to throw herself against the closing door. It didn't stop them from locking her in.

"It seems I misjudged you, Mr. Meredith."

"And I gets my old job back?"

"We'll see." Bates turned to Bridget, who now pressed her face between the narrow bars set in the door. "Pretty little thief, isn't she?" He stroked her cheek.

Meredith laughed.

Bridget staggered back, her head whirling from this sudden turnabout.

"Make yourself comfortable, my dove. We won't get to your trial until after Christmas, what with the hanging and all."

"No!" she shrieked.

Meredith pressed his greasy face to the bars and spit in her face. "You nearly cost me my job."

The warm spittle slipped down her cheek. She wiped it away with her sleeve and listened as their footsteps receded.

Bridget sank to her knees, cradling her face in her hands. Her worst nightmare had come to pass. She was in prison again. She had lost her baby and failed Cole. They would hang him, and there was nothing she could do to prevent it.

Cole heard someone coming. It wasn't time for his dinner and he had two days until his hanging. Perhaps it was the fancy attorney Sam had hired to defend him. Cole had told Sam that the cow was out of the barn and no use closing the gate now, but his old friend insisted there was money to spare since he'd hit pay dirt.

The only one he cared to see was Bridget. He wondered if they had reached Sacramento yet. Some stupid, irrational part of him still hoped she would visit him, even when he knew she would not. He'd served his purpose and was of no further use. Still, he had no regrets.

He'd done it. He'd reached her family and got them all down alive. It was a feat of which to be proud, and he was—very.

He glanced around the windowless room, seeing the

view from Broadner Pass in his mind's eye. What a glorious sight.

The ringing of heels on the stairs brought him back to his surroundings. The stone walls of the cellar below the state capitol came back into focus. The room was meant to store records but was solid enough to keep a condemned man. It had all the conveniences: candle, bed, blanket and bucket.

The visitor descended the final few stairs leading to his dungeon and he recognized the light tread of a woman. He stood and pressed his ear to the door.

The lock clicked and light flooded his dark world. He blinked up at the two people, hoping beyond reason to see Bridget.

"Hello, Mr. Ellis." He recognized the voice instantly.

His shoulders slumped. She had sent a proxy. "Oh, it's you, Mary. I thought…"

"It was Bridget?"

He had. Even though he knew that she had used him all along, the truth didn't keep away the longing and the hope. He loved her, fool that he was.

"It doesn't matter."

"Does it not? I had hoped otherwise." She studied him with a critical eye. "She wanted to come."

He nodded at the polite lie. If Bridget had wanted to come, she'd be standing there, not sending her sister to make excuses.

His jailor, Marshal Bates, kept a hand on his gun belt and motioned to the table and chairs in the adjoining room.

Mary took her seat, folding her hands as she waited for Cole to join her across the table.

"Mr. Ellis, I do not have time for niceties or dalliance." She turned to the marshal. "Mr. Bates, if you will excuse us?"

"Sorry, ma'am. After what your sister pulled, I just can't."

Cole sat up straighter. Mary had his full attention. "What happened?"

"Bridget tried to again secure your release." Mary's eyebrows raised pointedly. She said nothing to incriminate her sister but left no doubt as to how Bridget had tried to gain his liberty. She turned to his jailor. "Mr. Bates, perhaps you would be kind enough to step over there?" She indicated the far side of the room.

He pursed his lips, but did not move.

"I'm certain it is close enough to shoot us, if need be."

Bates scowled but moved to the wall, leaning against the crates of files.

"Where is she?" asked Cole.

"In jail." Mary scowled at Bates. "It was a trap."

Bates could not hold Mary's gaze. Cole felt his rage simmer deep.

Bridget was in prison. She was terrified of prisons. She'd told him that nothing except her family could have convinced her to even visit him on that brig. Yet she had come again—for him.

"Where are they holding her?"

"In the very same cell they had you, until her trial. She is in serious jeopardy."

He closed his eyes against the image of Bridget locked in that stinking cesspool. He glared at Bates, who smiled smugly at him, one hand casually anchored to the smooth handle of his revolver. Cole gripped the edge of the table.

Mary laid a hand over his wrist and he looked at her again, as if just noticing her presence. How did she know he was preparing to do something rash?

"Did Bridget tell you of her fear of prisons?" she whispered.

He nodded, thinking of Bridget in the workhouse.

"Did she tell you why she went to jail in Dublin?"

"Pickpocketing."

"That's a lie. She lies to protect her loved ones. It's something you should know. *I* was the pickpocket, Mr. Ellis. Me. I'd been teaching her, but wouldn't let her take the risk. It was my mark that went bad, not hers. He turned and saw Bridget. We ran, but she was smaller and could not run as fast as me. When they caught her, she never mentioned my name. Do you understand what I'm telling you? She went to the workhouse in *my* place."

Cole sat back as he tried to get his mind around this revelation.

"I owe her a debt that I can never repay. It was the least I could do to bring her west with us."

The resentment settled back in his belly. "And claim the child was yours."

Mary did not blink, blush or look away. Instead, she met his critical stare with one of her own.

"I did. It was the only way to protect Chloe from shame. A lie to protect those *I* love. But you blame her for trying to protect her child."

When she said it like that, it made him seem some kind of villain.

"I blame her for not trusting me."

Mary rolled her eyes. "Men! They are so quick to judge. Her father turned her out at the news. Did you know that? Right out in the street. And the man who got her with child?" Mary waved her hands in agitation. "He called her a whore. Can you imagine, after taking her innocence?"

Cole felt the irresistible urge to kill the man.

"What's his name?"

Mary pounded a fist on the table. "Now do you see the second reason why we lie to you? You fly off the handle, impractical. It's no wonder you are sitting in this cellar."

Cole returned Mary's scowl and noticed then how weak she looked. "How is George?"

The question destroyed her composure.

She clasped her hands and bowed her head. "Pneumonia."

"I'm sorry."

The flash in her eyes reminded him of Bridget and he almost smiled.

"You should be. Walking into a trap, when you know Bridget loves you. Of course she would try to save you, too."

Regret rolled in him and he spoke in low tones. "She doesn't know what love is. Love is honesty."

"You're mistaken, Mr. Ellis. Love is protecting your family, whether it's from the workhouse or from shame. Bridget understood that when she left our camp. George understood it when he tried to stay behind, and your wife understood it when she died rather than steal your chance at life."

Cole glowered. "Don't you speak about my wife."

"Did you tell Angela that you knew both of you would never make it out alive?"

He hadn't. Instead, he had pretended there was hope.

"You're no different than my sister, except she is not a hypocrite."

She was right. He was a fraud. He'd admired Bridget for her selfless courage and then condemned her for it.

"She did it for Chloe. What would you have done to protect Lee-lee?"

He would have killed. Understanding came to him too late. "She loves me."

Mary sighed. "Now you see the way of it."

Cole felt himself choking. "I'm sorry."

She smiled. "That may be just the thing. I thank you, Mr. Ellis, for listening."

Cole nodded and Mary stood.

"I have something for you." She reached into her bag. Bates came away from the wall.

"Hold it right there."

Mary gave him a look of exasperation. "Very well, you retrieve it."

"What?" asked Bates.

"Why, the *Transcript*. I thought Mr. Ellis might like to read the day's news."

Bates rolled his eyes and then retrieved the folded paper, slapping it before Cole with more force than necessary.

Cole pressed the pages flat with his hands. The headline stood bold and black across the page.

Local Hero Jailed After Daring Rescue

Mary pointed to a smaller headline farther down, her thin pale finger resting on the page.

Public Outcry Over Debacle Threatens Mayor's Reelection

Mary leaned forward. "Have hope, Mr. Ellis. The wheels are turning and many are with you."

He stood and clasped Mary's thin hand. "You have to get her out."

"I am endeavoring to do just that."

Chapter Twenty-Four

Bridget waited for Mary's visit, knowing she would come. Mary should have arrived yesterday, thanks to the wagon Mr. Giles had sent back for them when she first arrived in Sacramento. Today, when she heard Mary's familiar voice, Bridget found she did not have the courage to stand.

Cole had forsaken her and she was doomed for prison. There seemed no hope left in her world. Her only consolation was that her family would live and Chloe was safe in Mary's care.

Mary stood in the dark hallway before her sister. "I saw your Mr. Ellis today."

Bridget stood up and stumbled to the door, clutching the bars.

"What did he say?"

"He is regretful."

Bridget's fingers slipped from the bars. Cole regretful? It was a lie, some trick to fool her into false hope.

"He is! He told me to say he was sorry."

"Mary! How can you be so cruel?"

Mary gave her hands a squeeze through the bars. "He has forgiven you."

Bridget's breath caught at the possibility. She stuck her fifth finger out through the bars. "Is it true?"

Mary joined her fifth finger to Bridget's and nodded, solemnly. "True."

The joy lasted for several moments and then reality settled on her like the mist on a river. What did it matter, if he was to hang and she was to rot away behind bars?

She released herself from Mary and stepped back. Cole was to hang in two days. How would she live without him? "I wish I could see him, before…before…"

"Sam's attorney is hopeful of gaining a stay of execution. And Mr. Giles, from the *Transcript,* is speaking in five churches today. It is Christmas Eve and all are bound to be full up. Afterward he is holding a rally. You will hear it, I'm certain."

"Sam is a good friend to Cole."

"And Mr. Giles is a good friend to you. He still wishes to interview you, but the mayor won't allow it."

"The mayor is a coward."

"I do think so. The man's afraid and with good reason. I can smuggle your answers out to him. He has several questions."

"Go on."

Mary related his questions from memory and Bridget answered them.

"I'll come again tomorrow. Listen for the rally."

Bridget gripped Mary's hand through the bars and then withdrew. "How is Chloe?"

"Thriving now that we have cow's milk. She loves Mrs. Dickerson's biscuits."

Bridget smiled past the aching in her chest.

"And George?"

"The doctor says it is pneumonia. But the climate is so mild here, he is breathing easy already."

Relief washed through her. God had given her what she'd asked for. He had saved her family, rescued her little girl. Her smile faded as she considered the cost.

Bridget thought back to the day she'd met Cole and how readily she had been prepared to exchange his life for theirs. She had not cared what happened to him, if only he would help her.

Well, she had gotten what she asked for. God had showed her the value of a life, by making her love him with all her heart and then taking him from her.

Please, God, spare him.

Mary's voice roused her back to her tiny cell. "Don't give up hope, Bridget Rose. We are not licked yet."

Bridget nodded. It was an expression Mary had not used since they had left Dublin back in the dark days when there was no food, no work, no hope. But they had survived. She met Mary's gaze and saw a familiar glow of determination.

"I won't give up."

Mary left her then. That night, Bridget heard the crowd at the rally on the docks. They shouted and applauded. She knew Giles was a fine orator and was glad for his support.

On Christmas morning Mary came to her with news.

Mayor Barnnell had postponed Cole's execution. Bridget's elation lasted only long enough for her to note Mary's somber expression. She stilled, waiting for the other shoe to fall.

"I have it on authority from a source close to Mr. Giles that the mayor only means to delay until after he is reelected and then go on as before."

"When is the election?"

"November."

Their eyes met. Eleven months.

The days dragged on, with Mary's visit the only source of news. Sam had hired Bridget an attorney, but she had yet to see him.

It was not until well into January that Bridget comprehended that she was blossoming. The thought of bringing a baby into this dismal prison filled her with melancholy. Surely they would take the child away from her.

She revealed her situation to her sister on her next visit.

"You mustn't tell anyone," Mary said.

"They will know soon enough."

"It might hurt our cause."

Bridget had always deferred to her older sister, but she wondered if Mary was right about this.

"I would speak to the attorney."

"Bridget, why?"

She gave Mary a stubborn scowl and her sister sighed. "All right, then."

Horrace Covington arrived the next morning, unaccompanied. He was so tall that he had to crouch to peer into the gap in the door. When he did, his face reminded Bridget of an otter, all white and brown fur.

"Miss Callahan?"

There weren't so many women here that there could be any doubt, but she harnessed her sarcasm and nodded.

"I am."

He removed his hat. "Your sister sends her regards but is expecting the doctor this morning for her husband. I understand you seek an attorney."

"That's true."

"Before you begin, I must tell you that I am engaged by Mr. Samuel Pickett as counsel for his partner, Mr. Ellis. Your sister made a plea to Mr. Ellis and Mr. Pickett, and he agreed to pay for my services."

"How kind."

"I agreed so long as there is no conflict of interest, you understand."

"Yes." Sam was as good-natured a man as she had ever met. How generous of him to offer her help at this dark time.

Covington nodded. "Is it a court date you seek? I can certainly expedite that."

"It is rather more complicated, I fear." She told him her situation.

"I most surely will petition for your immediate release. Under the circumstances, it may be feasible and I believe we can keep this matter private."

He departed, only to return the following afternoon with a signed release. Bridget could not believe her good fortune as she stepped above deck for the first time in nearly a month and scanned the city.

"The conditions of your release include no contact with Mr. Ellis. Violation would lead to your reincarceration. You now have a court date in February but are in my care until then."

"Where shall I go?"

"Your sister has taken a room on I Street. I'm to bring you there."

He escorted her down Broad Street and round the back of a chemist shop.

"Top of the stairs." Covington tipped his gray felt hat and bowed at the waist.

"Thank you for everything."

He replaced his hat and took his leave.

Mary must have heard her on the stairs, for the door flew open and she rushed down to hug Bridget.

"There now, we are all together at last."

Mary seemed so joyful that Bridget was sorry she could not muster the same enthusiasm.

"George is waiting. He has a job. He's to start Monday as a wheelwright." Mary grasped her hand and tugged. "Come along."

The first thing Bridget saw upon entering the long narrow room was Chloe, sitting on a gingham cloth and chewing merrily upon a wooden spoon.

"Teething," said Mary.

Bridget scooped up her daughter, pressing her cheek to Chloe's. Chloe beat the spoon against Bridget's back in delight and squealed at her appearance.

"She's been asking for you."

"Ge-ge!" said Chloe, in her best attempt at Bridget's name.

Bridget's heart ached.

She turned to face Mary. "I want her to call me Mama."

"But Bridget, that's impossible."

"No, it's not. I'm tired of lying."

"But you have no husband."

"I could say he died on the trail." Another lie. She grimaced.

Mary hesitated, staring at her sister as if measuring her determination. "If you are sure."

The silence stretched between them. Mary never let it go on too long.

"You'll want to wash." She tried to scoop Chloe from Bridget, but Bridget held her a moment too long. Mary tried again and Bridget let her go. "I have a basin and pitcher past the curtain. There's a clean dress, as well."

"A dress?" They'd left everything behind. Bridget suddenly noted her surroundings, taking in the new curtains, pots on the stove, a woven rug by the hearth. She cast Mary an appraising glance.

"Sam has given us a loan. He's a dear man."

Bridget suspected his partner, Cole, was the true benefactor.

"Oh, and Mr. Giles has been here twice since word came of your release. He left his card. He's keen to interview you about our ordeal and doubly curious to know the reasons for your release. But I'm not sure it's wise. Too many questions that can't be answered."

Bridget scowled, but instead of contradicting her elder sister, she marched behind the curtain to wash and change.

She spent the rest of the day playing with her daughter by the hearth that her sister provided. Once she had thought this was all she wanted in the world, but now she was no longer satisfied.

The following morning she took Chloe and went to see Mr. Giles. His efforts, coupled with Mr. Covington's, had stayed Cole's hanging. Bridget was beyond grateful.

"But there is more to be done," Mr. Giles said. "The man is a hero and we treat him like a criminal. I am gravely concerned. The mayor means to leave him to rot and he can do it. Ellis is convicted and now faces two more counts of horse theft."

Bridget held Chloe on her lap, jiggling her knee occasionally. Her child seemed content, gnawing on her own fist. "Isn't there anything I can do?"

"Your story will help, particularly if you emphasize that your family would have perished if not for Ellis."

"That's true enough."

"The public is with us in sentiment, but we need them in the streets. We need a touchstone. Something to tug at the heartstrings. I'm certain we will latch upon something as we explore your tale."

Bridget began to tell of the journey. She admitted she had freed Cole.

"In desperation and after all the others had turned their backs," added Giles.

She confessed to striking the groom, rendering him insensible. Giles hesitated.

"You're taking a risk. They could charge you with the crime of horse thief. It's a hanging offense."

"They'll never hang me."

"Because you are a woman? You are likely correct, but it's foolish to take such a gamble."

It wasn't the only reason. "It is the truth."

"I wouldn't stake my life on it," said Giles.

Bridget mustered her courage. She knew exactly the touchstone Giles needed, if only she was brave enough to take this step. To save Cole, she must reveal her secrets and expose her daughter to scorn. Or she could stay silent and watch Cole die.

Something inside her toughened. She found the strength to do what was not easy but was right.

"They won't hang me, Mr. Giles, because I am carrying Cole Ellis's child."

Giles's arms shot out as he braced himself on the table. His face paled and his eyes opened wide.

"Are you certain of this?"

"I am." She smoothed her hand over the buttons at her neckline, trying to calm her pounding heart. "And Chloe, she is not my niece—but my daughter. It is why I took such desperate measures—to save her."

Giles leapt to his feet. "Great blue blazes, it's the story of a lifetime." He rounded the table to stand before her. "And you will admit to this, allow me to print the story in my paper?"

"If you think it will help him."

Giles paced from the window to his printing press and back again. On the third trip he began to mutter to himself. He sounded like a politician preparing a speech.

He stopped before her, pressing his hands to the desk as he leaned forward. "He must marry you."

Bridget's voice became a strangled thing. "What?"

"It's what we need. He'll have to agree. Will you do it, Miss Callahan?"

It was her dearest wish—a longing, really—to marry Cole. She'd never thought he would have her. Now Cole would be forced to marry her. It wasn't right. Her head sank.

"He doesn't know."

Giles coughed. "But he must, and then he will do the honorable thing."

She brushed a hand protectively over her daughter's head, sweeping back the curly red hair. "He doesn't know about Chloe, either. I was afraid to tell him. Afraid of what he might think of me."

Giles patted her hand. "It is an obstacle, granted. But not insurmountable, by any means. I believe with all my heart that this is what is needed to tip the scales of justice in our favor. We could even appeal to the governor. We will argue that the mayor is on a vendetta. But you must be married, Miss Callahan. It gives you substance and, more important, it gives you a legal right to act on your husband's behalf."

Bridget tried to imagine Cole's reaction to this news. He hated lies and she had lied to him from start to finish.

"But I'm prohibited from seeing him," said Bridget.

Giles scoffed. "By whom?"

"A judge. It is part of my release agreement."

"We'll go see this judge this very day, madame. He cannot keep you from Mr. Ellis, not when you have a claim. If need be, we will involve the clergy."

Bridget wished for just one moment she could step back to the instant before she had revealed her secrets. Now everything was spinning out of control.

She thought of all that Cole had done to save her family and how she had repaid him with lies.

Now she might secure his freedom. But to gain his release, he would have to wed her, entering into a different kind of prison. She leaned forward and pressed her lips to the top of Chloe's head. What to do?

To marry him under such circumstances…the anguish threatened to drown her. She loved him, but knew full well that he did not love her.

"Come along, Miss Callahan. We have business."

Chapter Twenty-Five

"That Giles is a menace," said Covington, shaking his satchel as he entered Cole's cell. "The man had no right. I'll sue him for defamation of character." He tore back the flap of his worn leather case and slapped a copy of the *Sacramento Transcript* on the table.

Cole eyed the headline. "What's this?"

Mother Desperate to Save Her Child

Bridget's name, Chloe… He snatched up the paper as ice crystals formed in his blood. They knew. Somehow they had discovered her secret. "But how?"

"What?"

"How did they learn of this?"

Covington waved a hand in the air. "She told them! The woman has no shame. Imagine telling a newsman such things. I gained her release, as you desired, and surely would have gotten her acquitted—"

"She's out?" He held his breath waiting for his answer.

"Yes, yes, but listen, please. She has learned of your fortune and seeks it. Mind me now, for she is a fortune hunter. The only positive development is that she claims to have helped you steal the horses. Is that true?"

Cole was on his feet. "She what?"

Had the woman lost her mind?

"Oh, now you see what we are up against. But that's not all. They've run an evening edition. The man's a damned zealot." Covington withdrew a second paper. Before he could extend it, Cole ripped the pages from his hand.

Mother Begs, Free Unborn Child's Father

Cole's heart stopped as he read the first sentence.

January 24, 1851. Broadner Pass survivor Bridget Callahan finds herself in a delicate condition and seeks a reversal of Judge Jonathan D. Hardy's edict banning her from speaking to Cole Ellis.

He clutched the paper and then staggered against the table, knocking his chair to the floor.

"What—is this true?"

"How should I know? The woman claims to have had relations. If you tell me it is slander, I shall restrain her and that hothead Giles."

Cole thought back to their night in the cabin, when he'd held her in his arms and loved her until dawn.

"It's possible."

Covington scratched beneath the whiskers on his

chin. "This is difficult, most difficult, as I have represented you both. Mr. Pickett will just have to choose whom I am to represent. But I was your attorney prior to becoming hers. She will need to find other counsel. I don't believe they can force you, if you are unwilling, and I might still be able to keep her away."

"No." He was desperate to see her, had thought of nothing else since learning of her daring attempt to free him. Covington thought she was a fortune hunter, but he did not know her. Cole tried to reason why Bridget had done something so irrational.

"Are you certain she *told* Giles?"

"Yes."

Then she had a reason—a very good reason. She hadn't been willing to tell him about Chloe, but now she had told everyone and revealed that she had lain with him. It made no sense. "I don't understand."

"Giles has some harebrained idea that he can turn popular sentiment toward your case. He's appealing to the governor. Says the mayor is acting out of revenge, not justice. I wish for once the man had consulted with me. This could be disastrous."

Cole began to comprehend, but still he could not believe it. Had Bridget revealed her secret to try to save him? It seemed impossible, but not when he added in her attempt to break him out of prison.

"She did it for me."

Covington cleared his throat. "She is after your gold claim, Mr. Ellis. If she can force a marriage, she will be your only heir."

Cole did not believe it. The woman was many things, but not a fortune hunter.

"It is the only reason I can fathom for a woman to publicly humiliate herself. Had she asked me, I would have advised against this rash course of action. It may still be possible to buy her off."

He met the man's red-rimmed eyes. "She's not after the money. She's trying to save me from hanging."

Covington's brow wrinkled as he considered this. "It is possible, I suppose."

Cole stormed across the room and clutched the latch, forgetting his position until he found the door locked.

"You have to let me see her."

"Impossible. No contact, as a condition of her release. She has agreed not to come within fifty feet of you. If she violates this agreement, she could be reincarcerated."

"Another reason she told them, so she could see me."

"And it just might work. Clever, really, and very daring."

"Can you take her a letter?"

Covington rubbed his thumb over his mustache. "Under no circumstances. I am still her counsel and a letter constitutes contact."

Her new attorney, Mr. Lynn Gutherie, was as round as a barrel, with a florid face and jowls to rival a bloodhound. He stood beside Bridget, presenting her case to alter the agreement forged by Mr. Covington on her behalf.

"Miss Callahan," said Judge Hardy, "I do not approve of your shenanigans. You have used your condition to escape justice for a crime that you very clearly did commit."

Bridget lowered her gaze to the floor, feeling her ears tingle as blood rushed into her face.

"However, I am not a man to punish an unborn child for the crimes of the mother. Thus I have given you your release. But this request violates the conditions of our agreement, an agreement that you yourself signed."

Gutherie waddled forward. "Your Honor, my client's previous attorney did not bother to explain the conditions of her release. Had she known she was signing away her right to see the child's father, I am certain she would have had pause. The agreement is unreasonable, as it violates her right to see the man who has done this to her. You give this couple no opportunity to correct the issue of the child's legitimacy, for how can they do the honorable thing if they cannot meet?"

"By proxy," snapped the judge.

"But Your Honor, many consider the man a hero, wrongly jailed by a vindictive and vengeful man using his high office to run roughshod over the legal system."

The corner of the judge's mouth twitched and a very unattractive smirk rose. "And who happens to be a Republican, while you chair the Democratic Party."

Gutherie waved a hand as if dismissing his concern. "Inconsequential."

"We will agree to disagree on this. To what end does she seek to see Mr. Ellis?"

"Why, who can say the mysteries in a woman's heart?"

Bridget forced herself to keep her head bowed in a

posture of contrite submission, stifling the urge to kick the judge in his shins.

"Indeed."

Bridget felt his eyes upon her and looked up, very discreetly.

"Many women, more modest women, would have gone to great lengths to keep their shame secret."

Gutherie planted a fleshy hand on the table beside the judge. "Would you?"

The men exchanged knowing glances and the judge's somber expression slipped. He studied Bridget and then Gutherie.

"She might just pull this off."

"With your assistance, Your Honor. Party politics aside, you must admire a woman willing to submit to public scorn to achieve her aim."

Hardy did not take his glittering eyes off her.

Her attorney continued, his voice smooth and sweet as honey. "These are unsettling times. The mayor does not have the backing he once did. Might I suggest that it would not hurt to have a friend in both camps, when the time comes for reappointment."

Hardy's mouth twitched, as if he meant to smile and then suppressed the urge. "Miss Callahan, whatever else you might be, you are an audacious woman. I will allow you to visit Mr. Ellis and further, I will marry the two of you, whether he is agreeable or not." Hardy nodded at Gutherie. "Now that, sir, is a headline."

Chapter Twenty-Six

Cole's counsel arrived in the morning with surprising news.

"The governor intends to review your case."

Cole blinked in astonishment. "But why?"

"No one is more taken aback than I, I assure you. But that blabbermouth Giles seems to have roused the city. He has even touched the hearts of the fairer sex and they, sir, have the ears of their husbands. I should think the circumstances that Miss Callahan finds herself in would be repugnant to any respectable woman, but they are steadfast."

Cole resisted the urge to throttle the man for insulting Bridget. *Respectable women, indeed.*

"You do not ask why they unite? For you—Mr. Ellis. For you."

"What?

"You—the dashing hero, the deliverer of women and children and conqueror of the Cascades." His counsel had his finger raised to the ceiling as he delivered his oration. "They have become *your* champion, and do you know who is the ruler of this gaggle of hens?

"Mrs. Julianna Barnnell, wife of His Honor, Mayor Barnnell." He and Cole exchanged a look of understanding before his attorney continued. "It can only help your cause. Her involvement is a source of embarrassment for His Honor." Covington beamed. "Under the circumstances, it would be most prudent to take care of that little matter with Miss Callahan."

"You talking about me marrying her?"

"Indeed."

"I'd say that's up to her."

Cole held out hope that Bridget wanted to marry him. But deep in his heart he recalled that she had walked out of the safety of camp in order to help her family. She had also taken the blame for a crime that sent her to the workhouse. Was she now engaged in a similar act of self-sacrifice? Was she willing to marry a man she did not love to save his life?

The notion of wedding a martyr grieved him, because he knew he was hopelessly in love with the little firebrand.

"You are agreeable?" asked his counsel.

It shamed him that he was willing to let her do it. She had managed to get him out from under the noose. Now he faced an exceedingly long prison sentence, yet to be determined.

He imagined Bridget in the firelight, how she had given herself to him and how, at the time, he thought she felt something for him. Now he just didn't know.

"Mr. Ellis, your decision?"

"I'll marry her."

"Very prudent."

Cole glared.

"I'll make the arrangements. I think Mr. Giles should be a witness. I have come to terms with the man and concede that the press does have its uses."

"I'm marrying here?"

"I think it would help."

"Fine." He thought of his first wedding, to Angela, in the white clapboard church in Brunswick, Vermont. He had gone forward into matrimony certain that Angela loved him with all her heart. Now he would face another bride, one whose heart was not so open. The two women were as different as dawn and dusk. How was it possible to love them both?

But he did.

Covington rubbed his hands together in anticipation. "Very good. Leave it to me. I will send word as to when the ceremony will take place. Once the ladies out front hear, not even the mayor himself can stop us. The mayor's wife is a hopeless romantic and childless, poor thing." He grinned broadly. "Perhaps she would act as a witness."

Covington rapped on the door and the guard released him. He was so caught up in his mission he did not even turn back to issue a farewell.

Cole spent the rest of the day pacing.

The mayor's wife, Mrs. Julianna Barnnell, would not hear of Bridget marrying in a plain wool dress. She arranged for a dress and dressmaker to alter a frothy lace gown to fit Bridget's diminished body.

On the day before the wedding, Mrs. Barnnell arrived at ten in the morning, precisely, with her maid, dressmaker and assistants. The maid, Katie, was Irish as well, making Bridget more uncomfortable with the situation.

The mayor's wife opened a box and her maid drew out the bustle and hoops. They fit perfectly, thanks to the drawstring waist.

From a second box, Katie lifted out the gown. Bridget gaped at the miles of white satin and lace trim, and the seeded pearls that adorned the bodice.

Mrs. Barnnell clasped her hands together and sighed. "It was my dear sister's dress. The style is not current, but the workmanship is exquisite." She held the dress up to Bridget and frowned as she noted the disparity in the size of the dress compared to the woman. But she rallied quickly. "Oh, you'll look lovely once we take it in."

"It's white," said Bridget.

Katie glanced at her and then blushed, understanding Bridget's objections completely.

"Well, of course," said Mrs. Barnnell.

Bridget met the woman's gaze and lifted a brow.

"Oh, I see. Don't be silly. It doesn't matter in the least."

It mattered.

Bridget glanced down at the sea of sugary lace and forced a smile. She had no more business wearing white than she had marrying a man against his will.

"You must indulge me. I have spoken to Mr. Giles. He plans to have your likeness in the newspaper. You must look a proper bride."

"I'm not proper."

Mrs. Barnnell waved away her concern as if it were a gnat. "Traditional, then."

She signaled the maid and the dress was gathered and lifted over Bridget's head.

"Oh, dear," said her benefactor. "I should say you will not need a corset."

It seemed hours that Bridget stood while the women pinned and chalked the dress. At last the invading army of milliners left her in peace, but the morning of the wedding they returned with a hairdresser, who carried several irons.

Bridget had seen to her own hair since she was old enough to hold a comb and did not take kindly to this stranger messing about. By the time the woman had finished, Bridget had a scorch mark on her neck. Bridget studied herself in the small glass. Her hair was neatly parted and lay coiled on each side of her head like two sticky buns, dripping white ribbon icing. Worse still were the large, unnaturally tight ringlets that bounced beside her ears like Irish sausages.

"There now." Julianna glowed. "Aren't you beautiful?"

Mary pressed a hand to each shoulder and leaned forward to whisper in her ear, "The veil will cover it."

Bridget tipped the mirror until she could see Mary's sympathetic face and smiled. She took one more look at the dreadful result of the woman's efforts and felt nauseated. She had to swallow back her trepidation.

"Now the dress," ordered Julianna.

"If we could just have a moment," said Mary.

"Oh, certainly. I'll be right outside."

Bridget stood to face her sister.

"I've never seen a more melancholy bride."

"He doesn't love me. He told me so. Cole only agreed to escape the noose."

"It's a better reason than many I know. But I think you are wrong about his feelings. Did you ask yourself why he came all that way to save us—kept on when others would have quit?"

"Because of his promise."

"No, Bridget. He did it for *you*."

She saw that Mary believed this and so there was no point in arguing. "Let's get on with it."

Mary pressed her lips together as if holding something back by force of will. Then she lifted the dress from the narrow bed.

Bridget stripped out of her old gown and then burrowed through the silky underskirts like a groundhog until she emerged at the neckline.

"I'll call them," said Mary.

Complete with lace veil and frothing dress, she descended the back stairs of the apartments she now shared with Mary and George. The mayor's private carriage awaited in the street. The irony of riding behind Barnnell's new carriage horse was not lost on her, but she had little time to enjoy the brief moment of victory before the carriage pulled up in front of the white stone columns of the courthouse and capitol.

There was a crowd at the steps. Bridget peered out, trying vainly to see clearly through the haze of white lace hanging before her eyes. What were they all doing here?

She had thought they might insult her as she passed, but they did not.

She clutched the borrowed white fan and small prayer book in one hand, moving to the edge of her seat.

Mr. Giles waited, stepping forward to help her descend and then offering his elbow. She felt a catch in her throat as she saw he planned to fill the role vacated by her father. What would her father think to see her now?

Her head bowed. He would be ashamed of her notoriety and the scandal she had caused. It was another black mark against the name of Callahan. Would word reach him? She shivered at the thought.

"You are a most beautiful bride," said Giles and patted her trembling hand, now resting stiff as wood in the warm crook of his elbow. "I have engaged an artist. I think a likeness of the bride will only serve to bring more sympathy to our cause."

How could she object?

Her mother's words came to her mind. "A lady's name appears in the news only three times—on her birth, her wedding day and the day she dies."

How many times had Bridget's name blanketed the paper? She swallowed back the bitter taste in her mouth and cleared her throat.

"Of course."

"He is just inside. The judge forbids the artist at the ceremony. Says this is circus enough." His voice revealed how pleased he was.

Bridget's stomach rolled as they arranged her on the inner steps. Was Cole just inside the thick doors before her?

Mary adjusted her veil to reveal her face and then draped it so it ran down the marble steps like cake icing.

Bridget studied the twitchy little man in the gray felt hat who now stood scratching charcoal frantically over the top page of a pad of paper. He worked for several minutes and then turned the page, took up a new position and began again. He did this twice more. Bridget's back ached and she began to tremble from holding her position so long.

"Nearly done," he squeaked.

Mary moved behind him and her mouth dropped open as she looked from Bridget to the rendering. Her nod of approval was Bridget's assurance.

He flipped the pad closed and tipped his hat to her, leaving a smudge of charcoal on the brim. "That should do." He smiled at Giles. "I'll have a plate for you by this afternoon."

"No later," warned Giles.

"Yes, yes." He scuttled away, reminding Bridget of a rat fleeing a ship.

Bridget groaned as she descended the three steps to stand in the entrance chamber beside Mary.

"I'll just see if they are ready," said Giles, disappearing through the courtroom doors.

"Married by a judge," whispered Mary. "You should be married by a priest in church."

"Mary, please," said Bridget. "I have little to say about it."

"But you will marry in a church, when you can?"

"He's Protestant. I doubt he'd agree."

Mary's eyes widened at this. She could never marry in her church. Not unless he converted.

Giles returned, moving at a fast walk. "They're bringing him up now."

Bridget's heart raced as Mary lifted the veil back into place. Dread settled over her as she wondered what Cole would say, what he would think.

Hadn't he told her that he would never wed again? That he could not bear to take the risk of suffering such loss again. Yet she had forced him, by revealing her shame to all. She rested a hand over her still-flat stomach. There, safe and warm, his child grew by the day.

Giles held the door and Bridget stepped through, her underskirts rustling like dry leaves blowing over the ground.

She spied the judge, sitting stiff and dark as a raven behind the raised dais.

Mrs. Barnnell moved to the left to stand before him in some mock version of a church wedding. Still, it was binding. There would be no escape for either of them. The child and the civil ceremony would hold them. Wouldn't they?

She grasped Giles's elbow with more force than necessary, clinging to the rough weave of his jacket as he marched her forward to stand before Judge Hardy. There they stood silent, ready for the ceremony, save the groom.

Bridget's skin grew moist as she pondered Cole's absence. They just had not yet brought him from the holding cell. It was not his choice when he came and went.

But what if it was more? What if he preferred that prison to this one?

A soft cry escaped her. Mr. Giles patted her hand.

"Just a few minutes longer, I assure you." His face was a blur beyond the veil.

She was glad for it, as it kept them all from seeing the tears welling in her eyes.

The door to the left opened noiselessly. Next came the rattle of a chain.

All heads turned toward Cole. Bridget craned her neck, trying vainly to see him clearly. He wore a clean white shirt, but no coat. His beard was gone, but what of his expression? She could not make it out.

The clink came again and she saw his wrists were shackled to a length of chain that looped between them, forcing him to keep his hands before him.

They had him trussed like a turkey. Her heart twisted in her chest. This was wrong. She stood dressed like some upper-class debutante while he came bound and chained as if to his execution.

The guards flanked him, gripping his upper arms as they walked him to his place beside her. They stepped away, but not far. Marshal Don Bates stood by the door, his hand resting easily on the pistol strapped low on his hip.

Cole gawked at her. "Bridget?"

Her own tears choked her word. She tried to speak, but emitted only a strangled cry. She nodded her answer.

He bowed his head. "I'm sorry."

The tears fell then. She could not help it. They coursed down her cheeks and into the lace collar fastened by Mrs. Barnnell's cameo brooch. He was sorry—sorry to be her husband, sorry for their forced marriage, sorry not to love her.

The judge cleared his throat and began the ceremony. His clipped, dour tone made it seem more admonishment than joining. He came quickly to the conclusion. Cole stood silently beside her. How she longed to take his hand. She glanced toward his hands and saw again the shackles. He stood straight and still, staring at the judge.

Was he thinking of his last wedding?

Of course he must be. On that day he must have been happy and nervous. Had Angela worn flowers in her hair?

Bridget felt more unworthy than ever in her life. He was a good man with a heart as big as the mountains, but life had rewarded him with her. He deserved better. He deserved to be happy. But how could she presume to step into the shoes of a woman he loved?

She could not. She was a liar, thief and worse. He had been right about her all along. She sniffed, trying to keep back the tears, and Cole glanced her way. She lowered her chin, hiding her shame in the white lace that mocked her true nature.

The judge did not ask for Cole to kiss her. Instead, he directed them to sign the license. Cole offered her the pen. Her fingers trembled as she scrawled her signature in coarse, uneven letters. The pen fell from her hand and Cole lifted it, dipping it once and then drawing off the excess ink at the side of the well before adding his signature. The strong even curves and neat letters showed that he had had some education.

Mrs. Barnnell stepped forward to sign as witness, as arranged by Mr. Giles to strengthen his headlines. She bubbled with delight as she added a looping slanted signature to the page. Mr. Giles came last and the deed was done.

Mary drew back Bridget's veil. Bridget gazed at

Cole, her vision clouded now only by tears. He looked as if he did not know her. His eyes were wide and his brow wrinkled as he peered.

"Bridget?"

"What is it?" she asked.

He shook his head as if trying to rouse himself from a nightmare.

"All right," said Judge Hardy. "Bring him back down."

The guards moved forward, grasping Cole's arms. They marched him off and he went, looking back at her as if he had never seen her before in his life.

The door closed behind him and tears erupted from her. She swayed. Giles clasped her arm, guiding her to a bench.

"Bring some water."

Water? As if she needed that. What she wanted, and could never have, was a husband who cherished her. And what he wanted was to have a woman he could trust or, better still, no woman at all.

Mary kneeled before her. "You have saved him."

Bridget's head sank even farther.

Chapter Twenty-Seven

They removed the shackles, deposited Cole back in his cell and locked the door. He sat alone upon the bunk.

It was the first time he'd seen Bridget since they'd taken him and he had not even recognized her.

But how could he? She was wrapped up in slippery white fabric that hugged her ribs and narrow waist, then billowed out about her in the shape of a bell. He thought of her in her boy's trousers, boots and wool skirts tucked up into her belt. That was the woman he knew, not that lady who floated before him as if she had no legs. What had they done to her?

During the entire ceremony, he'd wondered if it was really her beneath that veil or if this was some trick. Then Mary lifted the lace curtain and a stranger stood there, ribbons dancing about her neck and her lovely, wild hair subdued.

She was crying. That was plain enough. Bridget had done what she had to do to save him. Because he had rescued her family, she had sacrificed her reputation in a bid to earn him his freedom. Back on the mountain, when he had loved her, he had not been able to do the honorable thing. Now he had. He had given their child his name.

A child.

The idea washed him in dread. He had not wanted this, not ever again. What if the child died, as well?

He felt the pain already, anticipated it like a blow. Lee-lee's death had torn his heart to tatters.

But if his heart was dead, he could not feel these things for Bridget, could not have this terror over the child.

He wanted them—both. But already he was afraid of losing them.

"Oh, Bridget, why did you have to open that lock?"

The *Sacramento Transcript* reported the details of the wedding and included a lovely etching of a mournful bride. Bridget's tragic image stirred indignation in the women and righteousness in the men.

The governor's staff could not handle the number of irate citizens flooding his office with petitions for Cole's release. It took only two days for the governor to reach a decision. He summoned the mayor to his offices.

At noon the following day, the two men stood on the steps of the capitol to make their joint announcement.

The *Sacramento Transcript* reported the governor's exact words.

"Mr. Ellis acted with true valor when others refused to take action, risking his very life to save the lives of others, among them an innocent babe. Had he not requisitioned the horses from the livery, the stranded family would surely have perished. We owe Mr. Ellis a debt of gratitude. Due to his extraordinary heroism, the sentence is reduced to time served."

There was no mention of the mayor's carriage horse, but the paper did say that Mrs. Barnnell stood proudly at her husband's side as the crowd cheered the announcement.

Mr. Giles lowered the paper and grinned, first at Mary and then at Bridget, who sat with Chloe on her knee.

"What it doesn't say is that when Barnnell tried to speak, he was booed off the platform. The man's reelection will be an uphill battle."

"What about Cole?" asked Mary.

"He will be released at two this afternoon. The entire town will be there to see your reunion."

Bridget went cold. "Oh, I—I don't think…"

"My dear," said Giles, "you must go. He is your husband."

She dropped her eyes, toying with the silky hair on Chloe's head. "He didn't choose to marry me."

"He did. I was there."

Bridget met his gaze. "It was a shotgun wedding. You know it."

Giles flushed. "Still and all, he is better for it. See now, you're a pretty wife and strong as steel, and he owes his child his name, in any case."

All true, so why did Bridget feel sick? Because just once in her life she wanted a man who loved her. She wanted what Angela had.

Fairy tales. She was a woman who had seen things that should have made her more practical about the world.

Perhaps it was those very things that made her ache so desperately for what she had never had.

Mary rested a hand on her knee and gave her sister a squeeze, then turned to Giles. "We'll be there."

Bridget pressed her lips together, but said nothing.

Giles held Bridget's gaze, answering Mary, but speaking to Bridget. "I'm counting on it."

Mary saw Giles to the door.

"And thank you again for all you've done. You are a true crusader."

The door closed and Mary pressed her back to it. "We must see about getting you ready."

Bridget thought to object.

"The entire city will be there, Bridget. They'll all be watching. The least you can do is comb your hair. You look like a madwoman."

Bridget slid Chloe to her hip and walked to the washbasin. Then she settled her daughter on the dresser, where Chloe splashed in the bowl as Bridget washed her own face and dragged the comb through her hair.

Mary insisted she wear the new caned-gauze bonnet George had given his wife, choosing the gray shawl for herself.

When they left the building, Mary reached for Chloe. "I'll take her."

Bridget turned away. "They know about her, Mary. There's no need to hide any longer."

"I still think it best if—"

"She's mine, Mary."

Mary stiffened. Bridget rarely contradicted her sister

and Mary seemed affronted. At last Mary lowered her arms, folding them before her.

"It is one thing to read about it, quite another to have it thrust in your face. I should think you'd want public sympathy."

"Well, I don't."

"Have it your way, then." Her sister's voice dripped with disapproval.

Mary dragged her shawl over her shoulders and smoothed her hair, reminding Bridget of a hen straightening ruffled feathers.

The starch went right out of her. "Mary? I can't thank you enough for taking care of us. You've been with Chloe since the moment she was born." Bridget thought of her birthing. She had sent word to their mother, but she had not come. Not that they expected her to after her father had told her she was dead to them. But Mary had defied him, taking Bridget in and seeing her child into the world. "I can't ever thank you enough."

Some of Mary's clipped tone dissolved. "Perhaps you can return the favor."

Bridget cocked her head, not understanding what Mary meant. She certainly didn't need looking after, not with George thriving and with more work than he could manage as a wheelwright. They'd have their own shop in no time.

"I'll be having my own confinement soon."

Bridget brightened. For a moment all the despair and heartache went right out of her and she understood the new radiance in her sister's face.

"Oh, Mary!" She clasped her hand. "Oh, I'm so happy for you both."

"George has already chosen the name. If it's a boy, he wants to name it Ellis. If a girl, then Ellie, in honor of your husband."

Her husband. Bridget could hardly believe it. She didn't feel like a wife.

"Come along, then." Mary clasped her hand and led the way.

At half past one the sisters marched down I Street to the courthouse. Seeing the crowds somehow stiffened Bridget's resolve. She lost her sorrow in favor of stubbornness as she passed, putting on a brave face.

Murmurs passed through the crowd. "There she is." "That's her." Children pointed and adults gawked.

Mary stayed at her side, as she had always done. George met them at the steps, taking a flanking position on Bridget's right while Mary took the left.

"You've got your family here, Bridget Rose," said Mary.

"You'll always have us," said George.

The mayor stood with his wife at the top of the courthouse steps, along with the governor, Judge Hardy and Marshal Bates. The only one missing was Cole.

"Ah, here comes the bride," said Governor Tisdale, grinning broadly. He spoke in a loud voice, meant to be heard by all. "Let me shake the hand of the bravest woman in California."

The crowd cheered. It was not the welcome Bridget had expected.

Tisdale turned to Bates. "If you will bring the groom, I will sign the clemency papers."

The marshal disappeared and then emerged holding

Cole's arm as if to prevent him from breaking away from the herd.

Tisdale beamed. "It is my honor to see that justice is served here today. This man has proved that sometimes the ends do justify the means. He has saved these three souls and, by doing so, perhaps many generations to come. He is accused of violating the law, but who among us would not do the same to rescue a beloved daughter or wife or son? Justifiable, I say, and so I am proud to sign this paper." He motioned and an aide rushed forward with a pen, freshly dipped. Another held the paper, tacked to a board. "I exonerate Cole Ellis and declare him a free man."

A man in the front of the crowd hollered, "He ain't free, Gov. He's married!"

The crowd laughed and the joke was repeated, spreading backward like a receding wave.

The governor laughed as well and signed the release.

Tisdale spoke to the heckler like an old friend. "I hope he finds his current arrangement preferable, for I think I have never seen a lovelier bride than Mrs. Ellis."

Bridget felt herself blush clear down to her roots as Tisdale offered his hand. She clasped it and he kissed the back of her hand before passing her off to Cole.

His touch was tentative. Their eyes met. She could read nothing from his expression except the strain he felt.

She could not even speak past the lump in her throat. She held Chloe in one arm and Cole's hand in the other as the crowd went silent, trying to catch their words.

Cole leaned close to her. "Bridget?"

The same heckler shouted again.

"You going to talk her to death or kiss her?"

Cole wrapped an arm around her waist, pulling her in close, and then dipped to press his lips to hers. She melted in the warm sunshine, barely hearing the cheers of the crowd.

When he released her, she was dizzy.

She heard a familiar voice and turned to see Mr. Giles of the *Transcript*.

"Mr. and Mrs. Ellis, do you have anything to say to the people of Sacramento?"

Cole pulled Bridget to his side. "Yes. Thank you one and all. Now, if you will excuse us…"

Hats flew in the air and the crowd surged forward to slap Cole on the back, kiss the bride and coo over Chloe.

Sam and George stepped forward to clear well-wishers out of the way, but it still took a full forty minutes for the party just to reach Seventh Street.

The men wanted to buy Cole a beer and the women wanted to invite Bridget to call. The couple declined all offers as Sam ordered them to follow him. Chloe fell sound asleep on her mother's shoulder. Bridget could not see where Sam was headed, but soon found herself inside a building.

She glanced about and recognized the lobby of the Imperial. They did not pause but were ushered up the stairs to a suite of two rooms. When they crossed the threshold, Sam, George and Mary remained standing in the hall.

"We will see you tomorrow," said Mary. She smiled and then kissed them both on the cheek. Mary stepped forward and extended her arms.

"You'll let me take her now?"

Bridget noticed the difference. Mary did not issue a directive to be heeded, but rather made a request.

Bridget smiled and allowed her to gently lift Chloe from her arms, cradling the sleeping child to her bosom.

George shook Cole's hand. "Take good care of our girl."

"Best of luck," said Sam, slapping Cole on the back and then stooping to kiss Bridget's cheek.

And then they were off.

Cole closed the door and turned the key.

The silence hung heavily in the air. Both tried to speak at once.

"Shall we—"

"Are you—"

They broke off.

"You first," he said.

"I'm grateful to you for giving our baby your name. But I don't want a husband whose sole reason for having me is to avoid something more miserable than marriage to me."

He said nothing for a moment and she felt like a fish thrown up on the riverbank, unable to breathe and unable to escape. His brow wrinkled as his gaze pierced her. If anything, it made him more handsome. She could not stand the scrutiny and so, with trembling fingers, she untied the bonnet strings and laid the hat aside.

If only this were her wedding day and this man loved her. The ache of longing came so strongly that it threatened to buckle her knees. She clutched the chair back for a moment, feeling his eyes upon her.

"Bridget?" His voice was low and made her insides tighten with want. "I've a question."

He laid his broad hands heavily upon her shoulders and he turned her until they stood face-to-face. His bare palms sent heat through the thin cotton of her sleeve, torturing her. It took all she had not to step into his arms. She held on to her pride, forcing herself to remain upright as she lifted her chin to meet his gaze.

She tingled all over as she looked into his blue eyes, recalling his touch, his scent, his kiss.

"Why did you marry me?"

She did not hesitate. "To save you."

"Is that the only reason?"

She glanced away and then back. How could she answer that? To tell the truth was to lay her heart open to be broken. *Never tell a man you love him.* Her mother's advice scratched through her mind, harsh as nails on a slate. *Once you tell him, he'll use it against you always.*

She thought of her mother's unhappiness. Then she looked back into Cole's eyes. His expression seemed expectant, almost hopeful. Could it be possible that—that he loved her, too?

Bridget thought of all the risks she had taken—freeing him from prison, facing the mountain a second time, telling the world of her shame. But somehow all those perils paled in comparison with what she was about to do. She had told him once and he had mocked her. The shame of that still burned.

He had told her often that love was trust. Did she dare believe him, after all her experience said otherwise?

Was he asking her to trust him now?

She closed her eyes to gather her strength. Then she met his gaze squarely and spoke in a surprisingly steady voice.

"I did it because I love you, and that's the truth of it."

His smile broke slowly, spreading across his face until he beamed like a lantern. His grip tightened.

She cuffed him in the rib cage with her open hand. "Well, say something."

He shook his head, still grinning like an imbecile. The smile transformed his features. His eyes glittered as if he held back tears. The starch went out of her as worry took hold.

"Cole?"

His hands slipped down to grasp her waist and he lifted her high in the air, whirling her in a circle.

The instant her feet touched the ground, he captured her in a crushing embrace. "I believe you."

She wriggled, trying to escape. "Is that all you have to say?"

He held her tight, refusing to let her go, and used his thumb to tip her chin until their gazes met.

"No, it's not all. I would have married you without the threat of prison and without the baby. I love you, too, Bridget Rose."

"But you do want the baby?" She held her breath as she waited.

He hesitated and she felt her joy melting like ice chips in August. He clasped her hands and led her to the bed, where they sat facing each other. Did he feel her trembling?

"I want it, Bridget, with all my heart. But sometimes that is not enough."

Her confidence returned with her understanding. "Sometimes it *is* enough."

"I'm afraid of losing you both, as well."

There, he had said it, the truth of his heart. Bridget stroked his cheek. "I'm too stubborn to die on you, Cole. You should know that by now."

He tried to smile and failed. "But what if—"

She pressed his face between her palms, forcing him to look at her. "It's what makes life precious—the risk. Not knowing how many days we share is what makes each one dear. You were brave enough to face the mountain twice. Surely you are brave enough to face our marriage."

"I'm not."

"Well, then, I'll have to be more careful crossing the road."

His jaw dropped in incredulity as she grinned at him. And then he laughed. She joined him and he drew her into his arms and hugged her.

"I've never met anyone like you." He stroked her back and she pulled away to look up at him. His expression turned serious again. "You've given me what I thought to never have again—a family. I can never thank you enough. You're a wonder, Bridget Rose."

"Not a thief and a liar?"

"That, too. But I find those to be endearing qualities."

"Well, then we're well matched."

He lifted one dark eyebrow. "You gave away your secret."

She could not hold his gaze, and said nothing. She did not regret the choice, for it had saved him. But she did worry about Chloe and what the consequences would be for her child.

"You traded it on the chance you could save me."

She nodded.

"It's why I want to adopt Chloe and give her my name."

Bridget gasped and threw her arms around his neck, crushing herself against him. "Oh, Cole, I can't thank you enough."

He held her tight. "Well, you could try."

She drew back at the coaxing tone of his voice and noted the wicked, lustful glint in his eyes. Her body tingled all over, just from that look.

"Mr. Ellis, you are a scoundrel."

"Mrs. Ellis, you are a scoundrel's wife."

She offered her mouth to his. He swooped, taking her with passion as he lowered her to the bed. She opened for him and his tongue slipped within, rousing and teasing.

He pulled back to gaze down at her, all playfulness gone from his expression. "You brought me back to life, Bridget Rose."

She rested his large hand on her flat stomach. "I'd do the same for any of my family."

His look turned grave. "Perhaps we should not…" He glanced at the mattress.

"Oh, no! I was robbed of my wedding night once already. Not a second time." She grasped him by the collar and pulled.

He tumbled next to her, making the bedsprings squeak. It was the beginning of a symphony that went on throughout the rest of the day and well into the night.

* * * * *

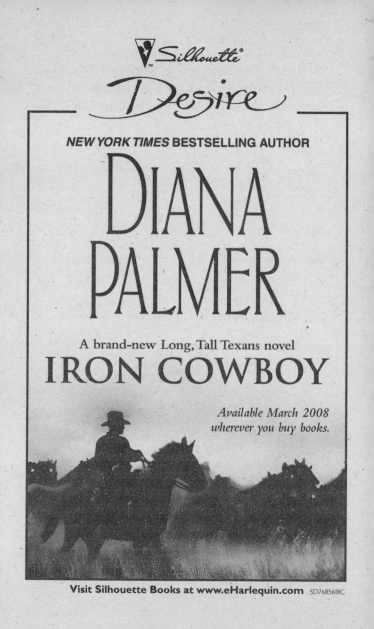

Silhouette® *Desire*

NEW YORK TIMES BESTSELLING AUTHOR

DIANA PALMER

A brand-new Long, Tall Texans novel

IRON COWBOY

*Available March 2008
wherever you buy books.*

Visit Silhouette Books at www.eHarlequin.com SD76856IBC

HARLEQUIN®
Super Romance®

Bundles of Joy—
coming next month
to Superromance

**Experience the romance, excitement
and joy with 6 heartwarming titles.**

BABY, I'M YOURS #1476 by *Carrie Weaver*

ANOTHER MAN'S BABY
(The Tulanes of Tennessee)
#1477 by *Kay Stockham*

THE MARINE'S BABY (9 Months Later)
#1478 by *Rogenna Brewer*

BE MY BABIES (Twins)
#1479 by *Kathryn Shay*

THE DIAPER DIARIES (Suddenly a Parent)
#1480 by *Abby Gaines*

HAVING JUSTIN'S BABY (A Little Secret)
#1481 by *Pamela Bauer*

Exciting, Emotional and Unexpected!

*Look for these Superromance titles in March 2008.
Available wherever books are sold.*

In the first of this emotional Mediterranean Dads duet, nanny Julie is whisked away to a palatial Italian villa, but she feels completely out of place in Massimo's glamorous world. Her biggest challenge, though, is ignoring her attraction to the brooding tycoon.

Look for

The Italian Tycoon and the Nanny

by **Rebecca Winters**

in March wherever you buy books.

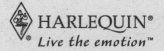

www.eHarlequin.com

HR17500

JENNA KERNAN

Every bit as adventurous as her heroines, Jenna is an avid gold prospector, searching America's gold-bearing rivers for elusive nuggets. She and her husband have written several books on gem and mineral hunting. Her debut novel, *Winter Woman*, was a RITA® Award finalist for Best First Book.

Jenna lives with her husband and two bad little parrots in New York. Visit her on the Web, www.jennakernan.com, for news, contests and excerpts.

HHBIOKERNAN08

COMING NEXT MONTH FROM

HARLEQUIN®
HISTORICAL

- **TAMING THE TEXAN**
  by **Charlene Sands**
  (Western)
  Clint Hayworth wants revenge—and he'll be damned if he'll allow his
  father's conniving, gold-digging widow to take over the family ranch!
  But something about her is getting under his skin....
  *This is one Texan in real need of taming—and Tess is just the woman
  for the job!*

- **HIGH SEAS TO HIGH SOCIETY**
  by **Sophia James**
  (Regency)
  Ill-fitting, threadbare clothes concealed the body of an angel, but what
  kind of woman truly lay behind the refined mask? Highborn lady or
  artful courtesan, Asher wanted to possess both!
  *Let Sophia James sweep you away to adventure and high-society
  romance.*

- **PICKPOCKET COUNTESS**
  by **Bronwyn Scott**
  (Regency)
  Robbing from the rich to give to the poor, Nora may have taken
  more than she expected when she steals the earl's heart!
  *Sexy and intriguing, Bronwyn Scott's debut book heralds an author
  to watch.*

- **A KNIGHT MOST WICKED**
  by **Joanne Rock**
  (Medieval)
  Tristan Carlisle will do whatever it takes to secure the lands and
  fortune that will establish his respectability in the world and fulfill his
  duty to the king. Even if it means denying his attraction to a Gypsy
  posing as a noblewoman...
  Join this wicked knight on his quest for honor and love.